THE ANGER

CHRONICLES

THE ANGER CHRONICLES, BOOK ONE

JESSIE PREISENDORFER

A NineStar Press Publication

www.ninestarpress.com

The Anger Chronicles

© 2024 Jessie Preisendorfer

Cover Art © 2024 Melody Pond

Edited by Elizabetta McKay

First Edition, September 2024

ISBN: 978-1-64890-803-3

Also available in eBook, ISBN: 978-1-64890-802-6

CONTENT WARNING:

This book contains sexist language, profanity, discussion of physical assault of a minor (off page, past); underage drinking and drug use; anger management issues; teenagers dealing with depression; therapy; and running away.

Shay, fourteen and queer, just got placed with her fifth foster family in three years. Of course, she's always angry or about to be, who wouldn't be? This latest foster family, a rabbi, an accountant, eight-year-old twins, and a big black cat offer Shay another chance at being part of a family.

Shay is the new kid at school for the third time in one year, which is bad enough, but being in eighth grade just complicates things, especially when Shay develops a crush on the cute girl who runs the art club. As much as she tries to stay above the school drama, Shay is sucked into it after she makes yet another anger-fueled bad decision that gets caught on video and goes viral. One bad decision essentially ruins her school life and a budding relationship. It jeopardizes Shay's placement with the Morgensterns just when they're finally getting closer.

When Shay gets an apology letter from her estranged father, recently released from prison, she realizes she needs to make a choice. Should she stay with the Morgensterns, or should she give her father another chance? Will her anger issues continue to sabotage any chance at stability?

To Reggie and all the kids in the foster system, past, present, and future. We see you.

CHAPTER ONE

<u>Things that suck about being a foster kid (incomplete)</u>
1. Changing schools
2. Being perpetually behind in school (see #1)
3. Not knowing the rules and breaking them anyway
4. Being the "outsider-est" outsider everywhere, even at home
5. Having to pretend to like everyone in the new family

ALL OF THE above happened to me this past year. Three times. There was more that happened to me this year. I was placed with three different foster families, went to three new schools, ran away from one super shitty caseworker (twice), met some stereotypical mean girls, and had a starring role in one viral video that ruined my life.

Things didn't completely suck 100 percent for once in my shitty life, when, by good luck, which I never had, I met the Morgensterns. (You should know that I don't believe in luck. I don't know how else to explain that my placements usually suck, but this one doesn't. I'm partially at fault for my bad placements— I have "anger issues," according to my social worker, Rhonda the Craptastic, and I make pretty bad choices, if I'm being completely honest.)

One more thing. I almost died from the smell of bacon drifting into my room. Absolutely starving, I started down the stairs to find the bacon in my brand-new placement and tripped over a big black cat on the landing. Grabbing the railing to prevent plunging to my death, I stopped and sat with this huge cat next to me, staring at me. I tried to remember when I had eaten last—I guessed Thursday. And today was Saturday? Maybe?

I couldn't stop thinking about the peanut butter sandwich I'd eaten under the train tracks. This was how much of an idiot I was. I could have taken the whole loaf of bread and a jar of peanut butter, but no, I packed one whole sandwich to sneak out of my last foster house. Not even an apple or anything. Idiot. (You should know that I'm not an idiot when it comes to school. I'm okay at school, when I go to school. I just "lack common sense," according to Rhonda the Craptastic, who can rot in hell.)

Happy family sounds rose up from downstairs. That made me so angry I forgot about being hungry for, like, a minute. I wasn't angry at the family sounds or the family. It wasn't their fault my shitty social worker called them at midnight last night to come pick me up. I was just angry in general. I didn't even know why. (You should also know I'm usually angry.) Sometimes, it got my attention, like now—it was there, right below my skin. Just as quickly, I only felt hungry again; the anger had slipped back beneath the surface. I heard a door open behind me.

"I hope you're hungry. Mrs. Morgenstern always makes a nice breakfast on weekends. I hope Spock didn't bother you. He doesn't usually like people. He's not as hefty as he seems. He's under tall." Mr. Morgenstern laughed at his own corny joke as he made his way down the stairs, stepping carefully around Spock, the huge black cat.

I remembered Mr. Morgenstern driving home. He could barely see over the steering wheel. Sitting on the stairs, I thought, He's under tall too.

He stopped at the bottom of the stairs. Here comes the pep talk. But he simply said, "Come on in when you're ready. I'll save you some bacon."

I was so hungry. So hungry. But I was sitting on the stairs in another new house. With a new family. And new rules. And eventually, new drama. Then a new new family. A burst of laughter came from the kitchen. Suddenly, I was more tired than hungry. So tired. Too tired to even be angry. I went back upstairs to the room on the third floor and crawled back into bed.

CHAPTER TWO

WHEN I WOKE up again, it was pitch-black, except for the light beside the bed. I was even hungrier than before, which I didn't think was even possible. I had to try to find food. I was an expert at stealing food—you had to be sometimes when you were the extra kid, and there wasn't always enough. A couple night lights in the halls helped me find my way to the kitchen, where a light remained on over the stove in the silent house. Good. I was too hungry to be too careful.

I opened the fridge and found a plastic container with a sticky note on it that said, "Shay." Yup, that was my name. I took out the container. Inside was a huge piece of chocolate cake. I almost drooled onto my shirt. I didn't want to hunt for a fork, so I ate it with my hands. It was the best thing I'd ever eaten in my life. As I washed the plastic container in the sink, Mr. Morgenstern walked in wearing a fluffy robe, Spock trailing behind him. I froze, waiting to get yelled at for being up, for being in the kitchen, for eating between meals. My face got hot. I got pre-angry, which is when I get angry at people before they have a chance to get mad at me. My anger was the reason I had to leave family #4. My anger was also the reason I had to steal a peanut butter sandwich, which I ate under some train tracks.

He was more startled than me. "Oh. Hi, Shay. Good, you found the cake. Let's have some milk." He opened the fridge, took out the milk and a cake-sized round plastic container, then gestured to the cabinet behind me. "Grab two plates and glasses from there."

I got out two plates and glasses. He opened the container—the rest of the chocolate cake. He cut two pieces, put them on plates, then placed one in front of me. I'd already had a piece of cake. He was probably testing me to see if I was greedy enough to take a second piece. I took a step back, peering at him. He smiled, which I decided was genuine.

I had to say, I was an excellent judge of smiles. I've seen my share of good ones, bad ones, fake ones, real ones. Fake ones like some teachers gave when they got a new kid in the middle of the year, already knowing we were way behind. Real ones like the good social workers gave when they checked in and it was actually going well. The secret was the eyes. If someone smiled with their eyes, it probably wasn't a fake.

Mr. Morgenstern smiled with his eyes. I could tell it was genuine. "You missed dinner. Have a second piece." I thought he'd begin the probing questions about school, my family, my previous foster families. Why did foster families even ask about the previous families? The social workers (whose smiles turn fake during those last visits) have told them everything. But Mr. Morgenstern took more interest in his cake. I just ate more cake and drank my milk.

He poured some milk into a bowl on the floor for Spock. "I'm not supposed to give him milk, but I can't resist his inscrutable smile."

I didn't know what "inscrutable" was, but I didn't ask. I was probably supposed to know. It was probably a vocab word they covered during a week I was switching schools. Changing schools sucked. (See item #1, top of the list.)

The cat purred loudly. I was about to ask how old Spock was, but Mr. Morgenstern got up, gathered the plates and glasses, and put them in the dishwasher.

"Good night, Shay. If you get bored, there are some books and a TV through there." He pointed to a doorway. He smiled at me before he went back through the door to the stairs.

Spock sat, watching me. I went through the door to the room with the books and TV. He followed me.

I flicked a light switch, which turned on a desk light, revealing a large room, crowded with two couches, two lounge chairs, bookcases filled to overflowing, and a desk. A TV on a table sat in the corner. (I will admit that I like to read.) Being a foster kid wasn't cool. Being a foster kid who read was the most uncool thing ever.

Here's what was cool, at least in the schools I've gone to: Fighting, smoking pot, partying, posting weird stuff on social media. Those were the cool things the cool kids did. Here was what I've learned from experience: Fighting got you suspended, which was bad because foster kids risked being returned to the group home if they had "repeated behavior issues" at school. Besides, I didn't care enough about anything to actually fight about it. Also, I couldn't afford pot, no one invited me to parties, and I didn't have a cell phone anymore. Plus, once you were cool, there was a ton of pressure on you to stay cool. Trust me. It was harder staying cool than getting cool. So, I really didn't care about being cool. Good thing because I was a foster who liked to read.

Reading was the best way to escape my life. In two of my foster houses, there was only one TV and, of course, the foster kids never got to control what we watched. But I could always read, living someone else's life, in some other place, in a book.

In foster house #2—the house with the Garbage Family—there were a lot of books. The Garbage Parents also read smarty-pants magazines and threw parties for their smarty-pants friends. The only decent thing about foster house #2 was that they had good books. That was where I started reading a lot.

So, when I found this room in the Morgensterns' house, I was a little relieved. Even if they turned out to be Garbage People, too, at least I'd be able to read. I went over to the bookcase that held a ton of books with symbols on the spine. I opened one that had a worn, cracked leather cover but couldn't read the language inside. Next to a globe that mapped outer space instead of the

Earth, I found a bunch of science fiction books. I grabbed the one labeled *Dune*, which had a desert on the cover.

I turned on the light next to one of the large, inviting chairs, grabbed the blanket from the back of the chair and settled in. Immediately, Spock jumped up and curled around in a ball, right on my feet.

CHAPTER THREE

SO, THIS BOOK, *Dune*, don't even get me started. It's amazing. I can't even begin to describe it. This isn't a book report, but you should read it if science fiction, revenge, mysticism, politics, and extreme environments interest you. Oh, and giant worms that live under the sand, waiting to swallow people whole.

I must have read for a couple hours because when Mr. Morgenstern popped in eventually, I noticed it was light out.

He said, "Good morning. What are you reading?" I showed him the book, which got him excited. "Dune! I haven't read that in years! What do you think?"

I told him I thought the Bene Gesserits were cool. He beamed.

"My niece, Anna, wanted to be a Bene Gesserit after she read this. She's a lawyer for Planned Parenthood now." He nodded at the cat, who stared back at him. "Spock doesn't usually tolerate anybody. Breakfast is in about an hour. Your backpack is in your room if you want to change."

I realized how gross I was, wearing the same clothes from the night I got here. It'd been a day (or two? Ugh, three?) since I last showered. I folded the blanket, put it back on the chair, and headed upstairs. Halfway up, Mrs. Morgenstern came out of a room. She had to be almost a foot taller than Mr. Morgenstern and as narrow as Mr. Morgenstern was wide.

She said, "Good morning, Shay. I'm glad you're here. There are towels in the closet in the bathroom for when you want to shower. There is shampoo and conditioner in the closet, too, along with extra toothbrushes. Help yourself. There's plenty of time before breakfast."

I nodded, "I think I will. Thanks." I returned to my room, pulled out some clothes from my backpack that passed the smell test, then went back to the bathroom with towels, shampoo, and conditioner. After, I made my way back downstairs to the kitchen, where Mrs. Morgenstern was at the stove. She turned, waved, then continued flipping pancakes, making bacon, and buttering toast, all at the same time.

"Hi, Shay! Breakfast is almost ready. Would you set the table?" Without waiting for me to answer, she gestured to a cabinet over the counter. "Plates are up there. Forks and knives are in that drawer." She pointed. "Five place settings, please. Put two by the bench."

I did as requested.

Mrs. Morgenstern poured some batter on the griddle, then turned, spatula in hand. She smiled at me. (Smile judging: genuine.) "The boys will be here in a minute. They'll want to know everything about you. The secret is..." She lowered her voice, turning her head to see if anyone was close by. I checked, too, then realized she was joking. "...they won't remember anything you say, so if there's anything you don't want to tell them, make up the answer. They mostly want your attention."

I'd never had an adult tell me to lie to a kid before, but it turned out to be good advice.

Suddenly, two boys burst through the kitchen door, locked in a struggle over what appeared to be an action figure with a Barbie head and a fish bottom. I guessed they were about eight years old. They were completely identical, even dressed the same. Then, they saw me. Everything came to a complete stop, and then mayhem erupted as they came charging over to me.

"I'm Nathan / I'm Eli." They both reached out to shake my hand. I knew it was a contest, so I couldn't shake either one first. I held out both of my hands in fists. Immediately, they put theirs into little fists to bump mine at the same time.

"Are you Shay? What grade are you in? Where are you from? What's your favorite color? Are you in high school? Is chocolate your favorite? Are you Jewish too? Can you tell us apart?"

Then, they stopped, waiting as if they actually expected answers. I couldn't help it; they were pretty cute. I laughed out loud.

"I told you." Mrs. Morgenstern laughed, flipping pancakes.

The twins continued to wait for answers.

"I'm in eighth grade," I said, answering the easiest question.

They turned to their mother. "Did you put bananas in the pancakes? Can I have toast instead? Is that Shay?"

Mrs. M. said, "Nathan, can you pour milk for you and your brother and Shay?"

Nathan darted to the refrigerator, declaring, "Shay is sitting next to me on the bench."

Eli said, "Me too," as Nathan poured three glasses of milk.

Nathan said, "There isn't room for all three of us on the bench, dummy."

Eli yelled, "I'm not a dummy" before bursting into tears. He ran to the door, right into his father, who was coming in. Eli pushed past him, out of the kitchen.

Nathan's lower lip trembled, his eyes filling with tears. I didn't know what the big deal was. I figured maybe it was because they were fighting over sitting next to me.

"What happened?" asked Mr. M. I immediately apologized for causing trouble.

Mrs. M shook her head. "It wasn't you, Shay. Nathan, tell your father what happened, then go apologize to Eli."

Nathan's eyes spilled over as he blurted, "I called him a dummy. I'm sorry. I forgot I'm not supposed to do that. He's not a dummy. I'm the dummy."

Mrs. Morgenstern put her hand on his shoulder. "You're not a dummy, Nathan. No one is a dummy. Go apologize. Tell him breakfast is ready. There's rye toast for him."

Nathan put the milk on the table and left the room.

I knew it was still probably about me. I apologized again. Then I offered to eat in my room to make it easier, explaining that I did that at foster house #3; none of the foster kids ever ate with the real family.

They exchanged a look. Mrs. Morgenstern said, "Whatever you want, but we have plenty of room."

The boys came crashing back into the room, laughing.

"Boys, on your bench," Mrs. M said. "Shay, your seat is across the table. We'd prefer you to eat with us, but after one meal with the boys, you may change your mind. Heck, we may join you."

Mr. Morgenstern casually gestured to the chair across from the bench.

I took the chair as the boys quickly sat on their bench, quietly staring at me. Mrs. Morgenstern brought over a large plate of pancakes and a plate of bacon, which smelled similar to regular bacon but wasn't. Then, she brought over a small plate with buttered slices of rye toast. She began piling pancakes and bacon on Nathan's plate as Eli helped himself to toast.

Once everyone began eating, Nathan asked me, "Where are your parents?"

My mother died of a drug overdose; my loser father was in prison. I almost told the truth to this nosy kid, but I paused as my face got red, my first bite of pancake halfway to my mouth. Suddenly, I couldn't eat because my mouth had gone dry with pre-anger. Pre-anger never leads to anything except anger. I didn't want to snap at a little kid. Not on my first day. Gotta make nice with the real kids.

Good thing I was an expert deflector—of conversations, arguments, feelings. I asked him, "Did you make that Barbie-head doll?"

Nathan jumped up and grabbed the doll off the counter. He shoved it to me across the table. "It's not a doll. It's an action figure because I'm a boy."

I turned it over in my hands. It was actually pretty cool-looking. I nodded at him. "This is pretty cool-looking."

Nathan smiled broadly. I'd saved it. I hadn't snapped at one of the real kids. *Nice work, Shay.* Then I beefed it.

"Beefed it" meant to ruin something. My good social worker (the one before my current piece-of-shit social worker) used to say that to me—"Well, Shay, you really beefed it here"—when I screwed up at a placement. I didn't know why I beefed it with Nathan. Maybe I still stung about the parent question. I teased him. "I have it now, and I'm a girl. Does that make it a doll?"

Mr. Morgenstern snorted with laughter, quickly turning it into a cough.

Nathan looked at his father, then back at me. Kids were really good at picking up on subtle shit; he knew there was an edge to my teasing. He held his hand out silently. I hesitated, as though I was going to keep the doll. Which I wasn't, of course, but I still hesitated handing the kid his toy back. Pre-anger drained slowly; I hated myself for it. Everyone turned to me, so I handed it back to Nathan. "It's an action figure," he said quietly.

Then, Mr. Morgenstern said, "Pancakes are divine, hon. Thanks."

Eli chirped, "Great toast, Mom!"

They either didn't notice what I had done, or they were trying to pretend it hadn't happened.

I decided to play along. "This bacon is different. It's good but different."

Eli said, "It's turkey, but it smells like regular bacon! We're Jewish, but we can eat pork, but we like turkey bacon better. Do you like turkey bacon better? Are you Jewish? We're Reform. Are you Orthodox?"

He waited. It got quiet. These twins and their tag-team awkward questions. But Queen Deflector was ready.

"This turkey bacon is good."

Eli turned to Nathan. "I told you she would like it." Nathan made a face at his brother.

After breakfast, I tried to help clear the table, but Mrs. Morgenstern stopped me.

"Not today," she said. "We'll get you on the chore list next week. But for now, unpack. Settle in upstairs. Okay?"

That made me super uncomfortable. I wasn't used to doing nothing. "I'm used to doing the dishes and cleaning up after meals."

Eli said, "Were you a maid at your last house? Did you have to clean the bathroom? Stinky!"

Nathan chimed in. "We have to put our clothes away after Mom washes them. We're like maids too."

This next part was a good example of how much of a baby I could be. I got really upset about being called a "maid." My face got hot again as I skipped right over pre-angry to regular angry. My grandma had been someone's housekeeper. Every night she'd come home exhausted.

I yelled, "I wasn't a maid," then followed this up by storming out of the kitchen. Super cringe, right? As soon as I got to my room, I berated myself for yelling at the real kids. I sat there mentally beating myself up for a while because they'd move me back to the group home again if I kept yelling at the real family children. I didn't want to go back to the group home. I really didn't. Not yet.

A few minutes later, there was a knock on the door. I didn't want to talk to anybody, so I ignored it.

After a couple seconds, Eli said, "It's Eli. Can I come in?"

Sigh. "Try to control yourself, dummy," I said to myself. "Sure," I said out loud.

He came in and stood just inside the door. He was scared of me. Made sense because I was a monster. "Sorry I asked if you were a maid."

"Aww, Eli, thanks. That's not why I got upset. It wasn't because of what you said. But thanks."

He stood there.

Then, I saw he was holding a piece of paper. "What's that?"

Eli walked over to the bed and handed it to me. "I'm dyslexic. I'm in a special class for reading at school. I only found out this year."

"Oh. Okay. Is this your school work?"

He climbed up onto the bed. "Homework."

"You had homework over the weekend?" I asked. He nodded. I shook my head. "That stinks. Do you need any help?" I checked the paper. "Find the nonsense words. I think you got them all."

He shook his head. "Nathan had to help me find them. I'm not that good a reader. I just want you to know I'm dyslexic."

I didn't know what to say. "Oh. Okay. Thanks for letting me know."

He was waiting for me to trade secrets with him, so I found one that wasn't nearly the worst.

"Um, you should know this about me. This is my fifth foster house."

Eli sat there for a few seconds. I could see he was thinking. Then he asked, "Is that a lot?"

I didn't want to scare him, but I also didn't want to lie or deflect right now. "Kind of a lot."

"Oh. Okay." Eli was just a kid, but I didn't catch any judgment or disapproval in his voice. He hopped down, clutching his homework paper. He pointed behind me and said, "He doesn't like anybody," then left.

I turned to see that hefty cat, Spock, sitting on the bed, squinting at me. I couldn't read him at all. Suddenly, I knew what "inscrutable" meant.

CHAPTER FOUR

(YOU SHOULD KNOW that #1, I lie a lot, and #2, I am an excellent liar. The first person I lied to at this placement was Mr. Morgenstern. Or rather, Mr. M.)

"Call us Mr. and Mrs. M," he said. "To save time," he said, laughing at his own corny joke. It was so dumb that he laughed at his own jokes. THAT was the funny part, in my humble opinion.

The next day was Sunday, so it was pretty chill. It turned out the boys were getting over colds. Identical twins got identical germs, I guessed. I wasn't worried about getting sick because I'd spent enough time in group homes to develop a pretty strong immune system. Lunch was canned noodle soup (which I love), made even better because Mrs. M buttered saltines for the twins and me. It was delicious. I didn't even know you could butter saltines.

Immediately after lunch, I told the first lie of the day, the one to Mr. M. The twins were working on science projects for school with Mrs. M, and Mr. M was planning to visit his mother in a nursing home. The twins couldn't go because of their twin colds. When Mr. M asked if I wanted to go, I quickly said, "No." Then, The First Lie. "Because I have a sore throat." Lies were more believable if you added the right amount of detail. I added, "I probably caught the twins' cold." Totally believable, right? I lied because I didn't like being around old people. I wasn't sorry about lying. (I never am.)

Old people stared at me; they couldn't tell if I was a girl or a boy or what just because I had short hair and no boobs. Also, there were always a lot of questions. Rapid fire, like the twins, except they wanted information fast.

"What do you want to be when you grow up? Where are your parents? What religion are you? Do you want to be Catholic? Is "Shay" a girl's name or a boy's name? Have you ever done drugs? Are you sure you don't want to be Catholic?" I was sure Mr. M's mother was as nice as he was. I really couldn't handle the questions.

I also had important plans for the day. My day would be almost entirely spent dreading the worst part of a new placement—the first day at a new school. It'd be a nightmare. Again. I was starting at the local middle school in eighth grade, plop in the middle of the year. Tomorrow, Mrs. M and I would register me for school and get me a uniform.

I spent most of the day in the library room, reading *Dune* while dreading school. Occasionally, I was called into the kitchen to ooh and ah about the science projects. Nathan was making a 3D model of the surface of the moon, so he was covered in flour and paste. Eli was doing a trifold about the life cycle of a frog, so he was covered in green marker and spent a lot of time hopping around the kitchen *ribbet*ing.

Right after dinner, Mr. and Mrs. M and I sat in the kitchen and talked about the rules. Every house had rules, but only some foster parents actually told you what they were before you got in trouble for breaking them. Anyway, the list:

The Morgenstern Rules

1. Homework gets done every day after school. (I can't wait to watch the twins do homework without fighting. Spoiler alert, they fight every day.)

2. Empty the dishwasher and help clear the table

3. Bedtime is at 9:00 p.m., but I can read until 10:00 if I want. (Kind of early, but whatever.)

4. Using the computer is fine, but they would monitor where I go online

5. I can share the TV with the twins as long as we don't watch anything too scary (Nathan scares easily.) or with cursing (Eli will curse.)

6. I have to clean my own room and bathroom. (My own room? My own bathroom? First time for both, so yeah, you bet they'll be clean.)

7. I get an allowance of 10 dollars per week. (Amazing. I

don't have to do anything to get it. If I don't do my chores or get in trouble, I lose TV and internet, not the 10 dollars per week.)
8. I have weekly appointments with a shrink. (Yuck, but whatever. My own bathroom!)

After the talk, Mr. M asked me how my sore throat was. I lied again.

"Still hurts." I didn't count that as a separate lie because it was the first one repeated. (I mean, I understand that I lied twice to this person; I'm just saying it's one total lie.)

I thought he was disappointed. Worse, I knew he knew that I was lying. It was weird to have been caught doing it. I thought maybe he wanted to say something else, but he didn't. He probably wanted to scold me about the lying but didn't have the guts. Mrs. M had a strange expression on her face, I figured it was probably disappointment too. Right on schedule. She must have known I was lying too. Whatever. It was one lie, twice. It was really starting to bother me that they caught on to me this easily.

She stood up. "Okay, Shay. That's it for the rules talk. Any questions?"

I shook my head, waiting for her to call me out on my lie. She didn't.

"Time for the twins to have their bath, and then it's bedtime. Shay, we have a few errands to run tomorrow, so maybe you should go to bed early tonight, you know, because of your sore throat." She totally knew I was lying.

Now, I felt bad for lying, which was immediately followed by feeling pre-angry for feeling bad. But who was I even angry at? I didn't know. I nodded with my head down.

"After we run our errands," she continued, "we'll stop at the Big City Diner for lunch. I love that place." She smiled at me (genuine). My face got hot from embarrassment at being caught in a lie. I tried to smile back but failed spectacularly—it was probably more of a grimace. "I'm glad you're here, Shay. See you in the morning." She left the kitchen.

Mr. M said, "Shay, we're adjusting too. If something makes you uncomfortable, let us know." He paused as if waiting for me to come clean.

I wasn't ready to reveal my terrible secrets to a stranger. Luckily, I came up with something so he'd leave me alone. "So far, so good. Having my own bathroom is cool, thanks."

I had to get out of there. "I'll go to bed and read for a while."

"Okay, Shay. Hope you feel better tomorrow."

I wondered if he meant about my anger, then realized he was talking about my sore throat. "Thanks."

I escaped upstairs to my own bedroom with my own bathroom, which I scrubbed thoroughly even though someone had cleaned it before I got here. Guilt cleaning, I guessed.

CHAPTER FIVE

EVERYONE WAS UP early on Monday. The twins were over their colds, so they were getting ready for school. I stayed upstairs until I heard them leave. Then I went downstairs.

"Good morning, Shay." Mrs. M smiled as she handed me a cereal bowl. "I hope you're not disappointed we're not having pancakes again."

"No, of course not. Cereal is great." It really was. Most times at the Berrys' (family #4), I showed up too late for milk and ate dry cereal. There was a whole gallon sitting on the counter today though. I sat there, crunching.

I lied to Mrs. M immediately as we got into the car to start our day. The worst part was, it was a stupid lie.

She asked, "So, are you looking forward to school tomorrow?"

I immediately lied. "Yeah."

First of all, it was a dumb question. No kid ever, EVER, in the history of everything, ever said "Yes" to that question. Even if some kid was corny enough to actually be looking forward to school, they'd NEVER admit it. Second of all, she deserved to be lied to because of asking that dumb question. She glanced at me, then backed out of the driveway. Ugh. Caught lying again. I was off my game.

Our first stop was a stone building that appeared to be a church.

"This is our synagogue. I have to pick up some papers. Come on inside if you want."

I followed her. We walked past a group of bundled up little kids outside playing.

"Good morning, Rabbi Morgenstern," one of the women monitoring the kids said.

"Good morning, Maya. How is your mother?"

"She's feeling better, thanks."

Mrs. M was a rabbi? That was kind of cool—she wasn't wearing a gown or a frock or a robe or anything. Her being a rabbi was sort of a secret identity. We went inside to her office. The small room held a wooden desk, two chairs, a coat rack, and bookcases on three walls. The desk had orderly stacks of papers on it.

"This is where I work, Shay. I'm the rabbi of this congregation. You know what a rabbi is?"

I nodded. "You're like a priest."

She shook her head. "Rabbis and priests are quite different, actually. I'm more of a teacher. I teach the Torah, which is Jewish law. And I'm the spiritual leader of this congregation."

She grabbed a few folders off the desk. "Want a quick tour?"

I nodded again. She showed me the synagogue. It was cathedral-like, with stained glass windows. I imagined people filling the space, sitting on the wooden benches, with Mrs. M leading them, standing up front. I thought it was kind of cool that she was in charge of this whole thing. She had a key to this closet that held ancient scrolls—that was pretty cool too.

After the synagogue, we stopped at the school administration building to drop off my paperwork for the Big First Day Nightmare tomorrow. The secretary sent us back to the Records Department after staring at us a little too long. I knew he could tell we weren't related. The lady in Records took the fat envelope out of Mrs. M's hands. She shuffled through the papers, and then her face changed.

Oh no. Pity. I got pre-angry and waited for the Records lady to make the sympathy "tsk" noise, do the pity tilt with her head, or say something overly kind.

She didn't do any one of those things. She did all three. "*Tsk*, Shay." Head tilt. Then, "You must be very brave."

Pre-angry to angry in one millisecond, I opened my mouth to say something, but then Mrs. M stepped in.

"We have an appointment in twenty minutes; if you don't mind making a copy of those papers, we can be on our way."

We didn't have an appointment in twenty minutes. Rabbi Morgenstern had just lied to the Records Lady. I gaped at Rabbi

M with my mouth still open. I shut my mouth.

Records Lady took the papers out into the main room. A minute later, we heard the copier. When I snuck a peek at Mrs. M., I was surprised to see that she looked mad. She turned to me.

"You look mad," she said.

"So do you," I blurted.

"Yep."

Records Lady came back, head still tilted in pity, smiling too kindly at me again. Mrs. M took the papers, shoved them back into the envelope, and handed them to me.

"Shay," she said, "please go wait outside."

After silently taking the papers, I walked out. Mrs. M came out a minute later, chirped the car unlocked, and we got in. She started the car and put it in reverse. Then she turned to me.

"I told her she was being condescending to you. You're fourteen, and you don't need adults treating you as if you're five. I didn't want to embarrass you or her. That's why I asked you to come out here."

I really wanted to tell her how surprised I was that she'd seen all those things. I also wanted to tell her, "Thank you," but that didn't seem enough. So then, I thought I would say, "Thank you very much," but I wasn't writing a thank-you note. By this time, I should have said something, anything. My pre-anger had melted into gratitude, but I didn't trust gratitude, so I said, "Okay."

She turned to me. I was afraid she'd try to talk to me, but she turned back and pulled out of the parking space without saying anything.

After a few moments, she said, "We have to go to your new school and check you in there."

"Okay," I said again because it was the only word I knew.

Consolidated Middle was located in a factorylike building. I half expected steam to be pouring out of smokestacks. I pictured students punching in at a time clock every morning, carrying lunch pails, wearing hard hats.

"You can walk to school tomorrow, or we can drop you off," Mrs. M said as we parked. "After that, I can either walk part way with you or tell you how to get here. It's pretty easy."

"Okay," again. Again!

Mrs. M turned to me and then away. Finally, she stopped on the sidewalk. "How many times have you done this? Switched school midyear."

I counted in my head. "This is my third time this year. Five times total."

"That's a lot of switching." She added when I shrugged, "This is a good school. Built like a factory, but it's a good school."

I said, "Okay," because that was my new favorite word.

At that point, a class came outside, screaming and tearing toward the playground. They were young, maybe sixth graders. We turned to each other; she rolled her eyes.

That totally caught me off guard. I went, "Ha!" and she smiled.

We got buzzed into the school. The smell hit me immediately—all schools smelled the same, a combination of disinfectant mixed with lunch. Middle schools also smelled like middle schoolers. (If you don't know that smell, you're lucky.)

When we entered the office, the secretary was on the phone. She gestured to two chairs.

A girl sat in one of the other chairs. She said to me, "What did you do?"

I was confused. "What?"

"Why's your mom here?" She thought I was in trouble.

"I didn't do anything. What did you do?"

The girl rolled her eyes. "I almost fought with this girl, Jamie. I told her to wait until after school, but she started running her mouth during science."

"Mrs. Morgenstern?" The secretary, Ms. Mozier, called us back through the swinging half door to her desk.

The girl said to Ms. Mozier, "Sure, take them first. I'm missing math class, but I guess that isn't as important as these people."

Ms. Mozier said, "Charlotte, you're not going to math today."

"Well, can you have somebody bring my books up here at least? They're outside Mr. Hamilton's class."

Mrs. Mozier didn't answer but picked up the phone and punched in four numbers. "Hi, LaTasha. Can you ask Mr. Hamilton to send Charlotte's books to the office? Thank you." Hanging up, she turned to the closed door to her left, then said loudly, "Principal Parkson—Mrs. Morgenstern and Shay are here. We'll be in the conference room." She led us into a room off the main office with a long table and padded chairs.

Mrs. M and I sat on one side. A really tall Black woman entered.

"Hi, Shay, Mrs. Morgenstern. I'm Principal Parkson." She reached over the table and extended her hand. I shook it. "Welcome to Consolidated Middle School."

The door pushed open, and a man entered. He was white and sizeable—both tall and wide—and had a huge stack of papers in one hand and a pen and a coffee cup in the other. He held the pen and cup so awkwardly that coffee sloshed around but didn't spill, like he was in a cartoon. He carefully placed everything down on the table. I held my breath as the coffee sloshed some more. Inside my head, I said a *whew* when the cup was level on the table.

"Hi, Shay." He smiled, giving me some serious eye contact. "I'm your guidance counselor, Mr. Stetson. Nice to meet you, partner." Except he said that last part with a fake cowboy drawl that made "partner" into "pod-nah."

Great. I knew I could expect more corny jokes from my new best friend, my guidance counselor. At least I knew how to play their game. "Nice to meet you, pod-nah," I said back. The adults smiled approvingly.

They registered me for five classes: math, science, social studies, language arts, and art. I was in some dumb homeroom, too, where everyone already knew each other because it was February.

"I'll meet you out front before school tomorrow to walk you to homeroom. Here's your schedule. You'll need four notebooks, pencils, pens. You know, school stuff. Do you have a uniform yet?

Bring shorts and a T-shirt for gym class on Thursday." Mr. Podnah sat back, speech successfully given.

"Oh. Ms. Peete," he continued, "the social worker, runs a girls' group on Fridays at lunch. I signed you up this week. Go, check it out once, you don't have to go back if you don't want to." He slid a paper over to me—my schedule: classes, times, room numbers—with a handwritten note at the bottom that said *Fri lunch, Ms. Peete, room 103 basement.* He said, "I'll try to remember to get someone to show you where room 103 is. If I forget, ask your science teacher."

Mrs. M asked about lunch.

Principal Parkson responded with, "Shay qualifies for free lunch and breakfast if she gets here by 8:15." She turned to me. "Tomorrow, come in the front door so Mr. Stetson can meet you. I'm glad you're here, Shay. Do you have any questions?"

I pointed to my schedule. "This says 'locker number.' Do you have lockers here?"

Principal Parkson nodded. "Yes. Mr. Stetson will make sure you can open your locker tomorrow morning. Anything else?"

I shook my head.

Mrs. M stood up. "I think that's it for now. Thanks."

Everybody shook hands as though the meeting had been a smashing success.

The girl in trouble still sat in one of those hard plastic chairs, now holding a textbook and a notebook on her lap while writing—it seemed very awkward.

She nodded at me. "Hey, hope you're not in too much

trouble."

I replied, "Not yet," and she laughed even though I was being totally serious. It was only a matter of time in a new school. Everybody wanted a piece of the foster kid.

Next, we stopped at the Big City Diner, where we had huge sandwiches. When the server asked if we wanted dessert, Mrs. M ordered coconut custard. I ordered blueberry pie because I'd seen it in the case when we walked in. It was really blue.

Mrs. M asked me if I liked blueberry pie. I lied.

"Yes, it's my favorite." I was suddenly a world expert on pie. She believed me. I was happy that I was still capable of telling a good lie. The server brought over the pie slices. Even though mine was blue, I didn't like it.

Mrs. M asked if I wanted to taste the coconut custard pie. It was delicious! Exactly how I imagined heaven would taste if I believed in heaven, which I didn't. It was creamy and coconutty—so good. Mrs. M suggested switching pies because she didn't like hers, so we did. I vacuumed that coconut custard pie into my mouth like the diner was on fire.

"Shay, have you ever had blueberry pie before?"

Moment of truth. I'd been caught in my lie. Again. The last bite of coconut custard heaven turned to sawdust in my mouth. I shook my head, my eyes filling up with stupid tears. I stared at the table.

"Hey," she said, reaching across, nudging my hand to get my attention. "Hey. It's okay. Why are you upset?"

I choked down the pie. "I used to be a better liar."

She threw her head back, laughing. Then, with a smile on her face, she said, "Okay."

I smiled back. Genuine.

*

WHEN WE WERE all sitting for dinner, Mr. M asked, "How was your day, Shay? Consolidated Middle looks pretty industrial, but it's a good school."

I thought it was funny that everyone kept apologizing for the school's appearance. "My day didn't suck." That was not a lie.

Mrs. M told him about lunch. He asked about dessert.

"It's the best part of eating at the diner." I told him how coconut custard pie was my new favorite pie.

"That's Mrs. M's favorite too," he said.

I flicked my eyes at her, realizing she'd given me her pie and lied about not liking it. She winked back at me. I was thrown off—adults weren't supposed to lie, but she had. Twice today. Once to spare the Record Lady's feelings, once to give me a piece of pie. I only ever lied to protect myself. Both of Mrs. M's lies were kind of nice things to do. I wondered if I could ever learn to use my Super Powers of Lying for good instead of evil.

CHAPTER SIX

I SETTLED IN the study after dinner, where Mrs. M was reading with the twins. Mr. M came in and handed me an envelope.

"Ms. Rhonda dropped this off at my office today."

I was annoyed. Rhonda always annoyed me. "It makes sense that my craptastic social worker didn't have the guts to give it to me in person."

"Craptastic," Eli said. The boys started giggling.

"Sorry." I'd given Eli his new swear word for the week. Studying the return address on the envelope, it took me a minute to figure out who it was from.

V. Turner. Holy shit, it was from my father. But it wasn't from prison; it was from Harrisburg. He was supposed to still be in prison, wasn't he? I remembered what Grandma had told me after my mom died.

"That loser will be in prison until you're in high school. If he ever gets out." No love lost there. She'd never had a nice word to say about my father. "He signed away his rights to you, so you don't ever have to see him."

Victor Turner. I hadn't thought about him for a long time.

"This is from my father."

Mrs. M nodded as the twins craned their necks, maybe to see what a real letter was.

"I don't know what to do," I said.

"You don't have to do anything," Mr. M told me. "You don't even have to read it. I can put it somewhere safe until you're ready."

Why would he write to me? My father. My Dad. Father. I didn't even know what to call him. Sperm donor, my mother said once. My grandma called him a POS, spelling it out way after I knew what it stood for.

Everyone stared at me as I stood there, holding the envelope. "He got locked up when I was five or six. I don't remember him much—my mom took me to visit once or twice but I mostly remember the snack machine in the visiting room. That was the second time he was locked up. Selling drugs." Mr. and Mrs. M nodded, the twins stared at me. It was weird to talk about him and weirder to think about him. I hadn't thought about him in a long time. I examined the envelope. I mean, what could he want? I opened it. There was letter inside, written on notebook paper.

Everyone was staring at me. I didn't want to scare the twins.

"Can I go into the kitchen to read it?" I asked, feeling weird because I wasn't sure if I'd read it or rip it into a million shreds.

"Of course," Mrs. M said.

So, I went into the kitchen alone with the scribbled letter.

It was full of apologies, but right at the end, he said he wanted to see me. That gave me a chill. *What if he wants to take custody of me? What if he takes custody and then gets sent back to prison?* I waited for my anger, but the only thing that came was fear.

I went back into the study. "He's sorry for messing up, and he's sorry my mom and grandma died. He's sorry for a lot, I guess."

When Mr. M asked if I was okay, I said, "Yes" because I knew that would make it easier for them. I wasn't though. Not at all. (Does that count as a lie for good because I was sparing their feelings?) I wasn't okay at all. I was scared. Then the anger started.

"Your mom died?" Eli asked, making my heart sink.

"And your grandmother?" Nathan had tears in his eyes. Ugh. I was the worst around kids.

I turned to Mr. and Mrs. M for help.

Mr. M said, "Shay's mother was sick. For a long time."

"Our friend Kevin's mom was sick," Nathan said, "and she died. We helped them sit Shiva.

"Did your mom and grandmother both have cancer?" Eli asked quietly.

Mrs. M took this one. "No, and we'll respect Shay's privacy and let her tell us what she wants to." From her expression, I knew I couldn't tell them about finding my mom in the abandoned row house, slumped on a gross couch, nor how long it took the ambulance to get there or how she was already probably dead when I found her.

I thought of some true things to say. "My mom's favorite color was red, and when she was a girl, she had such a beautiful smile she was a model for dentists' ads."

I didn't tell them all those beautiful teeth turned black before they fell out. I didn't tell them how we were all saving money in a cookie jar for her because this one time, when she was clean, she wanted new teeth, which cost a lot of money we didn't have. I went to add money to the jar once after babysitting a kid down the street, but the jar was empty.

Grandma saw me with the jar. "I hid it. I hid it all. You keep your money, Shay baby. You hide it." That was how I found out my mom was using again.

"That's cool." Eli smiled at Nathan, showing him all his teeth. Nathan did the same thing back. Then they had some (a million) questions.

"Did you sit Shiva when she died? Was your grandmother beautiful too? What was your grandmother's favorite color? What's your favorite color?" The questions meant the twins were onto other things than death.

"I like green." With that expert deflection, the twins were done with the questions. At that moment, I realized I didn't even have a favorite color. Huh. Such a simple thing not to have, which made me super sad.

I saw Mr. and Mrs. M exchange glances. They turned to me,

no frowns or anything. I was relieved they weren't mad. Every day, I upset the people in this family. They didn't deserve it. Mrs. M reached over to pat my hand. As she did that, I remembered, yes, Grandma was beautiful, so beautiful. I could see her face clearly. When Mrs. M reached out to me in support, I couldn't handle it. I started crying but didn't want to upset the twins AGAIN, so I coughed and spluttered, "Excuse me. I'll be right back" and ran out of the room. AGAIN.

I ran all the way up to my room on the third floor, right into my own bathroom. Avoiding the mirror (because gross, it would have been me with severe cry face), I splashed water on my face for about ten minutes. I was either embarrassing myself or RE-ALLY embarrassing myself around these poor people. They didn't deserve to have me inflicted on them.

Spock, the huge black, inscrutable cat sat on my bed. "What?" I asked him. "At least I didn't blow up at anyone for no reason."

I plopped on the bed next to him. He rubbed his head on my arm until I scratched it. "I have to go back," I said to the cat, who didn't respond. "They'll think I'm weird." The cat purred. "Glad you agree. See you later."

I returned to the study. The boys were watching a video while Mr. M peeled an apple for them and cut slices off. I slid back into my chair.

"Sorry about that." I tried to apologize but couldn't think of a lie.

The twins were quiet, which was awkward. After the twins

had their apple, Mr. M took them upstairs for bed.

Mrs. M asked if I wanted tea. I nodded. "Good. We can have a chat," she threw over her shoulder as she left the study.

A chat? That couldn't be good.

I knew they'd tell me they didn't want me to stay here anymore. Of course, they didn't. I was a mess—always on the verge of losing my shit—plus, I could blow at any second. I'd probably start crying again. I didn't recognize myself. All because of the fucking letter. I reread it over and over until Mrs. M came back and handed me a mug.

I took a sip. I tasted flowers.

Mr. M returned and took a cup. "Jasmine tonight."

Mrs. M said by way of explanation, "Can we talk about the letter?"

I nodded, wanting to say, *Sure, no biggie, I'm cool, everything's cool.* What I *actually* said was, "I understand if you want me to leave. I'm a mess and I keep scaring the twins. Now I may have to go live with my father anyway."

They sat there. Mrs. M got up—she had tears in her eyes—and came over to hug me. She put her arms around me. (This is so embarrassing.) I squirmed away from her and started crying.

"No, don't be nice. I can't handle it."

She went back to the couch next to Mr. M.

"Shay," he said, ignoring my outburst. "We want you to stay. The twins are fine."

My head spun. "Why do you want a messed-up kid like me living here?"

"We're foster parents. It's what we do."

At least they didn't say the usual lies: "You're not messed up, Shay," and the worst one, "We already love you, Shay."

I didn't understand them. At all. "I don't understand. You're so nice to me, and you don't even know me. I'm a liar and a bad person. There's a reason this is my fifth foster home."

Mrs. M had a worried expression on her face. "I'm sorry I tried to hug you. I just didn't know how to tell you we still want you to stay here. But we do."

Mr. M chimed in. "Of course, we do."

They needed me to tell them it was all okay. That their explanation of why they wanted a super fuckup around was a good one, believable.

"Okay. So, what if my father wants me to come live with him?"

Mrs. M shook her head. "Your father gave up his rights to you years ago. You may have to visit him, but you probably won't ever have to live with him again."

I handed them the letter. They read it together, concerned.

"Good, he's working at...Fortune Warehouse." Mrs. M handed it back to me.

I scanned it. "He drives a forklift." I squinted. "He's a terrible speller. He didn't say if he has a car."

There was a pause, my mind racing. I never thought about the day my father would be released. Would he come take me away? Was that legal? What if he took me but then got sent back to prison? What if I didn't want to go live with him? I didn't even know him. What if he was a total creeper?

I could tell the M's had the same questions I did. "I don't know what to think. He wants to see me."

Mr. M turned to me. "Do you want to see him?"

"I don't know. He's my father, so I guess. Maybe."

Mrs. M sagged a little. Was she disappointed? "It's totally up to you. We can take you to Harrisburg for a visit, unless he wants to come here. But again, it's up to you."

Mr. M also seemed disappointed. "Ms. Rhonda is coming over tomorrow night to check in. We can talk to her about your options then if you want."

"That's good news, right? That Ms. Rhonda is coming over. She may have more information about your father," said Mrs. M.

And I lie-nodded. That was terrible news.

Anger piled on anger, edging out my fear and sadness. Great. "Can't we call her instead?"

Mr. M shook his head. "She has to do home visits. You know, the usual drill."

I did know the drill. The social worker Happy Family Foster Home Visit Drill, where everyone is fake happy, everything is clean, no one is a creeper. I didn't realize the Morgensterns knew about the Happy Family Foster Home Visit Drill. "You know the drill?"

"You're not our first foster kid."

Really. This was news. I had a lot of feelings about that— relief and (oddly) jealousy, were right up there.

"We can tell you about Molly some other time," Mr. M said,

indicating that the topic was clearly off limits for the time being. Honestly, I was relieved they didn't want to talk about their other foster kid. Too much was happening already right now. Ugh.

"You should know that Craptastic Rhonda and I don't get along."

"She told me that when she dropped off the letter today," Mr. M said. "What happened between you two?"

I wanted to say that I would tell them about Rhonda some other time, just to be a brat, but instead, I said, "She's a human crap person who pretends to care but only listens to adults while pretending I don't exist."

"Shay, really? A 'human crap person'?"

"Yes. She's made of crap, she only eats crap, and she only does crappy things to people, like not ever calling back or checking in."

Mrs. M shook her head. "I don't know how to handle that. You won't tell us what she did."

"Just believe me when I tell you something. That's more than Craptastic Rhonda ever did."

"Okay, Shay. Okay. Tomorrow, we'll do the drill; we'll find out the rules with your father, okay?"

I wanted to believe it would be that easy, I really did. "Okay, thanks."

She picked up the remote. "Baking? It's bread week."

Mr. M and I nodded. They were watching this show where everyone baked while acting impossibly nice to one another. I imagined that, off camera, they were absolutely shitty, changing measurements on recipe printouts, swapping salt with sugar on someone else's table, turning ovens to the wrong temperature. It made the sugary-sweet way they acted palatable.

Mr. M turned to me in seriousness. "I want you to know she won't do crappy things with us around."

I didn't believe him, of course. I knew that Craptastic Rhonda's powers were too strong. (Spoiler: I was right to not believe him.) But I wanted to, in that moment. So, nodding, I picked up my mug. It was green, with trees and grass on it, an Earth Day mug. I realized I kind of really liked green after all. More than all the other colors? I wasn't sure, but I was sort of fond of this green mug with its flowery tea.

THE ANGER CHRONICLES | 47

CHAPTER SEVEN

TUESDAY WAS QUIET. Mrs. M and I went to the store, where we bought a ton of groceries, then returned home to put them away. I went upstairs for a nap because I was still tired all the time.

When Mr. M got home from work, he joined the twins and me in the study. We were still working on their homework, which, I had learned, was quite a process. Mrs. M had gotten them started after their snack, but then I volunteered to take over when she went to start dinner. We were almost done, even though we'd already taken several breaks.

Tuesday was quiet. Mrs. M and I went to the store, where we bought a ton of groceries, then returned home to put them away. I went upstairs for a nap because I was still tired all the time.

When Mr. M got home from work, he joined the twins and me in the study. We were still working on their homework, which, I had learned, was quite a process. Mrs. M had gotten them started after their snack, but then I volunteered to take over when she went to start dinner. We were almost done, even though we'd already taken several breaks.

A list of the breaks we took
1. Nathan needed to change his shirt because he was mad at Eli and didn't want to be dressed alike anymore
2. Eli needed to change his shirt because Nathan had changed his shirt
3. They burped at the same time, and we had to take a laugh break because it was actually pretty funny
4. Nathan had to change his shirt again because when he was laughing at the burps he drooled on his shirt, and Eli called him "gross."

I was doing a great job.

So far, the worst part of my day, my week, and my month happened later that evening after dinner. Mrs. M came into the study, where we were all watching TV.

"Shay, Ms. Rhonda is coming over in a little bit to check in."

Nathan said, "That's your social worker, right?"

Eli said, "She's craptastic, right?"

I nodded. "You're right Eli, but can you stop saying 'craptastic'?"

"Okay, Shay. Are you her boss?"

"I wish, Eli. Social workers are supposed to help foster kids adjust to new homes, new schools, and new families. Mostly, Rhonda ignores my phone calls. She pretends to take care of me while spending her time on other kids who don't cause her as much trouble."

Eli and Nathan looked back and forth at their parents.

Nathan turned to me. "Do you get a social worker when you're bad?"

"No."

Nathan stared at me. I don't think he believed me. I didn't blame him.

A little later, Mrs. M said, "My turn tonight. Okay, boys, bedtime. We have time for three books if we get moving right now."

The twins scrambled to their feet. As they left, Eli turned. "Good luck, Shay."

I gave him the thumbs-up. He acknowledged with a thumbs-up and chased his brother up the stairs.

Mr. M checked his phone. "Ms. Rhonda is on her way. We talked to her on the phone last week before we picked you up. How long have you known her?"

I thought. "About a year. After Ms. Kate quit, they assigned me Rhonda. Ms. Kate took care of me, so I trusted her. She believed me. Stuck up for me. Rhonda has a problem with me. She doesn't get me. She doesn't like me. I don't know why."

That was a lie. I did know why. I just wasn't ready to tell them what Rhonda's problem with me was though. I could tell Mr. M didn't quite believe that Rhonda was terrible to me, but he'd see. Why would he believe me? I was just a troubled foster kid.

"Well, let's get through this check-in as quickly as we can then." Mr. M went into the kitchen. I heard him filling the teakettle, making tea, which is the opposite of getting through anything quickly.

Mrs. M came back downstairs as the doorbell rang. Soon after, little thumps sounded from upstairs—the twins had climbed out of their beds to get a peek at a social worker.

Mrs. M opened the front door. "Hi. I'm Mrs. Morgenstern. Nice to meet you."

"Hi, I'm Rhonda Walker."

"That's Nathan and Eli." Mrs. M must have been pointing up the stairs. "Say hi to Ms. Rhonda, boys."

Together, "Hi, Ms. Rhonda."

"Hi, boys."

"Back to bed now."

The boys thumped back across the floor, into their beds.

Rhonda walked into the study with Mrs. M. I hadn't seen Rhonda in months, not since the Englands' house (foster family #3). Mr. M brought in a tray with mugs. He helped himself to a cookie off the plate as he introduced himself.

Rhonda and I eyed each other, just a little too long. "Hi, Shay," she said, just a little too enthusiastically, combined with a totally painted-on smile.

"Hi, Rhonda." I was as falsely enthusiastic as I could be, trying to remove that smile from her face. I followed up with "How are you," as more of a statement, as if I was on *Gossip Girl* being fake friends with someone who'd slept with my boyfriend, but I wasn't supposed to know, but I did. It worked. She stopped smiling and turned to Mr. and Ms. M.

"How's Shay doing? I saw that you only picked her up a few days ago."

"Shay's fine," Mr. M said. "She's registered at Consolidated Middle."

I chimed in, interrupting, "I can't wait. It's factory-shaped, but it has a great arts program." I didn't even know if there was an arts program, I simply wanted to be part of the conversation about me that was happening right in front of me.

The M's turned to me. They knew I was lying about the arts program. Consolidated Middle specialized in hormones, acne, and unpredictable mood swings. The M's hadn't known me for very long, but I was sure they also saw how differently I was acting. Good. This was who I was. I could be super fake sometimes, acting out lies about myself. I knew Rhonda knew I was acting. She came right at me.

"Well, I'm a fan of the arts, but Shay needs to be in a supported class for math." As if that wasn't enough information about my shitty math ability, she added, "Her math skills aren't very strong." She went on. "She's missed a lot of school because of her, you know, outbursts." That stung a little, but my pre-anger kicked in. I aimed at her weak spot.

"How's Mitch?" Then I explained to the M's. "Mitch is Rhonda's husband."

Rhonda tried to hide it, but I saw that I'd gotten to her because her face hardened. "We're still trying to work things out; thanks for asking." She wanted to say something else, but then I dug in a little more.

"They were separated the last time I saw Rhonda. When was that, October? Before I got moved to the Berrys'?"

Mrs. M said, "Shay." I think she was trying to stop me, but my anger had kicked in and was now fully in charge.

"Oh, it's okay. I don't mind that I didn't see my social worker once while I was at my fourth placement in a year. She was awfully busy with her—what do you call it, Rhonda, your case-load? But aren't I part of your caseload?"

Mr. M said, "Shay." His voice had a tone. I glared at him. "Please, Shay."

I didn't understand why Rhonda could get away with not doing her job, but I was in trouble for pointing it out.

"Shay, I'm on your side," Rhonda said, which caused my anger to finally spill over.

"You're not on my side! You ignore me. You don't believe me. You don't even like me."

"But, Shay," she started. I really hated when someone said your name over and over, trying to calm you down. It didn't work. "Shay, we can work this out. Calm down. Don't have another out-burst. Let's make a good impression with these nice people, Shay."

"It's okay, Rhonda—" Mrs. M started.

Calm down?

"Rhonda," I said, cutting her off. "Tell them what you told the Garbage People. Tell them you said I was unmanageable. Tell them about how you said no families would want me anymore."

Rhonda said, "Shay, you've had some difficult placements. It hasn't always been your fault."

Mrs. M was upset. "Can we have a conversation? Shay, please sit down." I was standing, my fists clenching and unclenching.

My anger exploded. "It's not fair! I hate this! Every damned time!" I ran out of the study, ran out of the house, and kept running.

"Shay!" Mr. Morgenstern called after me, but I didn't turn around. I ran down the street. Even though I didn't know where I was, I kept running. I hated when adults always took each other's sides. Kids were always wrong, even when they were right. Even when adults did terrible things, no one believed the kid.

I ran until Consolidated Middle rose up in front of me, all factorylike and imposing. I stopped running and slumped against the fence, where I immediately started crying. Really sobbing. I never cried, but here I was, being a little baby. Ugh. I'd really fucked everything up. Again. Typical me and my anger, destroying everything all the time.

Now that the Morgensterns had seen the real me, no way would they want me to live with them, much less be around their kids. I'd be plopped back into the group home for sure. I'd never go to the factory-shaped middle school with the fake arts program. My anger, which had fucked me in the past several times, had really fucked me up good this time.

And then the cop showed up.

CHAPTER EIGHT

I WAS SUPER busy, sitting on the sidewalk, leaning against the fence around the factory-school, wiping my runny nose on my sweatshirt when a cop car drove slowly past me. At least I'd stopped crying. The cops were no friends of mine, so I got up and started walking.

"Hey, kid. Kid!"

I stopped.

"There's a curfew on school nights, you know."

"I know." A lie. I didn't know. I'd lived here for about ten minutes. How could I know there was a curfew? Then I lied again.

"My cat ran away." Here came the important detail to make the lie more believable. "His name is Spock."

"Where's your coat? Where do you live?"

Now I was in a bind. I didn't know the street where the

Morgensterns lived, or any streets, actually, so I took a shot. "I live on Maple."

The officer stopped the car. "You're pretty far from home. Get in, kid. I'll take you. The cat'll find its way home. They always do."

I wasn't stupid—I knew how cops treated runaway kids. I knew the horror stories. At the same time, I was freezing. Who ran away without a coat? This dummy. First, I only took one sandwich, then, three days later, no coat. I was the absolute worst at running away. (*Sorry, Eli. I know we don't say "dummy."*) The thought of never seeing Eli and Nathan again made me start crying. In front of a cop. Super dumb. Also, apparently, I'd gotten a little attached to the twins. The main rule of being a foster kid: Don't get attached. Never get attached. Damn. I was the worst.

I opened the door and slid into in the backseat. It was a familiar view.

"What's the address on Maple?" the cop asked as he started driving.

Pick a number. "One twenty-three."

The cop met my eyes in the rearview mirror. The car stopped. He turned in his seat. "You're crying."

Officer Obvious, right?

"What's the deal, kid?"

I didn't say anything. I didn't want to return to the M's house, with smug, separated Rhonda there.

"Okay, kid. We'll go to the station. Figure all this out." He turned away and started driving. The radio squawked, but I didn't understand what was said. He responded into his handheld microphone "Got her right here. Give me the address." More squawks. "Got it. I'll take her there; you give them a call and let them know I have her."

Apparently, the Morgensterns had called the police. Officer Obvious, here, would get a bonus (probably extra doughnuts) because he'd found me. Except I wasn't planning on returning to the Morgensterns'. No way. They'd be mad for sure. I'd be back in the group home the next day. Before he could start driving again, I pulled at the door handle. Nothing happened. I pulled harder.

"Doors don't open from back there."

Shit. I knew that already. Dumb.

"Kid, are you fighting with your parents?"

"My parents are dead." Half a truth, half a lie, but it worked.

"I'm sorry about that. So, who are you staying with?" Officer Obvious pulled the car over so he could face me. "I'm trying to help. You can't stay outside tonight. I got an address, so that's where we're going."

I'd stopped crying (yay), my tears replaced with anger. I fumed silently. He stopped trying to extract information from the witness and drove to the Morgensterns'.

"Wait here," he said after pulling up. As if I could get out anyway.

He went to the front door and rang the bell. Mr. and Mrs. Morgenstern appeared, craning their necks, trying to see me in the cop car. I slumped down. Suddenly, they were at the car. The cop opened the door.

"Shay, please come inside," Mr. Morgenstern said. "Rhonda told us why you two don't get along. We'll talk to the agency to try to get you a new social worker."

"Please come inside, Shay," Mrs. Morgenstern added, then shrugged. "I don't know what else to say."

Why weren't they mad? I'd be mad.

Officer Obvious added his two cents. "Go back inside with these nice people tonight, and tomorrow, you can work things out. Otherwise, I have to take you to the group home by way of the station. But you have to promise me that you won't run away again tonight. It's too cold out here."

I didn't say anything. I was still mad at Rhonda, at myself, at everything. Officer Obvious pulled me aside and privately asked if I felt safe with the Morgensterns. No one had ever asked me if I felt safe before. In my whole life. I almost cried at the kindness contained in that small act. Who was I, accepting kindness from a cop?

But of course, the Morgensterns were safe. Super safe. I told him that I was safe. He handed me a business card.

"This has my cell number on it. I'm on night shift for the next two weeks, but you can call anytime."

I took the card, still shocked at the kindness. We walked to the Morgensterns'.

Mrs. Morgenstern said, "Shay, stay here for tonight. Tomorrow, if you don't want to stay, we'll contact someone at the agency."

"Not Rhonda," Mr. Morgenstern added. "We promise."

Officer Obvious handed a card to Mr. Morgenstern too. Turning to me, he said, "Please go inside, Shay."

Then something strange happened. They all stood there, waiting. It was weird, three adults waiting for me to make a decision. Very weird. Then I realized no one was wearing a coat. We were all freezing. I couldn't run away tonight; it wasn't smart. Tomorrow, I could find a new placement. Plus, the thought of spending another night on the third floor in my own bedroom wasn't awful.

"Okay. I guess let's go inside."

Mrs. Morgenstern was about to cry. Mr. Morgenstern put his arm around her shoulders as Officer Obvious stuck out his hand to shake hands with me.

"Promise me you'll stay inside tonight. It'll get even colder."

I nodded. Then, I shook a cop's hand for the first time in my life.

"It was nice meeting you folks," he said to all three of us as we turned up the walkway to the house.

"Thank you, Officer," Mrs. Morgenstern replied.

As soon as we got inside, we went into the study. Mrs. Morgenstern grabbed a blanket from the chair, opened it, and moved as though she wanted to cover me. She hesitated. "Are you cold? Do you want this? You must be freezing."

I nodded. Gently, she put the blanket around me. She took another off the couch for herself. Mr. Morgenstern had gone into the kitchen.

"I was really worried about you, Shay. It's cold and dark

outside, and when you ran out, I thought of all the terrible things that could happen."

I didn't know how to answer this. We sat there in silence.

Mr. Morgenstern came back in with a tray holding three mugs of hot chocolate and a jar of marshmallow cream. *These people with their trays of hot drinks in mugs.*

"Do you like marshmallow in your hot chocolate?" he asked. I shrugged. He scooped some out to float it in one of the mugs. "Try this."

I did. It was soothing, warm, and creamy, and the marshmallow topping was amazing. I actually forgot everything else for a minute. The M's shared a blanket on the couch as they drank their hot chocolate with marshmallow. We were the picture-perfect family, except for me—the problem foster kid with the anger issues who ran away.

Mrs. M put her mug on the table next to the couch. "Shay, Rhonda told us what happened at the Millers'."

Shit. My worst secret, revealed. Fuck Rhonda's big mouth. "That's why I hate Rhonda. She didn't believe me. Ms. Kate was the only one who knew I was telling the truth. Rhonda only believed what she read in the report."

"Do you want to tell us what happened?"

I shook my head.

"Okay, you don't have to, but we want your side of the story too." Mrs. M picked up her mug again.

No way, not tonight, maybe not ever. But I said, "Okay, someday" so they'd change the conversation.

"Shay, we want you to stay here with us," Mr. Morgenstern said. "We all want you to stay, but we have to talk about the running away. Apparently, you've run away before."

Fuck Rhonda.

Mrs. Morgenstern tag-teamed him. "It can't be an option if you stay here. Because of the twins. If you staying here doesn't work out, that's one thing. We can explain that. But running away will make them think you're abandoning them. They won't be able to understand that."

As far as getting scolded went, it was pretty tame, in my experience. As far as pep talks went, it was shitty. Abandonment? I didn't want to tell her what real abandonment was or how it felt, but her talking about me doing that to the twins broke my heart, so I had to explain.

"I couldn't stay here another second with Rhonda; I just couldn't. You don't understand."

"As foster parents, we understand that earning the trust of a foster kid is tough. Tougher if the kid has been through some shi—" Mrs. Morgenstern caught herself, then continued. "Some shit. There is no denying that you've been through some shit. I don't expect you to trust us immediately. But I promise you, Shay—we will never lie to you. We will make mistakes, but we will always act in your best interest."

I almost reminded her about the custard pie lie but didn't because she was trying to be sincere.

I sat there.

"Okay," Mr. Morgenstern said. "I don't know why you ran

out tonight. But it scared us a lot. I want you to understand that. We don't know you, but we do care about you."

At the silence, I guessed it was my turn to talk. I said, "Okay, okay" so it wasn't my turn anymore.

Then we sat there for about a hundred years. No one talked. Very awkward. I picked up my hot chocolate, but it had cooled. Now I was responsible for not abandoning the twins AND making sure these grown-ass adults didn't worry about me. It was too much. I put the mug back down.

"I don't think I can handle this."

"Okay." Mrs. M was sad. "It's up to you. We can't make you stay."

"Why would you want to have me around anyway? I'm obviously messed up. I freaked out on Rhonda. Plus, I'm so dumb; I ran away in February without a coat and got caught in about three minutes. Why would anyone want to be around me even?"

Mr. M's face got all red. He stood up, which was almost comical because he was *under tall*. "Stop that. You're not dumb, Shay Walker. Rhonda isn't a great social worker; that's not your fault. You got harassed at a placement, and no one believed you. That's not your fault. The twins think you're funny and interesting. You're great with Eli. I enjoy talking about *Dune* with you. We're foster parents. If you were flawless, we'd never have met you."

Mrs. M put her hand on his arm. "You're a teenager, and you've had a hard time. But no teenager in the history of the world has ever been flawless. We knew that when we agreed to foster you. We want you to stay."

Another hundred years passed in silence as we all waited for me to speak. They wanted to know what my plan was. I wanted to stay. Then, I wanted to leave. In waves, not in parts. My whole being wanted to leave one moment; the next moment, my whole self wanted to stay.

I didn't know what to say, so I said, "Turner."

"What?" Mrs. M asked.

"Turner. My last name is Turner, not Walker. Rhonda's last name is Walker."

They gaped at each other.

"Mr. M called me Shay Walker, you know, during his speech."

They gaped at each other again and, oddly, burst out laughing. I didn't think it was that funny, but it was a little funny, plus it got me out of answering the question.

"I'm sorry, Shay." Mr. M apologized. "I have no excuse."

"It's fine. You just met me. I don't even know your address or your first names."

"I'm Ravid. This is Miriam, my wife. It's nice to have you here, Shay Turner."

I decided to go along, even though I was still completely undecided about everything. "Nice to meet you Ravid and Miriam." I stuck out my hand. They both eagerly shook it. I guessed they thought I'd decided to stay because their faces relaxed.

"Tomorrow, if it's okay with you, Shay, maybe you don't go to school. We can begin the process to find you a new social worker; you can settle in a bit more. Mr. M will be at work all day;

the twins will be at school. I have to go to the office for a few hours, so you'll be alone here, unless you want to come with me."

Were they allowing me to stay in the house by myself? I couldn't believe it. It was a Test of Trust, obviously. But more important, I didn't have to start school tomorrow!

"Sounds great," I said quickly. "You'd let me stay here alone?"

"She'll be alone here?" Mr. M agreed with me. Neither one of us trusted me.

"It will only be for a few hours," Mrs. M said.

Mr. M was obviously the more realistic of the two. I mean, I might steal all their... I scanned the room for something to steal. Books. They had books, but I didn't see anything of real value. Well, I'd get a chance to scope around more for stuff to steal tomorrow because Mrs. M had won this discussion.

I wasn't always a thief, but I needed to know my options. Then I found out that they thought I was crazy.

"Shay," Mr. M began. "We got an appointment for a therapist we want you to start seeing."

I didn't know what to say. What did one say when one's foster family called them crazy?

Mrs. M tried to help. "You may have some issues with anger." *Ya think?* "And we really want you to stay here, but your anger scares us."

I couldn't stop my sarcasm. "Maybe then *you* should see a shrink if you're so scared."

My sarcasm removed the gentleness from Mr. M's request.

"We'd really prefer you to talk to someone if you're planning to stay here."

Oh wow. The Big Threat. I was immediately angry. Really angry. But a part of me realized they were right. Which made me even angrier. Fuck them.

Maybe living with my dad wasn't such a bad idea. He wouldn't kick me out. He couldn't. He owed me. I wouldn't mind as much if I screwed up around him. He was a screw up. He'd understand. It couldn't be any worse than living here. Plus, he was a former addict—he understood about anger, stress, and all the accompanying shit. I wondered if he'd want to regain custody of me. I decided I would to try to go live with my father. He probably wouldn't be as disappointed in me as the Morgensterns were bound to be. Decision made—I'd live with my father. My anger cooled a little. My stay here with the Morgensterns was now officially temporary.

Until I could get to my dad's, I had to stay somewhere. This place was way better than the group home. If you've never shared a bathroom with eight other teenaged girls, you didn't know how amazing it was to have your own. I had to agree to the M's terms and see a shrink for as long as it took to get to my father's apartment.

"Okay. Fine. You win. I'll see a shrink."

One quick glance passed between them, during which I think they had a whole conversation without speaking. Someday, I wanted to be able to do that, make eye contact with someone and have whole sentences run between us silently.

Mrs. M said, "You have an appointment tomorrow with Dr. Carol Webster."

"Wow that was fast. You must think I'm really crazy."

"The appointment was already made when you came here. We didn't get a chance to mention it." Mr. M was a bad liar compared to his wife.

We drank cold hot chocolate in awkward silence. Actually, awkward didn't even begin to describe it. I was the best at turning things into the worst.

Finally, I said, "I think I'll head up to bed." That way, I could lie awake all night stressing out about seeing a therapist and worrying about if my father was a loser, a creeper, a drug addict, or all three.

They both said, "Good night, Shay."

I took my mug into the kitchen, washed it, dried it, and put it away. They were talking quietly in the study, probably about me. I thought about listening in but didn't want to know what they were saying, so I went upstairs.

I climbed into bed, thinking about how Mr. M didn't trust me to stay in the house alone yet, which I thought showed good instincts on his part. Why would anyone trust any foster kid that quickly? Mrs. M was obviously trying to show me that she trusted me in the hope I would trust her in return. That's not how it worked.

People tricked people into trusting them all the time, then screwed them over when they needed something. Which one of them would screw me over? In my experience, it was inevitable.

At least Rhonda would be out of the picture soon. No one cared what I wanted, but the M's probably only had to ask politely to get Rhonda out of my life. The good news was I didn't have to go to school yet.

It took a while, but I fell asleep after Spock curled up with me and started purring. I had the weirdest dream—in it, I was crying. At school. In front of the entire school, including Rhonda the Craptastic. I was carrying Spock in a cat carrier that I'd taken from the M's. Obviously, it was the dream of a crazy person. I didn't even like cats.

CHAPTER NINE

I WOKE UP super early. It was sort of dark but sort of light outside. This time of day always made me sad. The cat was curled at my feet. He stretched, then curled up on my lap. I wondered if my father would let me get a cat. We sat there for a while until it got a little lighter outside. I listened to the family morning noises with Spock.

By the time I went downstairs, the twins and Mr. M were gone.

Mrs. M called from the study, "Good morning, Shay."

I peeked in. "Good morning."

"I'm leaving in half an hour to go to the synagogue for a couple hours. You can come or not; it's up to you. I'm letting you know so you can decide. Your appointment is at 3:30."

Ah yes. My appointment with the esteemed Dr. Carol

Webster, therapist extraordinaire.

"Okay." I went into the kitchen for breakfast.

(This might surprise you.) I went to the synagogue with Mrs. M. It wasn't because of religion or anything. I didn't want to snoop around their house for items to steal. Mostly, I really didn't want to sit around all day alone, dreading the shrink, school, my father—basically everything. Mrs. M was definitely surprised when I said I wanted to go with her, almost as surprised as I was. She was also pleased and smiled. *Genuine.*

At the synagogue, I wandered around for a while. Then I read in an empty classroom, where Mrs. M found me.

"Let's go have snack with the day care."

I was all about snacks—I practically jumped out of the bean-bag chair.

I was impressed when we walked into the day care. All the littles sat in tiny chairs at little tables with little plates in front of them. The adults (Miss Midge and Miss Beth) were distributing snacks. Mrs. M gestured that I should take an empty seat. I was way too huge for the chair. All the little faces stared at me. One kid smiled shyly at me. I smiled back with a little wave. Then, all the littles wanted me to wave at them. Beth put some grapes on the plate in front of me.

"Thank you," I said. Almost as one, the littles said, "You're welcome!" I cracked up.

The snack was grapes, veggie straws, little cheeses, animal crackers, and juice boxes. Not too shabby. The little next to me needed help with her juice box. Suddenly, they all needed help with something and came to me instead of the adults.

Midge said, "Shay, you're great with the kids. Want a job this summer?"

I almost said *yes* but remembered I'd be living with my father by then. I shrugged in response.

After snack time, I stayed around to help clean up and ended up reading at story time. Mrs. M came by when it was time to leave. I had two kids on my lap and three more sprawled out in front of me. I'd just finished reading *Stellaluna*, my favorite from before everything turned to shit.

She said, "Say goodbye to Shay, kids."

"Bye, Shay!" was followed by hugs from all the littles. The kid who waved during snack time came over. He stuck out his hand very seriously. After I shook it, he marched away to play.

As we walked out, Mrs. M said, "You're really great with kids."

"Thanks. Kids are easy. They don't expect anything except snacks and fun."

Next on the agenda was my shrink appointment. We drove to a huge, fancy house made of stone, with an enormous porch and massive trees in the yard. All the houses on this block were this fancy.

Mrs. M pulled into the driveway. She pointed to the side door. "That's the entrance. I'll be waiting for you out front in an hour." She wasn't coming in with me. Now I was pre-angry.

"You're not coming in with me?"

"Do you want me to come in with you?"

Not now I didn't. "No, it's fine." *I'll get through this alone.
Like I do everything.*

She said, "Shay," as I put my hand on the car door handle.

Here came the pre-shrink pep talk.

"I think you're really strong. Resilient."

You also think I'm crazy. I knew I should thank her, even
though I thought she was full of shit. "Thanks." I opened the car
door, got out, and went to the door.

A fancy wooden sign said, "Dr. Carol Webster." Underneath
another read, "Please come in and have a seat."

I entered a small waiting room: two chairs, a small table
with magazines, and a fish tank. I smelled food cooking and heard
a TV. The shrink's family must be home. I wondered if she had any
kids, maybe even a teenaged daughter. What would they do if their
daughter had so many mental problems she needed a shrink?
Where did a shrink send her daughter? To a friend? How would it
work?

A door opened. There she was, my new shrink. (I should tell
you that I made a terrible first impression on Dr. Carol. Everything's fine now, but whew, this first time was a doozy.) She came
out to greet me, wearing a fancy white silky shirt, a silky scarf
around her neck, and black pants. She was white, middle-aged—
probably around thirty—and had high hair, all poufed up. Her
glasses hung on a chain around her neck.

"Hi, Shay. You can call me Carol or Dr. Carol." She stuck out
her hand, which I shook as professionally as I could.

"Hi, Dr. Carol." I wasn't planning on getting attached, so I used her title. That way, she'd

know I had boundaries. "Nice house."

"Thank you. Do you want a bottle of water?"

I said no, silently judging her for destroying the planet.

She led me back to an office with two couches, a desk, and wide windows filled with plants. She gestured to two chairs. "Let's sit here. Get acquainted with each other."

We talked about basic information for a minute or two. Mostly, she was trying to prove to me that she was "cool" and "nonjudgmental." Also, she'd read my case history. Five foster families, lots of family drama before that, blah blah blah. I knew I had to handle her carefully—she was a professional. She could probably smell a lie from a mile away. The best strategy would be a few lies mixed in with some truths. She wouldn't know what hit her.

When she asked why I thought I was there, I already wore my Lie Game face.

"My anger." (Truth.)

She asked, "When did it start?"

"The Millers. Foster family number two." (Truth.) "One of the real family kids stole money from Mrs. Miller's brother, who was visiting. They blamed it on me." (Lie.) "I got punished and grounded." (Lie.) "I was super mad because no one believed me." (Truth.)

I stopped talking. Here was where I'd find out if she believed any or all of it. If she asked me a general question (for example, *What was your punishment?*), she believed me. If she asked me a detail question (*How much money was stolen?*), she probably didn't.

But she didn't ask me any questions at all, which threw me. I thought what I'd said was interesting. If I was her, I'd have asked at least one question. She was a shrink seeing a kid with anger issues but had no questions? No curiosity at all? She must be a terrible shrink, I decided. Then I got mad because this was shaping up to be another waste of time. Not that I had anything better to do, but I'd be mad every second I was here. As often as I get mad, you'd think I'd get some enjoyment out of it, but I didn't. I didn't enjoy any of it.

Then, we had a terrible conversation.

"Do you think your anger is a problem?"

"No."

"You don't? Didn't you run away from the Morgensterns' last night because you got angry?"

Shit. All the adults were discussing me behind my back, again.

"You already know, so why ask me?"

"Ms. Rhonda called me last night. She thought it was important we start working together."

"Rhonda the Craptastic hates me so anything she does is the opposite of what she should do for me."

"'Rhonda the Craptastic,' huh? That's clever. Have you come up with a name for me?"

"Sure, let's talk about you. That's a great use of my time. My name for you is Rich White Lady. Who's paying you to waste my time here?"

"The state pays for my services with foster children. Don't you think you should know some more about me before you give me a nickname?"

"Naw. I'm good. Are we done yet?"

"Not quite."

We sat there in silence for a minute or two. I wanted to run screaming out of the room, but when I was mad, my stubborn streak occasionally became a useful tool.

"So, Shay, in these visits, we'll work on your anger."

"I'm not coming back."

"Why not?"

"I don't want to lose my anger. It protects me when no one else does."

"Give me an example."

"When I realized Rhonda was a shitty social worker, I got mad. I stopped believing she would ever take my side. I stopped being disappointed by her."

"Your anger prevented you from being hurt."

"Not hurt, disappointed."

"Who else has disappointed you?"

In my head, I screamed, *Everyone*. I didn't say it out loud, but immediately, I had tears in my eyes. I was furious with myself for that. *Well played, Rich White Lady. Well played. You are indeed a worthy adversary.*

She knew she'd struck a nerve and probably guessed I wasn't happy about it. She went to her desk, then came back and handed me a notebook as if I was in a teen drama movie. "This is for you to use to write down when you get angry."

Was. She. Kidding.

I slammed the notebook on the table, fuming. "Are you fucking kidding me?" *Pick your battle now, Rich White Lady. Redirect my tone or my language. Either way, I win because I'm in control; we're not talking about my anger anymore.* But she was a fierce competitor.

"My job here is to help you stay out of the group home. That's all. Whether you stay with the Morgensterns or with another family or with another three families until you're eighteen, your anger will be your main enemy. If you can't manage it, you'll age out of the foster system, sharing a bathroom with five girls in the group home."

Wow. Ouch. Her bit about sharing the bathroom hit home. Deeply home. *Damn, Rich White Lady.*

We sat there. I wasn't ready to concede complete defeat yet, so I tried to act salty.

"So, I should write 'I got angry on Tuesday'?"

She tilted her head at me. She knew I was being defiant on purpose. "No. I think you know what I mean. Write what was happening, how angry you got, who you were mad at—you know, details. That way, we can figure out what makes you angry."

"I already know what makes me angry. People. People make me angry." I picked up the notebook. "Do you want me to write that?"

She laughed. I wasn't trying to be funny, but I kind of was.

She sat back and studied me. "Do you want to tell me what really happened at the Millers'?" She'd known I was lying about something getting stolen.

It caught me off guard; I couldn't prevent reacting as my face burned. I stared at my hands as I scolded myself silently. *No no no. Just tell her you weren't lying. You can do it.* Turned out, I couldn't do it. I was too weak. I hated myself. Minutes ago, I'd met this Rich White Lady, who was already inside my head. Ugh. I really was the worst liar.

When I thought about what had really happened at the Millers', I started crying in front of yet another stranger. I was a mess of a person. Ugh.

She silently pushed a box of tissues across a table to me, which I ignored, wiping my eyes on my shirt. I sat there, staring at the floor.

"That's probably in my file," I said. "You could just read about it instead of making me say it."

She nodded. "I did read it. And I certainly don't want you to repeat what he said to you. I want to know why you lied about it to me."

"'Cause it was gross." I wiped my nose on my shirt again. "And I don't want to say it. I don't even want to talk about it. Ever."

She got up again and got a pen from her desk. She handed it to me. It was a fancy pen, one of the kinds you have to click. "I love these pens," she said, obviously changing the subject, of course.

I clicked it and scribbled on the first page of the notebook. The pen glided across the paper, a Fremen riding a sandworm across the desert. I shook my head. "Thanks, but I can't take this."

She tilted her head a little. "Why not?"

"It's too nice." I got choked up, repeating, "It's too nice."

She studied me for a long second. "Sometimes, it's easier to write when you enjoy the actual writing part. Put the pen and notebook somewhere safe and write whatever you want. It doesn't have to be about your anger. You can share parts with me or not; it's up to you."

"I'll never write down what Billy said to me," I vowed (and have kept that vow to this day).

"Oh, that's perfectly okay—he said terrible things to you. It's up to you what you write."

She believed me? Was that even possible? No. It was a ruse.

"You believe me?" I couldn't help asking.

"Of course," she answered as if it was that simple. "Why wouldn't I?"

"Because I'm an excellent liar, and maybe I wanted to get him in trouble."

"Shay, you are indeed an excellent liar. You certainly have some good reasons to lie. You should know, however, that you have a 'tell' when you lie. Poker players have tells when they're bluffing—they stare at their cards or shuffle their poker chips. You have one too."

She was a professional, that was for sure. More important, this piece of information was concerning to me.

"What's my tell?" I had to fix this. Quickly.

"You look down at the floor when you lie."

I was shocked. It was such an obvious tell. I would definitely have to work on that. I was about to start at a new school. All my tools needed to be sharp and ready.

As if she was reading my mind, Dr. Carol said, "So you're starting school this week. Let's talk about surviving the rest of eighth grade."

At the end of the time, we said goodbye. I walked out with the notebook and pen.

Mrs. M picked me up. "How'd it go?"

I one-word answered her. "Fine."

She wanted more, but I couldn't.

The rest of the afternoon and evening were also fine, except for the dread of school. The dread began as a small nugget of doubt in the early afternoon but turned into an all-consuming mind-sucking brain drain that ruined everything it touched, including sleep.

When I finally turned off my light, my dumb brain kicked into high gear. I worried about my locker, lunch in the cafeteria, getting to my classes on time, and, of course, being the New Kid in February. I should have been an expert by now, but it got worse each time. I tried to tell myself it wouldn't be that bad—I might even enjoy it. But I couldn't lie to myself. It was going to be awful.

CHAPTER TEN

MY ALARM WENT off, but I had gotten almost no sleep. Everything was in slow motion. I was already super depressed mixed with anxious. First day of school. Again. I washed up, got dressed in my uniform (which was super weird), and went downstairs. A new backpack sat, propped in my chair—green, with shoulder straps, a water bottle holder, and zippers that actually worked. Notebooks, a pencil case, and a binder from some accounting seminar weighed it down.

Mr. M said, "That's yours for now, Shay. If you want a different one, we'll get one this weekend. The binder is from my job—we forgot to grab you one, so we'll replace it."

"Thanks, this is great. Just great." I really meant it.

Then the twins came down for breakfast, with uniforms that matched mine. We were triplets. Their pants and shirts were a size too large, so I guessed they would grow into them, with belts to keep their pants up. They were very cute. I'd never dressed the same as somebody else before. Weird.

"Shay," Mr. M said. "What's your favorite takeout food? We'll do something special tonight to celebrate your first day."

I turned to the twins. "You guys want pizza?"

They started jumping up and down and cheering. I turned back to Mr. M.

"I love kale salads. How about kale salads?" It got silent. I winked at the boys and smiled, so they knew I was kidding.

They started chanting, "Pizza! Pizza!" and the M's laughed.

"Pizza it is. Let's go boys." Mr. M kissed Mrs. M goodbye before leaving. Really nuclear-family stuff. I watched this show as a complete outsider.

Mrs. M handed me a paper bag. "Peanut butter, some cookies, carrot sticks. We can get different food if you want."

I unzipped my backpack and tucked my lunch inside. "I've never packed my lunch before."

"Oh. Would you prefer the school lunch? I think it's..." She checked a calendar on the fridge. "...hot dogs, fruit salad cups, broccoli spears." Then she made a face and turned to me.

I shook my head. "I'm probably the only kid in America that hates hot dogs."

"No, the twins won't eat them either. Shay, listen."

I waited for her wise words of advice to a foster kid in eighth grade starting her third new school that year. What could she possibly say that would convince me that all the doomy and gloomy thoughts I'd been having weren't true?

"I don't know what to tell you," she said. "It's February, and it's eighth grade. If you make it back here in one piece tonight, we'll celebrate you surviving your first day."

I was glad she didn't try to sugarcoat it, but I would have appreciated maybe a little sugarcoating. Survive? Make it back in one piece? Was I going into battle?

Mr. Stetson, aka "Pod-nah," walked me to homeroom through the loud, chaotic hallway. Everyone was at their locker or yelling or running around. He high-fived a lot of kids while I got a lot of stares, of course. Everyone was wearing the same uniform, which was weird but also kind of cool. There were Black kids, Asian kids, mixed kids, two kids in wheelchairs, one kid with a dog with an orange vest. Then, I saw the girl from the principal's office yesterday, Charlotte, standing with a bunch of girls.

"Hey!" she yelled when she saw me. A lot of kids turned to see who she was yelling to.

Mr. Pod-nah waved her over and said, "Shay, this is Charlotte Dawkins—Charlie. Charlie, take care of Shay, okay? Be nice. She's in Mr. Hamilton's homeroom, same as you."

Charlie said, "You're new. That's why your mom was here yesterday. I didn't get suspended, as you can see."

Mr. Pod-nah held up his hand. "You will get suspended if you actually fight. So, stop cursing at Jamie in science. You two seem to be getting along fine now." He gestured to the group of girls Charlotte had been standing with. One of them, who I took to be Jamie, waved at us and immediately rolled her eyes before turning back to the group.

"She's a bitch," Charlie said to me, to which Mr. Pod-nah said, "Language" because that was what adults did.

"Well, she is," she said. "Come on, new kid." She turned to walk back to her group.

"She's Shay!" Mr. Pod-nah said loudly to Charlie's back.

I followed her as one of the teachers started herding kids into her classroom. Charlie and I pushed through the crowd to the last door on the left. Kids lined up outside the room, where a man with a clipboard stood.

"Mr. Ham, we got a new kid," Charlie said loudly.

Mr. Ham's annoyance flicked across his face for one millisecond. Then he said, "Hey, you must be Shay. I'm Mr. Hamilton, welcome to 240. Have you been to your locker yet?"

I shook my head.

"Charlie, take Shay to her locker, would you? Your combination is on your schedule. Be back here in five minutes." He went back to taking attendance as the kids walked into homeroom.

Charlie opened my locker for me, then stood there as I took out my notebooks, pencil case, and the binder. "You won't need all that stuff. We have an assembly first period. Just bring a notebook and a pen. Is that your lunch? I don't usually eat lunch. We're on diets. Was that your real mom yesterday?"

I knew she already knew the answer. "No."

"Foster mother?"

Whatever. She'd find out sooner or later. "Yes."

"Where's your real mom?"

"My real mom is a nanny for a royal family in France. When I fell in love with one of the sons, a prince, she sent me back here for a year to get over him." It was a plot from a *Sweet Valley High* book I read over the weekend.

Charlie laughed. Hard. "Okay. I get it."

We went back to homeroom. Mr. Hamilton pointed to the last seat in the last row. Perfect. Back here, no one stared at me. The loudspeaker chimed. It got quiet.

The kid in front of me turned around and whispered, "Hi, I'm Marshall."

"Marshall!" Mr. Hamilton yelled. "Announcements!" Marshall swiveled around. Mr. Hamilton focused on his computer as the announcements droned on.

Mitchell faced me again. "Who starts a new school in February? Didja get kicked out?"

Pre-angry now, but I couldn't blow this early on my New Kid debut. I decided to have some fun with Marshall. So, I told him a different plot. "No, I didn't get kicked out. I was at the mall one day and met a boy. He was part of a group that collected money for charity. We fell in love."

"Marshall! Turn around."

Marshall faced the front of the class, then leaned back and whispered out of the side of his mouth, "What happened next?"

"I gave up my designer dresses and purses to help raise money for his charity. Turns out it was a cult."

"What!" Marshall exclaimed loudly.

"Marshall!" barked Mr. Hamilton from behind his computer.

The bell rang. Everyone stood, but no one moved except the first row, who followed Mr. Ham out. We left homeroom, marching single file, alphabetical order (except me, of course) to the auditorium.

"What happened next?"

"My sister pretended to join the cult to rescue me. They figured out she was a spy and almost killed her." We arrived at the auditorium and filed in. Marshall was trying to sit next to me, but Charlie pulled me out of line next to her. Marshall tried to sit in front of me but got caught.

"Marshall, stay in line."

Maybe Mr. Hamilton didn't notice I was out of line. Or didn't care.

"Why are you talking to Marshall?" Charlie wanted to know.

"I was telling him my story of when I was in a cult, courtesy of *Sweet Valley High*."

Charlie laughed. "He's so dumb. But he is cute. He plays baseball."

"Do you like him?" I tried to imagine myself liking Marshall and failed.

She tossed her hair. "No. I had a boyfriend who's in ninth grade. I'm single right now. Have you ever had a boyfriend?" Then she followed with, "Anyone ever kiss you?"

I remembered Billy trying to kiss me at the Garbage People's house, getting mad at me when I didn't let him, and the nasty gross things he said about me, my mother, and my grandma. I remembered no one believing me when I told them what he did and being put in a new foster home two days later.

I got angry at Charlie's question. Instantly, the anger was lightning striking a dry forest. It took everything in me to not spew a flash fire at Charlie. My anger had a mind of its own. I couldn't speak, not even to find a lie.

"Are you blushing?" she asked as the lights dimmed.

A video started, the music blaring.

Charlie whispered, "Come with me," and stood up. I stood up. She gestured for me to follow her. I did. We walked past a teacher who weakly tried to stop us.

"Bathroom," Charlie whispered. The teacher nodded. We left the auditorium. "Stupid drinking and driving video. We see it every year. We can't even drive yet." We passed the bathroom and rounded a corner.

Charlie stopped. "Are you afraid we'll get in trouble for cutting the assembly?"

I told her the truth. "I don't care."

"Cool."

Then we cut the assembly. Down some stairs and out a door with a sign that threatened, "Alarm will sound if opened," in huge, red letters. A brick propped it open. Charlie pushed the door open to where two girls waited. I recognized Jamie, who nodded at me.

"Shay, these bitches are Jamie and Toya."

I nodded first at Jamie, who sized me up, then turned away without saying anything. Jamie was the kid who judged everybody by whether she thought she could take them in a fight. When she turned away, it signaled to everyone: I can take her. (Spoiler: she couldn't.)

Charlie shook her head at Jamie. I turned to Toya.

Immediately, I got a funny feeling in my stomach, as if I'd known her before or something. She had a short, natural cut and warm, brown eyes. My crush on Toya started right that second. (You should know I've had crushes on girls before. Boys too. Am I gay? Bi? What am I? It's exhausting to think about, so I don't.)

But Toya was cute, and I was hooked.

CHAPTER ELEVEN

"SHAY?" CHARLIE HAD said something. She was staring at me, expecting me to respond. But I wasn't listening to anything because I was distracted by Toya. Shit. Time for a lie.

"What? Sorry. I just remembered my lunch is in my locker."

Charlie was impatient. "I told you. We're on diets." The other three nodded. "We're planning our next cut day, next Monday. It's Jamie's birthday. We all cut school on birthdays. When's your birthday?"

I wasn't planning on celebrating my birthday by cutting school, so I lied. "I guess I missed it this year. January sixteenth."

Jamie said, "Guess we can't celebrate your birthday this year, new girl." There's a Jamie in every group. Always trying to prove herself as having the coolest things, the best hair, the skinniest body, the hottest boy, the newest phone, the best fists. Jamie was going to be annoying; I could tell. Turns out, I was right.

Let's agree that I was an expert on switching schools. Here was what I'd learned about the first day at a new school. The first day at a new school was filled with all sorts of decisions, none of them about actual school. Instead of thinking about doing class-work, getting caught up, or how to get to the next class, a new kid ONLY thought about where to sit at lunch, how smart or dumb to act in class, fending off questions about family, fending off questions about where they used to go to school, who to be friends with—cool kids, jocks, brains, losers, smokers—or staying solo. Starting midyear made it all worse.

Charlie, a girl with social power, had scooped me up as a friend. I knew it would be wise to keep her and her group on my side. I also knew Jamie was baiting me because Charlie had taken an interest in me, a new girl.

I said the next thing partly to show Jamie I wasn't afraid of her and partly to get Toya's attention. "I don't give a shit about cutting school on my birthday, Jamie." I emphasized her name be-cause she'd called me "new girl." I glanced at Toya. To my shock and horror, we made actual human eye contact, THEN SHE SMILED AT ME. I didn't smile back because 1) I didn't think my face could smile pleasantly right then, and 2) if I did, she'd know I had a crush on her, automatically making things weird.

Charlie said, "Jamie, stop being an asshole. You don't have to be an asshole all the time." Charlie was wrong—as it turned out, Jamie *did* have to be an asshole all the time. But she was one of Charlie's friends, so if I wanted to hang out with Toya (and I really,

really did), I'd have to put up with her "shenanigans," as my grandma used to say.

Grandma would not have wanted me to be in foster care. If she hadn't died, I wouldn't be. She really wouldn't have thought very much of Jamie, but I got the feeling not a lot of people did. You should know, my grandma was awesome. She tried to be nice to my mom, even though my mom was a mess most of my life. Grandma was super nice to me all of the time, even while she was taking care of my grandad at the same time. She didn't put up with "shenanigans" though.

"That's the bell," Toya said. "What's your next class, Shay?" Her voice was silky and soft.

This was a major crush, I realized. I also knew I'd probably make an idiot of myself if I wasn't careful. (Spoiler: I did make an idiot of myself even though I was careful.) I checked my schedule. "Science."

"I'll walk you to science," Charlie said.

"See you at lunch," Toya said. I felt my heart jump.

"Ha!" Jamie leaned over my shoulder. "You have math with Ms. Schunk and Ms. Lucy. It's learning support math." Jamie rolled her eyes.

I quickly faced her. "What are you saying, asshole?"

Jamie was surprised for a second, then said, right in my face, "I'm saying you have learning support math. Dummy."

With that, Charlie was between us. "Whoa, Jamie. You don't always gotta be an asshole."

Jamie laughed and sat back down, but the damage was

done. My weak spot had been exposed— Toya knew I was in a special-ed class.

Charlie walked me to science class. "I don't have science with you. I'm in algebra with the nerds this block. I'm not a nerd; I'm just good at math. After this class, we have lunch. I'll find you, and you can hang out with us. I want you to tell your France story to that bitch, Jamie."

"Language, Charlie!" yelled some random teacher standing in the hallway.

Charlie waved in acknowledgement. To me, she said, "She was my best friend, but she turned into a bitch."

Everyone in this group had some grievance with everyone else. Whatever. When I went to live with my dad, I'd worry about school. Here, I only had to get through the day. Survive, as Mrs. M suggested.

We stopped at a classroom where there was a weird smell. The teacher came into the hallway wearing a lab coat and goggles.

"This is Shay," Charlie said. "She's new. Mr. Ham told me to walk her to class."

Mr. Hamilton had not asked her to walk me to class.

"Hi Shay. I'm Ms. Winken. Your seat is at that table in the back with the boy struggling to put his goggles on." She turned. "Hold on, Marshall, I'll help you in a second."

Great. Dorky baseball kid, Marshall, was my lab partner.

"I'll write you a pass, Charlie," Ms. Winken said, "but this time, go straight to math."

"Okay, Ms. Winken. I promise." Charlie rolled her eyes at

me as Ms. Winken scribbled something on a piece of paper. "See you in the cafeteria for the feeding frenzy." Then Charlie left.

I headed toward Marshall, who was waving frantically at me.

Ms. Winken stood in the doorway, pointing with her clipboard. "Not that way, Charlie. Math is down the other hallway." As she watched Charlie, I watched her inner debate whether to keep yelling at Charlie. She shook her head and turned back to class.

Marshall, who practically broke his arm waving at me, kept waving until I was almost at the lab table. "Hi, Shay! We're lab partners today."

"Hi again, Marshall." For the life of me, I couldn't figure out why Charlie thought he was cute.

"Write down all the stuff on the board. Ms. Winken does notes checks every week."

I opened a brand-new notebook and dutifully wrote the date at the top of the page. Then, "Demonstration—Dancing Mothballs."

Marshall checked my work as if it was my first day in a school ever. He nodded. "Good. Write the objective too. All the teachers have to make us write the objective in our notes."

So, I wrote, "Students will be able to understand and explain density and buoyancy."

"You spelled 'bouncy' wrong," Marshall said over my shoulder.

"I spelled it right. It's buoyancy. It means floaty-ness."

"Oh. Thanks." He made the change in his notebook. I rolled

my eyes.

Ms. Winken shut the door when the ball rang. She didn't make a show of me being there, for which I was grateful.

"Dancing Mothballs" was super corny but kind of cool. The mothballs didn't really dance, but calling it "dancing mothballs" was probably an attention-grabber for the kids who knew what mothballs were, I guessed.

Here's what I learned
1. When you put mothballs in a beaker of vinegar, they sink because they're denser than the vinegar
2. Then they get bubbles of carbon dioxide on the outside from the stuff in them mixing with the vinegar
3. Then they get less dense because of the bubbles, and they float up
4. Then the bubbles pop, and they get denser and sink, etc.
5. They do this rise and sink thing until the mothball is gone or eighth graders lose interest or make too many jokes about moths having balls

Marshall was a fine lab partner who wasn't annoying at all. He only made one joke about moths having balls. (I won't write it here because it isn't that funny.) We got no homework in science, which was nice. Marshall said he'd show me where the cafeteria was. When the bell rang, we filed out with everyone else.

"Nice to meet you, Shay," Ms. Winken said as she hung up her lab coat.

"You too. See you tomorrow," I said back, as fake cheerful as I could.

Marshall led me to the cafeteria, but I could have found it from the noise level. As we went down the stairs, the yelling, shrieking, screaming, laughing, and music got louder. When we entered the cafeteria, it was as if a wooden club had hit me in all my senses. The sound level was so loud I couldn't hear what Marshall said to me when I stopped dead in my tracks. There were no windows, making the light all fluorescent and stark. Even though it was February outside, it was too hot inside. All those bodies really heated up the place.

I realized my lunch was in my locker, which was fine because I wasn't at all hungry. All I could smell was hot dogs and hormones.

CHAPTER TWELVE

THE TILED ROOM had long cafeteria tables with attached rows of seats that would fold up so the custodians could scrape and mop the muck off the floor after all the lunch periods. It was densely crowded with eighth graders.

Marshall got in a long line. "This is where we buy lunch. Do you buy?"

"My lunch is in my locker."

"Okay. I can buy you lunch today. Use my number."

Then Charlie showed up. "She's not eating your nasty lunch, Marshall. Come on, new kid." She grabbed my arm and dragged me away, heading to a corner where Jamie sat with two other girls, staring at their phones. Great.

They glanced up, saw it was me, and rolled their eyes in exactly the same way. Pretty impressive, I had to admit.

"Guys, Marshall tried to get the new kid to eat that nasty lunch. Isn't that gross?"

The other girls nodded, eyes still on their phones. Charlie plopped down next to Jamie; I sat next to one of the other girls. No one said anything. Charlie got out her phone and started scrolling, ignoring me. I sat there for a minute, getting angry. Why was I here? How much did I need this friend group? Why did Charlie bring me here only to ignore me? I stood up.

"Where are you going, new kid?" Jamie challenged me.

"I have to pee."

"I'll take you." Charlie stood.

"No, that's fine. I'm sure I can find it."

She wasn't used to being told "no," but she sat back down, eyeing me. "When you come back, we'll post something together. What's your Insta?"

"I don't remember," I said and walked away. The Nameless Phone Faces hadn't even looked up.

"Can't leave the lunchroom." One of the cafeteria aides stopped me.

Easily, I lied. "I just got my period. I need to go to the nurse."

The aide, who had what had to be worst job on the planet—standing in a screamingly loud, migraine-y bright, middle school–smelling cafeteria—handed me the laminated red pass that said, "Nurse."

"Thanks." I headed out.

Somehow, I ended up in the hallway with my locker opened. One of the many benefits of attending as many distinguished educational institutions as I had was that there wasn't a locker I couldn't open. I could open locked classroom doors, too, but that was a story for a different time.

I fished out my lunch from the backpack.

"Aren't you supposed to be at lunch? What are you doing up here with the Nurse pass?" It figures some teacher would be wandering around, yelling at kids who want to eat lunch instead of play the politics game of being the new kid in middle school. They probably got a bonus in their paycheck for every kid they hassled. This guy just got his bonus.

I shut my locker and turned to him, lunch bag in my hands, preparing my lie.

Then, as if conjured by magic, Toya stood in the doorway of a classroom. I pointed in her direction. The hassling teacher, satisfied that I belonged somewhere, wandered off.

Toya. Here she was. My mouth had dropped open.

"Hey, Shay," she said, then turned back to someone inside. "Ms. Prince, we're done with our rough draft. Can you check it?"

Ms. Prince came to the doorway. "You got it, Toya."

Toya pointed down the hallway. "Shay, the nurse is down that way. Do you need someone to walk you?"

I should have said, *Yes, can Toya walk me everywhere forever?* But instead, I mumbled something stupid. I don't remember what I said, but I do remember standing there with my mouth open.

Toya waved AND SMILED AT ME, then went back into the room with Ms. Prince.

First things first, I closed my mouth. Then I peeked into the classroom. Toya sat at a table with four other kids, their heads bent together as they worked on something. Ms. Prince read something at her desk as she ate a sandwich. She had a soda can on her desk. Teachers had to eat lunch too.

"This is good," Ms. Prince said to the group, holding up some papers.

I slipped away with my bagged peanut butter sandwich and wandered for a few minutes, evaluating the latest encounter with Toya with an eye toward improving my performance, which, by all accounting, was dismal. Toya remembered me; that was good. Standing there with my mouth open; that was bad. Some changes needed to be made in how I handled seeing her face-to-face—her face was a very good one but also very distracting.

The strategy I came up with
1. Don't let my mouth drop open like a fish
2. If it does drop open like a fish, close it
3. Speak to her

This was a good strategy, simple enough even someone as socially clumsy as me could do it. I went a little further—I would greet her casually yet purposefully. A greeting—that would do it.

Maybe *Hiya, Toya,* the next time I saw her. I could handle two words, right? But "hiya" was too casual, too bro-y. Maybe

Hello, Toya. Nope. Too fancy. Maybe *Hello.* Nope, too stuck up. Maybe just *Hi. Buenos días. What's up? 'Sup?* Ugh.

"Are you supposed to be up here during lunch?" Another teacher got his bonus. I rounded a corner without answering, escaping inside a girls' bathroom.

I ate my lunch there as if I was in a movie about bullying. I would eat my lunch in the bathroom every day if Charlie let me get away from her and the Nameless Phone Faces. A group of girls came into the bathroom. They sounded pretty young. It was obvious they were cutting class, which meant they would probably be in here a while. I left the stall and threw my lunch bag in the trash. Yep. Sixth graders. Ugh.

"You're awfully far away from the cafeteria," one of them astutely observed.

"Eating with all your friends?" a jokester chimed in. They all laughed.

Instantly, my pre-anger at Charlie, Jamie, this school, and myself boiled together. I got right in the jokester's face.

"I got out of lockup two days ago. I beat up a kid pretty bad at my last school. Get out of here."

"Naw," the jokester scoffed as her friends edged toward the door.

I stared her right in the eyes. "Get. The. Fuck. Out!"

She jumped a little but turned to leave. Then she said, "Imma get a teacher."

I shrugged. "Snitches get stitches..."

Jokester took off, her friends close behind. A stall door

opened to reveal a girl. She threw away her lunch bag.

"Thanks. They're really mean to everyone. Were you really locked up?"

"Get out!" I roared. She ran.

The girl from the stall made me mad. She acted as if I was supposed to defend her against some stupid sixth-grade bullies. *Get a thicker skin, kid.* I wasn't some hero on an antibullying campaign. I'd eaten my lunch in a bathroom stall because I was afraid of what Charlie would do if I didn't want to be her friend. I was no hero.

This was some first day of school. I headed toward where I thought the cafeteria was. As I got to Charlie's table, the bell rang, thankfully ending lunch. We filed out.

"Where'd you go?" Charlie demanded.

"I got lost."

Jamie laughed. "It's not that hard to find the bathroom." She pointed to the hallway next to the cafeteria where there were boys' and girls' restrooms. "Yeah. Charlie, maybe you should walk her to the bathroom next time. Whose turn is it to walk her to class now?"

I turned to address Jamie's attitude, but someone stepped between us again. One day, no one would be between us, but this time, one of the Nameless Phone Faces, of all people, came to the rescue.

"I have math in the class next to you, Shay. I'll walk you. Come on." We left the cafeteria in a wave of people. I was shocked that she would be nice to me. Then she took my arm.

"I'll walk you to math, but it's not because I'm being nice. I'm only doing this because I hate Jamie. She made out with Chris Jackson at Deja's party last week. What a bitch."

At least we both hated Jamie. Nameless Phone Face wasn't on my side, but now I knew something about Jamie that I could use. Sigh. Why wasn't there a class in navigating middle school? That was one I'd do the homework for.

Math class was fun. I've never said that before in my life, but MATH CLASS WAS FUN. Ms. Schunk and Ms. Lucy joked around with each other so much it was hard to believe we were even doing math. They acted as if I'd been there all year; the other people did too. We worked on combinations and permutations (I know, I sound so smart). Basically, if the order of numbers mattered, it was a permutation. We should really call our locker combinations "locker permutations" instead because you couldn't just enter the numbers in any order.

I was in a group with Olaf, who told me immediately that he was dyslexic (same as Eli), Martin, and Nessa, who had a service dog, James. I was allowed to pet James because he took a break every day in math. That meant he wasn't on duty. I didn't know why Nessa had James with her, but he was cute, and she was nice. The whole group was nice to each other. I realized I was taking a break in math class too. I was off duty too.

We did an activity in our groups to be presented to the class. Everyone worked on it together. It was Olaf's turn to be the recorder, which meant he had to fill out the group's paper. But he didn't want to; he said he was terrible at writing. He never wanted to write, it turned out. After I asked him to show me how to do it, he ended up doing most of it anyway.

Ms. Schunk and Ms. Lucy walked around to the groups, listening and answering questions. They mostly left us to work. Then the groups presented to the class. Martin and Nessa were the presenters today; the good news was that I was off the hook for that. The whole class clapped hard for every group after their presentations, as if the group had established world peace. So corny. It was a dumb group activity, right? But then my group presented. When everyone clapped, it was kind of cool. I might have smiled.

We did get math homework, but Nessa, Olaf, and Martin all wrote their cell phone numbers in my notebook in case I had questions. It was almost unbelievable how nice they were being.

Nessa got up. "I have to take James out for a potty break. Bye, Shay. See you tomorrow." I waved.

Maybe school wouldn't be completely bad. At least I had one class where I wasn't called "New Kid" and dealing with drama. I checked my schedule. Language arts next. Martin asked if I knew where I was going. I didn't.

He checked my schedule. "Oh. I know where that is. Ms. Schunk?" He raised his hand. She looked over from where she was working with someone. "Can I walk Shay to her language arts class?"

She raised her eyebrows at me in a question. I nodded. "Sure, Martin," she responded and turned back to continue helping.

The bell rang. Martin and I left class. We stopped at my

locker, where I checked my schedule.

"I haven't memorized my locker combination."

We both said "permutation" at the same time and grinned.

I got my notebook for language arts, and we made our way to class. My heart sank as I saw Jamie go into the room. "Shit."

"She's an asshole," Martin said quietly.

"I know. Well, thanks for walking with me. I'll see you tomorrow."

"Yep. Good luck," he said before quickly walking away, leaving me alone.

Shit.

CHAPTER THIRTEEN

I WALKED INTO language arts class to find mayhem. The teacher was writing on the board while at the same time yelling to the class over her shoulder.

"Get out your journals. Complete this prompt."

No one followed her instructions, of course. The bell rang. Hardly anyone sat down; no one got out their journals. She finished writing and turned, startled to see me. She yelled for everyone to sit down. Students started slowly taking their seats, talking and laughing. I stood there, waiting. She was obviously irritated, and Jamie was suddenly standing behind me.

"Ms. Moss, this is Shay. She's new. You should put her in Raymond's group."

Ms. Moss nodded gratefully. "Good idea, Jamie. Would you show her to her seat and get her a journal out of the closet?"

I followed Jamie to a group of desks at the rear of the room, where a girl and a boy sat. The girl rolled her eyes took her books off my desk, stowing them under hers. Jamie went to a closet in the room, where she got out a composition book. She slapped it on the desk in front of me before joining another group.

"That's your journal," Eye Roller said to me. "Write something in it using the prompt on the board."

The boy—probably Raymond—stayed silent. Why did Jamie want me in his group? And why did the teacher listen to her? She was probably a sub.

The prompt on the board said, "Who is the person from literature you would most want to meet and talk to?"

I immediately thought of Jessica Atreides, from *Dune*. Complicated, super strong, lots of secrets, devoted to family, and powerful reverend mother to thousands of followers. I would have asked her how she got so strong, what she missed the most, if there was anything she regretted—I had a lot of questions for her.

I opened the composition book and wrote the date and the prompt at the top of the first page. The other two kids in my group didn't write anything. I closed the composition book. It was still loud in the room, with kids yelling that they had to go to the bathroom, the nurse, and random questions. On the board, in the spot for today's agenda, it said "practice verb tense agreement" and then "silent reading." (Spoiler: It isn't ever silent.)

Jamie and the sub came over to my group.

"Hi, Shay. I'm Ms. Moss. It's not usually this loud in here." She was apologizing. I tried to think of something to cheer her up a little. Why was this my job?

"That's okay. You wrote a prompt and an objective on the board. Most subs don't even try that hard."

Her face hardened. The Eye Roller and Raymond laughed. "I'm Ms. Moss. This is my class. I'm not a sub." Oh great. Just great.

Jamie smirked. Ms. Moss stared at me. That was a bad mistake. I wanted to fix it, but then Jamie said the thing that made me the angriest I got today.

"Ms. Moss, Shay is new. She's a foster kid and hasn't been in a lot of school this year. She and Raymond should have a lot to talk about, you know, because they're both foster kids."

Raymond's head dropped to his chest. Eye Roller jumped up.

"That's a shitty thing to do, Jamie."

Ms. Moss did nothing.

I stood up too. "Get the fuck out of here, Jamie."

"Now, now, Shay. Wanda. Please sit down. Jamie was trying to help."

Jamie's smirk almost broke her face.

"Jamie, please return to your seat," Ms. Moss said, and when she didn't move, "Jamie, please."

Jamie finally went to her seat, smirking all the way.

"I'm grading your journals tonight," Ms. Moss said, walking away.

Wanda (Eye Roller) and I sat back down.

"I fucking hate that asshole," I said.

"Me too," Wanda said.

Raymond shook his head and then put his head down on his arm on his desk. I thought it was a good idea, so I did the same thing. Foster kid solidarity, right? We kept our heads down for the rest of the class until the bell rang. I left without saying another word. I didn't know where my next class was, but I didn't care. I couldn't spend another second in that room. Fuck Jamie.

I walked the halls, searching for my art class for a few minutes. The bell rang, but I was still wandering. I didn't care— couldn't believe this day wasn't over yet. I didn't know where I was in the school, but I came upon a teacher herding her students into class.

"You lost?" Another bonus for an alert teacher.

I admitted I was. We checked my schedule.

"Rachel!" she called. A girl appeared at her elbow. "Would you escort my friend Shay here to Mr. Reuben's room?"

She nodded enthusiastically. Sixth grade, I decided. They were always happy to run errands for teachers.

Rachel led the way, practically skipping. "You're way far away. Come on." She tried to chat with me about being new as we walked along. Where did I come from? Where was my old school? Did I eat the lunch?

I wasn't feeling chatty, so I fed her a constant stream of lies. Rachel stopped outside the closed door of my class.

"Here you are, Shay! I hope your French prince emails you soon."

Thanks, *Sweet Valley High*, for a veritable treasure trove of available lies for the gullible.

I knocked on the door. A teacher opened it.

"You must be Shay. Welcome. We're doing self-portraits in charcoal this week. I'll be over with your supplies in a minute. There's an empty seat at that table in the back." As I started past the tables, everyone glanced up, but no one said anything stupid. Then someone waved. My heart stopped.

Toya. Toya was in my art class. Every day, last period, I would be in class with Toya. My day would end in class with Toya. I *was* going to survive this day. I waved back and hoped I didn't appear too eager. She returned to her drawing. I went to the rear table.

The teacher put some stuff on my table. He was holding a camera. "Hold it," he said and snapped a picture of me. I was unprepared. He handed the Polaroid to me. "Use this as a template." Then he handed me a charcoal pencil. "Outline your facial features first." He pointed to a wall, where a series of pictures hung with instructions underneath. "You're on step one. We'll be doing this project for a few more days; take your time in the beginning. If you need help, find me." He named all the things on my table. "Charcoal pencil, stick charcoal, gum eraser. Don't use your finger to erase or blend. Any questions?"

Yes, I had questions. Did Toya know I liked her? Did she like me? What was her favorite song? Was she good at art? Was she as mean as Charlie? Did it matter to her that I was in a supported math class or a foster home? I didn't ask Mr. Reuben any of these questions. "No questions."

"Okay, then." He smiled. I was on my own.

Most students were working one or two to a table. Toya sat with another girl. I forced myself not to stare at her by watching the Polaroid develop slowly. I hated pictures of myself. I hated my stupid face and my stupid hair and my stupid non-boobs—not pictured in the Polaroid—but as long as I was self-hating, I might as well do the whole list.

Watching the picture develop was torture, of course. I forced myself to keep doing it. Yep. I was right, an awful picture. I turned it over, face down. One of the worst. I had my eyes closed because, well, I was me. If there was a way to ruin a picture, I'd do it. But my eyes being closed wasn't the worst part of the picture. The worst part was that I was grinning. Ugh.

The bell rang, ending art class with Toya. She smiled and waved at me as she left, talking with the girl who was at her table. I stood there, returning my art stuff to the tray.

Mr. Reuben carried art supplies to the closet behind my table. "How was your first day?"

"Up and down," I answered truthfully.

He nodded. "Yep. Sounds about right. Listen, I have an art club Tuesdays after school. If you want to join, stick around after class on Tuesday."

"I'm not much of an artist."

He laughed. "Don't worry about that. The club is about making art, not being great at it. I have kids drawing anime, doing 3D printing, working on projects for school."

And then he said the thing that got me into art club. "Your

friend Toya is in the club."

"She's not my friend. I only met her today."

"Oh, okay. Do you know how to get to your locker?"

I shook my head.

"Eighth grade lockers are down those stairs, then turn left. They're in numerical order."

I found my locker, (locker permutation) opened it, and managed to get everything packed before Charlie showed up. I wasn't hurrying, but I sort of was trying to avoid seeing her anymore today. No luck. Charlie appeared just as I closed my locker.

"Hey."

"Hey," I said back.

She took her face out of her phone. "How was the rest of your day?"

"Jamie is an asshole."

Charlie nodded. "Yeah. Told ya. She told me what she did in LA class. Did you really call Ms. Moss a sub?"

"I did." I shouldered my backpack.

She nodded approvingly. "Badass move. Didja get any homework?"

"Math and, I think, language arts."

"Don't worry about your LA homework. Ms. Moss gives you credit just for doing it. She takes late work, so don't listen when she says she doesn't. Let me see your math homework."

Against my better instincts, I handed her my notebook.

"Huh. Locker permutation. Okay. What's this?" She had turned to the page with Nessa, Olaf, and Martin's phone numbers.

"You don't need these." She tore out the page and crumpled it. "Dummies."

"Hey. You can't rip my notebook. Give it back."

She hesitated. Did no one ever push back with her? She slowly handed the crumpled paper back to me.

"Okay, okay," she said. "I just don't want you to, you know, associate with the wrong people."

Yeah, as if your friends are such prizes, I thought to myself. Then I said it out loud. "As if your friends are such prizes." I hardly ever said exactly what I was thinking, but I was tired and pre-angry, it came out. I thought she'd be mad, but her face fell.

"Yeah. My only friend who isn't a bitch is Toya. I think she's avoiding me half the time."

I liked Toya even more after hearing this. "So why do you have shitty friends? You're smart."

Charlie got mad. "Smart isn't shit. Don't say that. Go home, Shay. Call your dummy math friends."

"Don't call them dummies."

Charlie sighed. "Shay, give me that paper."

I hesitated, then handed it to her. She uncrumpled it, wrote something on it, and crumpled it back up.

"In case you need real math help. See you tomorrow morning. We meet out by the playground before the doors open." She walked away. I uncrumpled the paper. She'd written her phone number and, underneath it, "Your friend, Charlie."

Friends. Huh. This day was surreal, for sure.

I made it home without getting lost. When the twins got

home, we started working on homework together in the kitchen, but after about fifteen minutes, I went upstairs to take a nap until dinner.

Mr. M called up to me. "Shay? Dinner time. You coming down?"

I sat up. Spock jumped off the bed. "Be right there." I splashed water on my face. Then I smelled pizza—my reward for surviving my first day. Mrs. M was right. Survival.

I fell into my chair at the table.

"Tired?" Mr. M handed me the pizza box.

"Long day. Really long day."

The twins were chomping on pizza, so thankfully, they didn't have a million questions. I could see Mrs. and Mr. M did have a million questions, but they let me eat a slice in silence. When we finally talked about my day, I left out: cutting the assembly, almost fighting with Jamie twice, Toya, and the sub-not-sub language arts teacher. Eli asked about the science experiment, so I told them about the dancing mothballs. Mr. M had to explain what mothballs were. I told the twins about the mothballs dancing up and down in the vinegar.

Nathan, perceptively, asked if anything went wrong during the day. Was he digging? Maybe. He'd been a little prickly since I'd run away, even though I thought he and Eli were asleep when I did that. I told him some stuff wasn't great, but I was sure it would all work out. I didn't say that, yeah, I'd kick Jamie's ass at some point, the language arts teacher would stop kissing Jamie's ass, and I'd actually speak to Toya.

"What classes did you have again?" Mrs. M asked.

"Assembly first."

"How was it?"

I'd cut the assembly, so I lied and gave a thumbs-down. Eli gave a thumbs down.

"Boring. Then science," I said and gave a thumbs-up. Eli did too.

"Lunch." Me and Eli, thumbs down.

"Math." Up.

"Language arts." Down.

"Art." Up.

Eli said, "You're a mothball." He did the thumbs-up/down thing a couple times. Everybody laughed. He was right. My day had been a roller coaster. I was a dancing mothball.

CHAPTER FOURTEEN

THURSDAY NIGHT, I went to bed early, embarrassingly early. Right after the twins almost. I tried to read but couldn't. Not even the dread of school kept me awake.

When I woke up, I picked up my uniform—still in a pile on the floor where I had left it—and got dressed.

Everyone said good morning. The twins and I ate cereal before I walked to school. I managed to get to homeroom by way of my locker without seeing Charlie or Toya or anyone.

Charlie cut in front of a kid to stand next to me in the line for homeroom. "You didn't call me last night."

"And good morning to you, Charlie. I went to bed early."

"Did you call one of your math friends?"

Was she jealous? "I went to bed early. I didn't call anyone."

Satisfied, she went back to her phone. The line moved up.

Then I was sitting in homeroom behind Marshall.

He leaned back. "We're in social studies together, I think. You have it first, with Mr. Ham?" I nodded.

From the front of the room came, "Turn around Marshall." Marshall turned around but gave me a thumbs-up as he did.

The bell rang; some kids filed out as more came in. Someone approached my desk. "You're in my seat."

I went up front. Mr. Ham pointed to a desk in the middle of the room. "That's yours in social studies, Shay. Okay?" I nodded, sat down, got out a pen and a notebook, then opened it to the first page.

Social studies class was okay. No drama, no dramatic people, which was nice. Lots of notes because we were in the middle of a unit, but no homework for over the weekend, so that was also nice. In science, we read an article and answered some questions. After science, Marshall and I were heading to lunch when a girl stopped us.

"Shay?"

"Hey, Fran." Marshall knew her.

"I'm supposed to bring Shay to girls' group now," Fran said.

I had forgotten about girls' group but was ecstatic to get out of lunching with Charlie and the Nameless Phone Faces. "Sure," I overly enthused, which caused Marshall to snap his head toward me.

"Bye, Marshall," I said cheerily. "I'm going with Fran."

"See you, Shay," he said slowly, waving as he turned to continue to lunch.

"We can go to the cafeteria to get your lunch first," Fran said.

"Can we go to my locker? I brought lunch."

"Sure."

After I retrieved my lunch, Fran told me about girls' group on the way to the basement.

"It's a small group. We talk about dating, our parents, you know, stupid school stuff. There are a couple rules. You can't tell anyone anything that anyone says inside the group. You don't have to talk at all, but if you do, you can't lie. If you tell us that you're using drugs or alcohol or having sex or hurting yourself, Ms. Peete has to tell your parents."

I got a lot of information on our walk. When we got to room 103 in the basement, Ms. Peete met us at the door.

"Hi, Shay, welcome to the girls' group. I trust Fran has filled you in."

"She did, thanks."

"I'm Ms. Peete, one of the social workers here."

Ms. Peete turned to the girls sitting in a circle of desks. "Friends, this is Shay."

Everyone in the room actually smiled (genuine, all). A couple waved shyly. Everyone had name tags on their desks with pronouns next to their name. A couple girls were eating lunch from cafeteria trays, a couple ate out of paper bags. Two weren't eating at all.

"Take that seat over there," Ms. Peete continued. "We're only together for lunch period, so we eat as we talk. Chris is telling us about something that happened at a party."

I sat at an empty desk that had a folded blank paper tent. I wrote "Shay" on the tent and then, "she/her."

I expected to have to introduce myself and share, baring my innermost feelings, but I didn't even have to talk. It was actually okay to eat lunch and listen to a girl complain about older boys at her brother's house party getting drunk and being gross. Chris's (she/her) story was basically that some boy tried to kiss her. Of course, she didn't want to. She pushed him away. Then he got mad and told all his friends she was "begging for it." Ugh.

Ms. Peete didn't offer any advice but asked us what we thought. One girl, Ginny (she/her), said a similar thing happened to her last year. People were still calling her "slut." Apparently, this wasn't as uncommon as I thought, people trying to kiss people who didn't want to be kissed.

Another girl, Unique (she/her), said Chris shouldn't have stayed at the party if there was drinking, that "She could have stayed in her room." A couple of the girls nodded.

Fran (she/they) said, "But it was her own house. Can't she be in her own house?"

Amanda (she/her) said, "You could have told him you had a boyfriend. That way he wouldn't have tried to kiss you." We all laughed at her innocence.

"Of course, he would still have tried to kiss her," Lucinda (they/them) said, then added, "She should have kicked him in the balls." The girls laughed again. Lucinda's solution was the best.

Ms. Peete said, "I can't encourage you to hurt anyone, but maybe you could talk to your brother about what his friend did."

Chris nodded, but I knew she'd never mention it to him. Then Amanda told a story about not being invited to a birthday party of a girl who had been her best friend in second grade but moved away when her parents got divorced. Amanda was quite a delicate flower, emotionally, it turned out. I sort of wished my main problem in life was not getting invited to my second-grade best friend's birthday party. Then I tried to remember who my best friend in second grade was. Failing that, I finished my lunch while the group all chatted for a few minutes.

With a couple minutes left in lunch period, Ms. Peete said, "Friends, thanks to everyone who shared today. You can all head on up to your next class. See you all next Friday. Shay, stick around if you don't mind."

After everyone had left, Ms. Peete turned to me. "I read your file. Counseling is available during the school day if you're interested."

Wow. What the hell was in my file? I must really need mental health help.

"I know you're seeing a psychologist outside of school," she continued, "but I could also meet with you once every week or so," then added as an enticement, "You would get out of thirty minutes of a class." It couldn't be math, but any other class was fine.

That intrigued me. "Do you have any appointments during—" I checked my schedule. When was language arts? "—during fourth block?"

She checked my schedule. "Ms. Moss's class? Okay. I do have Mondays available during the second half of fourth block. I'll set the time aside for you and let Ms. Moss know."

She paused and, after thinking a moment, wrote me a pass. "In case she forgets." We both knew she'd forget. (Spoiler: She did. Of course, she did.)

I would get to leave language arts in the middle of class one day a week. I could fake my way through a conversation with a social worker to get out of language arts. I headed off to math as the bell rang. I only got a little lost, arriving at math as the last clang of the bell echoed.

MATH CLASS WAS FUN. (AGAIN, WHO EVEN AM I WRITING THIS?)

Language arts was fine. We had an actual sub, who kept control of the class as well as (better than) Ms. Moss had the day before. The sub put on a movie based on a Shakespeare play clearly not intended for children because of the sex, bad language, gratuitous gun violence, and drugs. In short, it was awesome. The class sat perfectly still and only occasionally yelled stuff at the screen. Raymond had his head down the whole class again. He was missing a pretty interesting movie, but I understood his mood. I really did.

Toya wasn't in art (boo!), so I didn't get to see her at all on Friday. On the plus side, I escaped the end-of-day locker drama with Charlie by speed-packing my backpack. I was as tired as if I'd spent a whole week in school, but it had only been two days.

My exhaustion was probably partly to blame for what happened Friday night. That, plus the fact that I was an idiot.

CHAPTER FIFTEEN

FRIDAY NIGHT, I had a fight with an eight-year-old kid. I was dumb for letting it happen too. It totally wasn't Nathan's fault, even though he started it. It happened when the family went to temple, which was interesting and peaceful. It was Shabbat, a holy day that began at sundown. The M's said I didn't have to go, but I wanted to see Mrs. M in action.

We got there early. Mrs. M kissed Mr. M and left us to go to her office to prepare. I went to the day care with the twins to hang out until it was time for the service. Mr. M came with us but left after a while and asked me to bring the twins to the temple when it was time. There were other kids there; some of the littles recognized me from the other day. I really enjoyed the day care. I realized I'd miss them when I went to live with my father. Weird, huh? I'd just met them.

Nathan, who'd been a little standoffish since I ran away, had returned to normal. In fact, when it was time to go to the service, both of them puffed up a little because they were in charge of me.

"This way. We sit up front," Eli said.

"Say 'Shabbat shalom' when the usher says it to you. It means peaceful Sabbath," explained Nathan.

"We have to wear a kippah, but you don't have to." Eli took a small circle of cloth out of his pocket and placed it on his head. Nathan did the same thing.

We walked up to Mr. M. He smiled. "Shabbat shalom."

"Shabbat shalom," both boys replied.

"Shabbat shalom," I said, adding a little bow.

He laughed. "Nice bow, but you don't have to do that. We're not quite that formal. This is the sanctuary." He gestured to the large room filled with people. "I'm ushering today, so I'll be in right before the service begins. The boys know where to go."

Nathan and Eli were bowing to each other. Mr. M and I looked at each other. He rolled his eyes. We both smiled.

The boys led me into the sanctuary as Mr. M spoke to someone behind us.

"Shabbat shalom, Ben," he said.

Ben returned the greeting. "Shabbat shalom, Ravid."

Everyone was dressed up. All the men and boys wore kippot. We went right to the second pew, the boys on either side of me. Mr. M joined us right before the service started.

The service was pretty cool. Mrs. M started the service from a table in front of everyone by speaking Hebrew. Then, a man sang a song that sounded sad. Mrs. M led the congregation in chants, prayers, and songs. Most of the songs sounded sad. Sometimes the people sang; sometimes, a guy up front, called the cantor, sang a solo. At one point, we stood up.

Eli whispered to me. "Next, we take a bow. You don't have to."

There were some other things too—swaying and chanting.

I'd been to lots of other religious services—Lutheran, Unitarian, and family #2 (the Garbage People) were super Catholic, so I went a lot when I was with them. Didn't do them much good though, all that confessing and kneeling. You could say I was pretty skeptical of the whole "god" thing. I hoped my dad wasn't some weird religion.

The cantor took these heavy, ancient scrolls out of a closet. Mrs. M read from them in Hebrew. It was very cool that Mrs. M was in charge of the whole service. When she raised her hands, everyone stood. She led the prayer, then waved her hands down, and everyone sat. Pretty cool.

After the service, we waited for her to say goodbye. Everyone wanted to tell her how nice the service was. The twins and I waited in the sanctuary. This was where the trouble started.

"That was a cool service. Your mom is in charge of the whole thing," I said.

Eli nodded. "Yeah. She does this Friday nights and some Saturday mornings but not tomorrow."

"Are you Jewish?" Nathan asked me.

"No. I'm not really anything."

Eli asked, "What do you believe?"

I shrugged. "I don't know. My family didn't really do religious things."

"Did your mom do drugs? Is that why you aren't religious?"

Wow, Nathan. Right out of the blue. I hesitated, which was a mistake.

I didn't want to lie, but I didn't want to unload all my baggage on these little kids right then. I wanted to do a lie that spared feelings, a Custard Pie Lie. I thought of a lie, but it wasn't a good one.

"No. She had cancer." They stared at me in horror. I knew the trick to getting them to believe this lie was to give them a detail, a specific type of cancer. Seeing their faces gave me pause. To make everything worse, which I usually did, I couldn't think of anything specific to add to the lie. Super embarrassing for the Queen of Lies. Then, I dropped my eyes. My tell. Shit.

Immediately, Nathan said, "I know you're lying." He went to stand by his dad, next to his mom.

Eli gazed at me, disappointed. "I'm sorry your mom died." Then he moved away from me, closer to Nathan.

Damn. Even the twins could tell I was lying. That was terrible for me. I'd lost my touch. The line of people greeting Mrs. M was almost done, so I joined her. The twins didn't look at me. My guilt kicked in, and then I got pre-angry. I was only trying to spare their feelings. Fine. I'd tell them the truth. It was awful, but if that was what Nathan wanted, I'd do it.

"What did you think, Shay?" Mrs. M said, taking off her

robes and sashes.

"It was nice. I liked the music; some of it sounded really sad."

"It's not as sad as it sounds—our music is written on a different scale than the Western music you're used to." She headed back up front. "I'll meet you all at the car."

"Let's go boys. Come on, Shay." Mr. M started walking out. The boys and I followed him.

At a loud *click*, I looked back. Mrs. M must have turned the lights out because only a couple were lit, including one over the closet where the scrolls were kept. The sanctuary was beautiful.

"So, Shay, do you have any questions about the service?" Mrs. M asked when she got into the car.

"What are the giant scrolls?"

"That's the Torah, our holy book. We read from it on Saturdays."

"What's the cover?"

Eli chimed in. "The cover is called a mantle. It protects the Torah."

"Why do you keep the Torahs in a closet?"

Mrs. M turned to Nathan to see if he wanted to answer. He just stared out the window, so she answered. "It's called an ark, not a closet, and it symbolizes the ancient Temple of Jerusalem."

Eli started singing something, with Nathan joining in. They sang almost the whole way home.

As we pulled into the driveway, Nathan asked, "How did Shay's mother die? She said it was cancer, but I know that was a lie."

Eli added, "It was probably drugs."

I saw Mrs. M and Mr. M share a quick glance.

Mr. M said, "We'll talk about that when we get inside."

Nathan said, "Can you make sure she doesn't lie to us again?"

"Nathan!" Mrs. M scolded from the front seat. I was really pissed at this kid. I couldn't even speak.

When we got in, after the kids had a snack, Mr. M took them upstairs for bed.

Mrs. M said, "Shay, you don't have to tell them anything if you don't want to. I think they've figured out some things though. Tell them whatever you're comfortable with..." She hesitated. "Nathan was resistant to having you come here. You should know that. He had a problem with Molly. She broke his trust pretty badly; that's why he takes being lied to so hard."

Great. When the real family kids didn't want you around, it was only a matter of time before you got sent away. All this made me want to live with my father even more. Fine.

Mrs. M was still waiting for me to say something. "I know you're upset. Nathan needs some time."

What about me? When do I get time? Oh, that's right. I'm just a foster. I nodded because I didn't want to snap on Mrs. M. It wasn't her fault one of her kids was a jerk. Then I snapped anyway.

"Guess I better tell them how I found my mom on a couch in an abandoned building."

"Did you really find her on a couch?"

"Guess I better tell them she'd been there for at least a day, maybe longer."

"Shay, that's awful."

"But Nathan is having a hard time, so I'll tell him something else, right? If you think he's upset because I lied, wait until I tell him the truth about how my mom died and left me alone." I was crying because I was mad. I was shaking too. That was new, the shaking from anger. Great. My anger was growing stronger. It had even more control over me. Perfect.

"Shay. Nathan doesn't need to know every detail. I'm sorry about your mom. That must have been awful. You don't have to say anything if you don't want." Was she upset? Whatever. I was angry, which meant I didn't have any room left to care. But I had to say something to save my skin. Couldn't have one of the real family kids angry at me.

"I have to say something. I don't want Nathan to think I'm a liar." Because I didn't want one of the real kids to be mad, because then I would have to leave before I wanted to.

"Then tell him the truth, but don't tell him the bad parts." She turned toward the stairs to go take care of her real kid, then said something that made me feel shitty for being mad at her and her kid. "I'd be okay hearing about your mom sometime, Shay. It's a terrible story. I don't want you to have to carry it around by yourself."

She did seem to really care. I almost started crying again but caught myself when she started up the stairs. I stood there for a few seconds, making sure I wasn't about to cry again before following her into the twins' room.

Mr. M sat on the side of Eli's bed. Nathan lay with his back to the room.

"Nathan," I started. "My mom did die of an overdose. It makes me sad to talk about it because it's terrible. I'm sorry I told you it was cancer."

He rolled over so he could look right at me. "I'm sorry your mom died. I don't like when people lie."

The kid was direct—more than most adults I'd met. "I know. I'm trying not to lie as much as I used to." I turned to Eli. "I lied to you, too, Eli. I'm sorry."

He said softly, "I'm sorry about your mom." Then, he broke my heart. "Do you miss her?"

I did miss her. All the time. All the time. But she'd been a mess. Sometimes, it was awful when she was around. When she was clean, it was nice. I could make her laugh. When I did, it was the best thing I'd ever done. When she was using, I missed her; when she was clean, I waited for her to start using again. Ugh, Eli. I was sad and angry at the same time.

"Yeah. I miss her." Then I just stood there. Dummy. I didn't know what to say that wouldn't be sad or angry. I gazed helplessly at Mrs. M. She gazed back at me, also speechless. Mr. M saved the day.

"Nathan, Eli, do you have any questions for Shay?"

Eli asked, "Do you have any brothers or sisters?"

"No. Just me."

Nathan said, "Have you told us any other lies?"

I thought about it for a minute, meeting his eyes. "I lied about school today. It was mostly terrible. Parts were okay, but most of it was bad. I don't want your parents to worry about me, so I said it wasn't as bad as it really was." He nodded.

"You don't have to go tomorrow. It's Saturday," Eli chimed in, then continued with, "That's some good news." I gave him a thumbs-up, which he returned. I did the same to Nathan, who also returned the gesture.

"Okay, boys and Shay. Who wants pancakes and rye toast for breakfast?"

"Yay! I do!" shouted the twins.

"Well done, Shay," Mrs. M said after we left the room. "You handled that well."

"Thanks."

She didn't see the turmoil inside my brain—anger and sadness battling it out for possession of my mind.

"Mr. M and I are going to watch a movie. If you want to join us, I'm making popcorn." I thought about it but wasn't sure I wanted to go all nuclear family right away, so I went upstairs to my own room. I wondered if I would have my own room at my dad's.

I smelled the popcorn, which made me want to watch the movie. But I couldn't summon the strength to make small talk. I wondered what my father was doing at that exact moment. Would we have family movie nights, just the two of us? What kind of movies did he watch? Would he let me pick once in a while? I fell asleep dreading Monday and the return to school.

CHAPTER SIXTEEN

SATURDAY MORNING WAS chaotic because the twins were excited about their friend Marcus's birthday party that afternoon. Apparently, there'd be a cake and games, so they were out of their minds all morning. Breakfast was spent with them telling me—in painful detail—about their last birthday party. They seemed to have forgotten last night's disaster, which made me wish I could do that to my memory sometimes.

Mrs. M and I cleaned up the kitchen while Mr. M took the boys upstairs to gather their laundry. "If you want me to wash your clothes, Shay, I'll put them through the cycle with the boys' clothes while Mr. M is at the birthday party."

"Oh, no, I know how to wash my clothes; you don't have to do that."

"Okay. When you're ready, I'll show you how to use the

Beast and the Beauty. That's the washer and dryer. The Beast has a mind of its own; it's a little tricky. The Beauty is new and wonderful. Plays music when the cycle ends, senses when to stop drying, energy efficient." She sighed. "When did I turn into someone who rhapsodizes about a dryer that automatically shuts off when the clothes are dry?"

After we finished cleaning up from breakfast, Mr. and Mrs. M took us all shopping. The boys would buy birthday presents with Mr. M, while Mrs. M had a list for me, which turned out to be quite a haul.

Here's a list of everything I got
1. A laundry basket
2. Two binders for school
3. Some cool erasable pens in different colors
4. Snow boots, a winter coat, gloves, and a hat
5. A hoodie, pajama pants, and a couple long-sleeved T-shirts
6. Socks, underwear, and a lamp for my nightstand

So much stuff. It was a little overwhelming. Mrs. M even wanted to get me more stuff.

<u>Here's what I turned down</u>

1. A second hoodie

2. Flannel sheets

3. An alarm clock

4. A reusable water bottle for school.

Told you—overwhelming.

Even with all the stuff we bought, we still got to the register before Mr. M and the boys. Then they showed up even more excited than before.

"Shay, check out these presents we got for Marcus. This is a coloring book, but it's not a regular coloring book; it's disappearing ink, so you can color it over if you want. And we got him a game, and we got him a puzzle."

"Wow, great stuff. Marcus will love it."

They beamed. "You got cool stuff too. Can I see your pens? Can I borrow the red one? Why did you get a lamp? Can I wear the hat?" We drove home with Nathan wearing the hat and Eli wearing the gloves.

When we got home, Mr. M took the twins to get ready for the party. Mrs. M helped carry my stuff to my room.

"Thanks so much for all the stuff, Mrs. M. I really appreciate it."

She picked up the coat, hat, and gloves. "I'll take these to the closet by the door. It's supposed to snow later. You're welcome, Shay. I'm glad you're here. If you want to do laundry today, let me know. I'll be working in my office. Will you be okay on your own?" I nodded. Her office was a converted closet near the laundry room, with enough room for a desk, a table, and a chair. But the door allowed Mrs. M to work in peace when the twins were home.

I put all my new stuff away. So much stuff. I organized my school stuff in my new binders and set up the small lamp on my night table. It actually felt cozier. Then I cleaned the bathroom. My bathroom. I also reread the letter from my father. I noticed he'd signed it, "Your father, Vic." Was it weird that he hadn't called himself "Dad"? Would that have been weirder? Would I call him Vic or Dad? I still hadn't decided what to write to him. My room was so cozy that, for a few minutes, I couldn't remember why I wanted to leave the Morgensterns.

I went downstairs and stopped at Mrs. M's office. "Do you want a cup of tea?"

"I would love one, Shay."

"Any special flavor?"

"Whatever you're having."

"I'll be right back." I made two cups of something called "Autumnal Harvest" that smelled appley spicey and carried hers back to the office.

"Ooh, excellent choice for a cold day. Thank you. What are you doing today?"

"I put all my new stuff away. Thank you again. I'm going to read in front of the TV for a while."

"Sounds good. Let me know if you get bored."

"It's actually nice to finally have a day without stress, but I'll let you know."

I read for a while, watched some TV, and drank my tea, enjoying the quiet. But after a while, it was too quiet. I thought I would be able to relax with not having constant stress, but it turned out I didn't know what to do with my mind. Not wanting to bother Mrs. M while she was working, I went upstairs to get the Anger Journal that Dr. Carol had given me on Wednesday.

Then I went back to the study. While watching some cooking show, I tried to write about my anger, but it was hard to remember all the times I was angry. Plus, what about the pre-anger times? I had a lot of those too. I was still embarrassed about getting mad at Nathan last night. I turned to a fresh page and made a list with two columns, labeling them Pre-Angry and Angry. Then I started filling it in. I realized these would be long lists. Really long. This made me sad, which made me angry.

"Add it to the list," I said to Spock, curled at my feet. He didn't respond.

"What list?" Mrs. M had come into the room. She stood in front of the books with the weird writing on them and pulled one out. I joined her. (Listen to how good I was at deflecting as I totally deflected her question into a question of my own.)

"What's the weird writing on all these books?"

"It's Hebrew. This is *Ha-Tzofeh le-Bet Yisrael*—a book of essays. I'm doing some research for a class I'm teaching that starts next week." She handed me the book. She pointed at the characters on the cover, naming them while she moved her finger right to left. Then, ignoring my expert deflection, she asked, "What list?"

Resigned, I told her. "You know I get angry—Dr. Carol gave me a journal to help me with it. I'm supposed to write down all the things that make me angry."

Mrs. M made a face. "And you're making a list?" She laughed when I nodded. "If I made a list of all the times I was angry, I wouldn't have time to do anything else."

I was shocked. "Really?"

"Yep. I don't always show it. Sometimes, I get angry at one thing, but it's because of something else. Maybe you should provide some context of the whole, you know, situation around getting angry."

I wasn't sure what she meant.

"The other night, you got so mad you ran out."

The reminder made me cringe internally, but she, of course, didn't see it.

"But there was a lot going on—the letter from your father, Rhonda being kind of a jerk, plus you'd just gotten here. With all that context, it's understandable you'd be angry."

Wow. She thought Rhonda was being a jerk too. I didn't say anything.

"What I'm saying is that you may want to include a little context with your list of angry incidents."

Oh. That made sense. "I guess I can include a little context. That way it's not only a list of all the times I got mad."

"Are you angry right now?"

I thought about it for a minute. "No. You're all being really nice to me. School, on the other hand, is a nightmare."

She laughed. "I'll bet it is. Anything I can help with?"

"Nope. Just trying to survive every day."

"Good plan. Well, I'll leave you to your journal. I have to plan some lessons on modern Hebrew literature."

I climbed back onto the chair, wrapping myself around the cat, who was stretched out across the whole cushion. I started writing about my first night here—finding the cake and meeting Mr. M in the middle of the night. It was easier to write that way—tell what happened instead of listing all the anger.

So, these are my Anger Chronicles. Enjoy.

CHAPTER SEVENTEEN

THE TWINS CAME in from their birthday party all caked up and hyper. It was cold but sunny out, so I offered to take them outside. I wore my new coat and hat. I'd never had my own brand-new coat before. When I said this to Mr. M as he was bundling up the twins, his face scrunched up. Was he about to cry?

"Well, Shay..." he started but stopped. I could tell he didn't know what to say. "It fits great." It's odd how often I evoked pity without even trying. Sort of a superpower, I guessed.

I saw Mr. M checking in on us from the front window. The twins had each brought home a rubber ball from the birthday party. We played three-way catch, and then they tried to play Keep Away from me. It started snowing as we went inside for dinner.

After dinner, I was introduced to Family Game Night, the most nuclear thing ever. I almost couldn't handle the nuclearity of it. The boys brought out a stack of games, insisting I pick one. I thought Exploding Kittens sounded interesting, causing the boys to flip out with joy. We had to make sound effects when we drew an exploding kitten card, and—I have to be honest—my exploding kitten noise was by far the best in this group. It was a good explosion sound that built up to a crash followed by a little "mew" right at the end. Not loud, just accurate. The first time I made the noise, Mr. and Mrs. M both stared at me. The boys lost their minds. Then I had to make the noise a few more times. It was fun to make Nathan and Eli laugh hard.

We played a few more games before it was time for the boys to go to bed. Exhausted, I went up to my room shortly after they did. All that lack of stress today or maybe all the nuclearity had added up. Either way, I simply wanted to be alone. I wanted to get caught up in my Anger Journal. Also, I was about to finish *Dune*. There were more books in the series, but I'd still be sad when this one was over. I sat in bed, wearing my new pajama bottoms and a long-sleeved T-shirt, with Spock at my feet, writing in my journal. Snow fell outside the little window of my room.

I wondered if my dad had cat or a dog. I wondered if we'd play games and if he'd enjoy my exploding kitten noise as much as the twins did. I made the exploding kitten sound softly, just for Spock, who simply squinted at me, inscrutable as ever.

"Not impressed? Okay. You're going in my journal, Mr. Spock."

He winked one eye at me. I winked back. Then I settled in to finish *Dune*.

*

SUNDAY MORNING, IT was still snowing. I went out to help Mr. M shovel the driveway in my new coat, hat, boots, and gloves. When we came back in, the table was packed with bagels, cream cheese, tomatoes, and onions. I had lox for the first time—salty, fishy, but good. Eli ate some but turned up his nose. Nathan didn't try it.

After brunch, Mr. M said I was invited to go with them all to visit his mother. He told me it'd be fine if I didn't want to go. The boys stared at me, so I said I'd go. Turned out to be one of the best decisions I made that week. Mrs. Morgenstern was funny and sharp as hell. I didn't know why she was in a nursing home. She played hide-and-seek with the twins, but the best part was that she didn't ask me any typical "old person" questions about my gender, race, or religion. At one point, Mr. M took the twins in search of snacks while Mrs. M took a call from someone and stepped into the hall.

Mrs. Morgenstern and I sat together. It wasn't awkward, not at all, which was super weird. She kind of reminded me of grandma but without the stressed panic and constant worry on her face.

"So, Shay, how do you like living with twin boys?"

"They're fun and really enthusiastic about everything."

She laughed. "That's a great way to put it. Enthusiastic. Who did you live with before?"

Here we go. The questions. The endless questions. Let's

relive your life failures, Shay. Why did you get kicked out of so many families, Shay? Why doesn't a family function anymore once you show up, Shay? Why did your family break, Shay? What did you do? I briefly considered a Custard Pie Lie to spare her feelings, but I had a feeling she'd see right through it. My lying skills were on a bit of a downslope lately. Plus, she'd eventually find out the truth from her son, Mr. M.

My other play when people probed too much was a piece of truth. The shock value of the truth plus the pity that always followed usually stopped the questions. My pre-anger helped me decide to flood her with truth.

"Well, Mrs. Morgenstern," I began, but she interrupted me.

"I'm Devorah. The twins call me Nana, but you can call me Dev."

Okay.

"Well, Dev, my mother died of an overdose. My grandma took care of me until she died. My grandfather can't take care of himself, much less me. My father was in jail until a few weeks ago." I stopped, hoping the questions would too.

"That sounds terrible, Shay. I'm very sorry." She sounded truly sorry. (Judgment: Genuine.)

"Why are you here, Dev? You don't need a lot of nursing." She smiled sadly.

"I came here to be with my husband. He needed care. A lot of care. When he passed, I stayed because I couldn't bear the thought of going back to our home to live by myself."

I guessed we'd both suffered some loss. I understood about

not wanting to go home. I thought about my first social worker, Brenda. We went back to my grandparents' house after Grandma died, after Pops was put in a home. It was dark and cold, and the smell—of them, of home—just about killed me. When we walked in, it made me want to run right back out. I turned to leave, but Brenda stopped me.

"Let's get your stuff, Shay," she said, so we went to my little room upstairs—Gram's old sewing room—grabbed a backpack, shoved in some clothes, and got the hell out. I've never thought about that day until now.

"Are you mad about something?" Dev asked.

"Oh, I remembered a homework assignment I left at school on Friday." The lie slipped right out. "Math homework."

Of course, she didn't believe me. (Told you my lie skills were slipping.) That unpleasant memory of going back to Grandma's house made me mad.

She shook her head. "Math homework. Ha. Don't bullshit a bullshitter."

I stared at her, my mouth dropping open. A grown-up had just cursed at me. But her eyes were smiling, so I couldn't help myself. I smiled back.

Mrs. M came back into the room. "I'm sorry, Dev. We have to leave soon. Mrs. Adler died."

Dev nodded. "Of course, dear. Tell Maggie I'm very sorry about her mother."

Mr. M and the boys came back in, their arms filled with snacks. "We got cookies and juice and water and almonds!"

Mr. and Mrs. M spoke quietly. Mr. M put his arm around her shoulders briefly.

"Sorry boys," he said. "We have to leave early today. You can each pick one snack to take home. We'll leave the rest here with Nana." The boys were clearly unhappy about leaving snacks behind but did as they were told and, remarkably, didn't fight about it.

We said our goodbyes. Mrs. M leaned into Dev for a hug, and they touched foreheads. Dev said something to her quietly. Mrs. M nodded.

The ride back was quiet, even though the boys talked about their snacks the whole way. When we got home, Mrs. M went to change and left after a brief goodbye. I set the boys up to watch a movie, then went into the kitchen to make popcorn. Mr. M sat at the table. He just sat there. It was weird seeing him not in motion. Spock sat at his feet, peering up at him.

"Hey, Shay," Mr. M said. "Thanks for starting the movie. I'll be right in."

He had a strange expression on his face. Kind of sad. Then I knew what the matter was. He was thinking about his mother. His mother was old, too, just like Mrs. Adler. I knew he was thinking about his mother because I was thinking about my mother. I pointed at the cat.

Mr. M glanced down. "Yeah, he's sort of an emotional therapy cat sometimes." On cue, Spock jumped up into Mr. M's lap.

I sat at the table. "Is Mrs. M doing rabbi things tonight?"

He nodded. "She has to help plan the funeral and comfort

Mrs. Adler's family."

He paused, then asked, "What sort of service did you have for your mother?"

I tried to remember and got sad when I couldn't. Then I remembered why.

"I didn't go to my mother's funeral. I was in the hospital. I had pneumonia."

"Oh, Shay, I'm sorry."

My Grandma's funeral had sucked. "My Grandma's funeral was small. There were at most five people at the funeral parlor. They said some prayers, I think. Pops, my grandfather, was crying. It was awful. Because he was in a wheelchair, he couldn't stand up on his own to see in the coffin. One of the funeral parlor guys helped him stand up, and he cried and cried. I stayed in the back the whole time. When it was time to leave, a nurse took Pops outside. Then they rolled the coffin out. I stayed inside. I didn't know where to go. Finally, Brenda, my social worker, came and said it was time to go home."

"But you didn't go home to stay, did you." It was more of a statement than a question.

"No. My grandfather went into a nursing home, and I went into a group home."

"You've been through some real shitty stuff, haven't you." Another question that was really a statement. Another grown-up cursing right to my face. I had quite the effect on people.

The microwave kept dinging about the popcorn. I shrugged in response to his question/statement.

Mr. M put Spock on the floor, got up, got a bowl, and poured the popcorn into it. "Mrs. M probably won't be home until very late tonight." He turned to the door. "Eli! Come here please."

Eli came into the kitchen. Mr. M handed him the bowl.

"Share with your brother."

Eli took the bowl and tried to leave, but Mr. M didn't let go of it. Eli dramatically rolled his eyes like an eight-year-old.

"We'll share, Dad. I promise."

Mr. M let go, and Eli went back into the living room.

Mr. M told me everything that would happen to Mrs. Adler, all the rituals that would take place for her family to say goodbye. Mrs. M was in charge of all of it. The final part was sitting Shiva, where people visited Mrs. Adler's family to pay their respects. Mr. M told me we'd go over sometime during the week. I wondered how many times the boys had sat Shiva.

I knew Mr. M was still thinking about his mother. He'd have to sit Shiva for her too. Eventually, Eli and Nathan would sit Shiva for him. It was a super dark thought, but it was sort of comforting to know the rituals would continue. I saw gratitude in his eyes.

"Thanks for the talk, Shay. I worry about Mrs. M when she has to do this part of her job. It can be difficult."

"No problem. I'll do whatever I can to help."

He nodded, and I got up and joined the twins in the study.

"What's Shiva?" I asked them.

"Ugh. You have to sit and be quiet and think about the dead person and their family."

"Most of the time I don't even know the dead person."

"It takes hours and hours."

"You can't bring toys, and you can't have snacks."

"And you have to wear a tie."

"And shoes."

"It's boring."

The twins had sat a lot of Shiva, apparently.

I spent the rest of the evening wondering about my funeral.

CHAPTER EIGHTEEN

SCHOOL ON MONDAY was not the usual Mothball Dance of up, down, up down. It was all down, a mothball that didn't want to dance because it didn't have any friends because it had been dropped in a new jar of vinegar every few months.

Here are the lowlights
1. I didn't see Toya all day except for art, and we didn't get to talk
2. I almost fought with Jamie at lunch
3. I wrote a letter to my father, which was stolen out of my locker (hence the fight with Jamie)

I pretty much spent the entire day in a state of anger. Charlie met me at my locker in the morning, and by "met me," I mean slammed my locker shut as soon as I opened it, as a joke. Ha ha. She could have crushed my fingers but, instead, stood there, laughing at my angry-face, demanding interaction.

"What'd you do this weekend, loser?"

I reopened my locker, wedging my foot in the bottom so I could get my stuff for class. "Let the spice flow and rode a sandworm."

"No, seriously. Listen, there's a party this weekend at this kid, Favor's, house. You gotta come. Favor's parents are out of town, but her aunt is staying with her. She's cool. She's, like, twenty."

I moved my foot. She slammed my locker closed again. "Sure, it sounds fun." I lied.

"Great," Charlie said, but her face was in her phone as she wandered off. I headed to homeroom. (You should know that I love parties except for the people. Music? Good. Food? Good. Drinks? Good. I drink, but I don't get drunk because I'm not stupid. The people at parties are stupid—that's why I hate everyone at parties.) If Charlie and her pack were planning to go, they'd blab about it all week. Next week, it'd be all about how drunk they got, blah blah blah. Damn, it was only Monday morning, but already everything sucked.

Instead of doing the reading during social studies, I wrote my father a letter in my notebook. I asked him about: his job, his apartment, what he did on the weekends, what he cooked, whether he had an email address, and finally, whether he still wanted to come visit. I didn't say that I forgave him for screwing up, disappearing, getting arrested, not being there for most of my life. I didn't say I forgave him because I really super didn't. It made me angry to even think about it, so I avoided that.

I put my social studies notebook with the letter in my locker. I wasn't sure I'd mail it. Even if I did, I wasn't sure I'd tell the Morgensterns about it. I thought about the letter all through science, where I probably failed a quiz. When I got to the cafeteria, I walked up to Charlie's table. Jamie, Charlie, and the Nameless Phone Faces all looked up at me at the exact same time. I really didn't understand the expressions on all their faces.

Their faces. I could see all their faces. They weren't on their phones. Jamie held a notebook—a blue spiral notebook, just like my social studies notebook. It had "Social Studies" written on it, just like my social studies notebook. It had my name on it, JUST LIKE MY SOCIAL STUDIES NOTEBOOK. White-hot anger filled my whole body.

I stuck out my hand. "Give me my notebook." I said it so quietly I was sure they couldn't even hear it, but they knew what I was saying. As Jamie started to hand it to me, Charlie spoke up.

"No."

They all smirked at me.

"Open it," Charlie ordered Jamie. She did. Right to the page with the letter to my dad. "Take a picture." More instructions to Jamie.

Jamie's head swiveled to me then back at Charlie. She took

out her phone to obey just as I flew at her.

I knocked the phone out of her hand and grabbed my notebook. She pushed me away with both hands. As I launched at her, a cafeteria aide shoved between us. It was over before anyone else in the cafeteria knew what was going on. The aide stood between us.

Jamie yelled as I walked away, "My damned screen is cracked. That bitch cracked my screen."

Clutching the notebook, I left the cafeteria, past the aide at the door, who didn't even try to stop me. I wandered around the school for a while, making me super late to math class. Ms. Schunk asked me for a pass, which I didn't have. She asked me to come after school to get the notes on what I missed. Sigh.

After math class, I asked Ms. Schunk if I could stay and get the notes with her next class, but she told me I had to go to language arts. I plodded down the hall to the room with Jamie and her cracked screen, getting there in time for Ms. Moss to step into the hall with Jamie.

"Ah, Shay. Come over here with us please." Ms. Moss was about to go into her teacher-as-counselor role. All teachers thought they knew the best way to resolve conflicts in their classroom, but all they really wanted was for us to be quiet. I walked over to them. Inside the classroom, chaos reigned. One kid was using the classroom phone (forbidden!), another drew inappropriate things on the board (naughty!).

"Now, Shay, Jamie says you broke her phone at lunch."

Wow. Ms. Moss was even worse at this than I thought she'd

be. This would be easy. "Jamie went into my locker without my permission and took stuff out."

Ms. Moss turned to Jamie. "Jamie, is this true?"

Jamie caught on. Of course, she did. "What about my phone?"

Back to me. "Shay, did you break Jamie's phone?"

"How could I? We're not allowed to have our phones out at lunch."

Back to Jamie. "That's true, Jamie. Did you have your phone out?"

I added, trying to piss Jamie off a little more. "Also, Ms. Moss—Jamie told me she didn't like the *Monkey's Paw*. She said it was stupid and obvious."

Ms. Moss had told us several times it was one of her favorite short stories. Jamie hadn't actually said that, but my lie turned out to be the winning shot in this little game. Ms. Moss turned to Jamie. She actually looked hurt.

Jamie blew up at me. "You lying bitch! You're fucking lying!"

When the teacher next door came over, I slipped into class. Jamie never made it in—apparently, she was sent to Ms. Moss's buddy room for disruptive students.

Wanda smiled at me. "Got her sent to the buddy room. Nice work."

Raymond smiled, too, though his vanished as he uttered his first words to me: "You've made a powerful enemy today." *The Simpsons* quote chilled me.

Wanda's smile vanished now. I put my head down on my

desk. Ugh.

Later, during art class, Toya nodded at me. That was it. Nothing else, only a nod. She wasn't even smiling. This day was really a piece of garbage.

To make things worse, at the end of the day, I had a detention with Ms. Schunk. I didn't care about the detention; I'd had a million before. I didn't want it to be with Ms. Schunk. When I got to her room, she asked who to call to let them know I was staying for detention. I needed to deflect this phone call.

Now, I liked Ms. Schunk. Lying to her would have been super shitty. I decided to gamble with the truth. I told her Jamie had gone into my locker and taken something. We'd argued about it at lunch, so I got mad and left the cafeteria, then got lost.

Ms. Schunk didn't try to play counselor or anything, just told me to stay away from Jamie. I agreed heartily, even as I knew there was no way I'd ever be able to avoid Jamie. I asked her not to tell the M's about the detention, promising never to be late again. She said she'd give me another chance but had to call because I was going to be late from school. She called Mr. M and said I was staying after to get help with math. A lie. I was shocked. I knew adults lied to kids, and kids lied to everyone, but adults lying to adults?

"Well, Shay, let's talk about what you missed in math today."

"What? I thought I was having detention."

"That, too, but I told Mr. Morgenstern you were staying for help. We're definitely doing math."

It turns out Ms. Schunk wasn't a complete liar. I was a little disappointed she wasn't a complete liar like me but also a little relieved.

The day got worse when I got home. Mr. M was there with the twins. Mrs. M was over at the Adlers'. The twins were having a snack and doing their homework in the kitchen. Mr. M took me into the study.

"One of your teachers called and said you'd had an issue with another student today." He paused. I guessed he was waiting for me to talk. Damn, Ms. Schunk had ratted me out for having a detention after saying she wouldn't. That was disappointing.

I told him the same thing I told her. "Jamie went into my locker and took my social studies notebook. We argued at lunch, and then I got lost on my way to math class. That's why I was late."

His brows knit in confusion. "Notebook? Math class? I'm talking about the phone. Ms. Moss called about a phone."

Oh. Ms. Schunk wasn't a rat. Ms. Moss was. That tracked.

"Jamie dropped her phone when I took the notebook she stole out of my locker." I was getting angry. No one cared that she had gone into my locker.

"Jamie said you knocked her phone out of her hands."

So now I had an important decision to make. Telling the truth (that I broke the phone) meant the M's would have to pay for a new screen. Or I could tell a lie (she dropped it). But that was a Big Lie. Plus, the witnesses (Charlie and the Nameless Phone Faces) would definitely say I slapped her phone out of her hands.

Here was the thing. I broke the screen. I did. I definitely knocked the phone out of Jamie's stupid hand because she was about to take a picture of the letter I'd written to my recently-re-leased-from-prison father to post it on social media, which would have followed me for the rest of my life. Yeah, I didn't want that to happen, so I slapped her weak-ass hand, her phone fell, and the screen cracked. The question was, should I lie to Mr. M? If so, how big a lie? Because I didn't trust my ability to pull off a Big Lie, I went small.

"She had my notebook. The phone fell when I grabbed my notebook out of her hands." I emphasized that it was *my notebook* because they didn't care that she had *gone into my locker*. I told him a Small Lie surrounded by truth, which was, in my humble opinion, believable by him while being totally manageable by me.

Mr. M stared right at me. I maintained eye contact, which was important because I really needed him to believe the Small Lie and surrounding truth of what I had said. I forced myself not to drop my eyes, which was my tell that apparently everybody, including children, knew about.

"Ms. Moss told me Jamie said it would cost about 150 dollars to repair it. I'll call Jamie's parents after we talk. I don't care about the phone. Well, I care a little about the phone. I want to make sure you're okay."

I assured him I was. He asked about the notebook. I told him I didn't know why she had it or how she'd gotten into my locker. (That's all true. Why did she steal that notebook? How did she get into my locker?)

"Ms. Moss said you almost fought with Jamie. Is that true?"

Yes, it was true, but Ms. Moss didn't see that part in the

cafeteria.

"Jamie got mad when Ms. Moss tried to talk to us about it, but we didn't 'almost fight.'" A little lie because I knew he'd freak out if I told the truth about how Jamie and I were about to fight. Twice.

"Okay, Shay." He paused. "What else do I need to know?" He waited.

At first, I didn't know what he wanted. Then I knew exactly what he wanted. He wanted the Big Truth. All of it. He knew I was lying, that there was more to the story. Now, I had another decision to make.

I could tell him the truth about the letter to my dad along with my intentions to move in with him. I could tell him I'd been in countless other fights, and if Jamie and I ever fought, I already knew her weak spots. I could tell him I was having fun in math class and didn't hate science or social studies either. Since tomorrow was art club, maybe Toya would be there, maybe she thought I was nice too. I could tell him I hoped every day that Charlie's crew would stop being mean girls for once, that maybe Nathan would stop treating me as if I robbed his piggy bank. I could tell Mr. M all of the Big Truths. I felt free at the thought of doing that, almost weightless. My eyes burned with the relief of it.

I opened my mouth to speak, but nothing came out—like a cartoon with the sound turned all the way down. I'd had these kinds of dreams, where I was screaming, but it was silent. Nothing. No Big Truth, not even a Small Truth. I wanted to scream all the Big Truths, but...not a word. He was listening to me, but I wasn't saying anything. I just couldn't. It was too much. Too many Big Truths had clogged up the pipeline. I was pissed at myself. This was why I was such a fuckup.

I could see disappointment all over his face while he continued to wait. Thankfully, we were interrupted when Eli came into the room.

Mr. M turned to him. "What's up, pal?"

"I'm done with my homework."

"Want me to check it for you?" I offered because I needed to get out of the study. They both regarded me with suspicion. When Eli finally nodded, we went into the kitchen, where Nathan was doing his homework. He could tell I was angry by taking one look at my face. He got down off his chair and left the room. I checked Eli's homework until Mr. M and Nathan returned to start dinner. I stayed for a few minutes, then went upstairs.

Mrs. M came home for dinner. After everything was cleaned up, we had a talk. Mrs. M was stressed and tired. She needed to return to the Adlers', but first, they had to deal with my mess because I was a fuckup. Our chat was a dancing mothball of up and down. Up—Jamie's parents told them the phone was insured, so they wouldn't have to pay for anything. Down—I was grounded for a week. Up—being grounded meant I couldn't go to the party at Favor's house. Didn't really want to go anyway. Down—they didn't say anything, but I knew they were really regretting taking me in.

After the talk, I asked them for an envelope and a stamp, explaining that it was for a letter to a kid from my group home. Mr. M gave me one, and Mrs. M headed back to the Adlers'. I went upstairs for some privacy. I tore out the letter to my father from my notebook, put it in the envelope, addressed it, then put the stamped envelope in my backpack. I'd make it as easy for the M's as I could. They were too nice to have to deal with me. I'd do them the favor of finding a new placement for myself before they had to. My father had made me, then abandoned me. It was up to him to fix whatever my problem was. My next placement would be my last, with my father.

Chapter Nineteen

TUESDAY WAS FINE. My stuff wasn't safe in my locker, so carried my stuff in my backpack to every class, even though we weren't supposed to. Not a single teacher said anything if they even noticed. There was no drama—which was unusual but really fine with me. In art class, Toya nodded and smiled at me, making my stomach jump. I think I smiled back, but it was probably more of a grimace due to my shock. When class ended, everyone walked out, including Toya. I sat at my table for one, waiting for art club. No one else came, so I almost left, but then Mr. Rueben noticed me there all alone.

"Art club starts in five minutes, Shay. Want to help me get stuff out? Grab a smock."

I put on a smock, then helped him put painting supplies on two rolling carts.

"We're working on a couple murals around school," he said as he handed me a can filled with paintbrushes of all sizes.

Kids started coming in, one or two nodding at us. They were a mix of sixth, seventh, and eighth graders.

"Murals today, Mr. Reuben?"

"You betcha, Misha."

When Toya walked in, my stomach flip-flopped. As per usual, I turned my bright red face away.

"Shay!" She came right over to me. "Come with my group today, okay?"

I nodded. Idiot. My mouth didn't drop open like a fish this time in her presence, so I considered that making progress. I only had to speak to her to accomplish a life goal. Toya turned away to talk with some other kids as I mentally berated myself for not speaking. A simple greeting would have been fine. Mouth check—still closed. Keep it together, Turner, I said to myself.

Toya started pushing one of the rolling carts. "Mr. Reuben, we'll get started in the eighth-grade hallway, okay?"

Mr. Reuben waved as he continued talking to another group of smocked students.

Toya introduced me to the kids who were following us out of the art room. "Mekhi, Brenda, this is Shay."

"Hi, Shay," one of them said. "We're off to the eighth-grade hallway."

"There's a mural of Malala there."

"Do you know who Malala is?"

I nodded at Brenda and glanced at Toya, who smiled, rolling

her eyes at the sixth graders.

We got to the eighth-grade hallway, which seemed larger without students everywhere. I'd walked down this hallway every day but never noticed the outline penciled on the wall—clearly Malala accepting her Nobel Peace Prize. In the background, lots of sketched-in girls cheered her on. Pretty cool.

"This is cool." I said, to Toya, finally crossing something off my Life Goals List. I opened my mouth to add *Can't wait to see it finished*, but with the nice smile she gave me, I, of course, lost all ability to speak. Eventually, I realized my mouth was still open, so I closed it. One step forward, two steps back on the whole Life Goals List thing.

Toya poured paint into some trays to start the sixth graders working on the mural. "Come with me," she said. "We're doing a special project."

We rolled the cart down the hallway and stopped outside my science classroom.

"Ms. Winken asked us for a rainbow design around her doorway. She runs the queer club."

My face suddenly got hot. I'd always known I was different, probably gay or bi or something. I really liked Toya, but I'd liked boys before. What was that? I just knew I wasn't the same as everyone else. Yet another way I was different. Everyone else was so sure of what they were and who they were. Here at Consolidated Middle, there was even a club for it. I knew the word "queer"—it sounded kind of scary. But maybe not too scary. Maybe it was safe to finally have a label for what I thought. Who I was. Okay, maybe

I was queer. I'd give it a shot—calling myself "queer."

Toya tilted her head at me. "You okay?"

Deflect. "Yep. There's no pencil outline. Are we going to free-hand this?"

She shook her head. "No. Today, we design. Next week, we paint."

My face stopped burning eventually. We brainstormed ideas for something besides a plain rainbow. She was super creative. Together, we planned a rainbow that started at the floor, very lightly, almost invisible, then got brighter as it reached the ceiling. As Toya started the pencil outline near the floor, I went back to the art room to borrow a stepladder to get to the ceiling.

I have to say, while we were working, I actually spoke to her. We had a conversation. Maybe it was finally calling myself "queer" or simply being around her; it got way easier. Art club was almost over, but we'd finished the outline a while ago and now sat on the floor, talking as if we were regular humans. I couldn't tell you what we were talking about, but it was easy.

Her phone alarm chimed. "Hey. We've got to get back to Mr. Rueben's room so the kids can clean their brushes."

We rolled the cart back to the sixth graders, who had done an amazing job of painting part of the mural.

"Gorgeous. Nice job." I said. They smiled and pushed each other.

We all went back to the art room to put everything away.

"See you next week, everyone." Mr. Rueben waved as we walked out. I didn't want art club to end.

Toya walked with me out the school door. She pointed to a car. "My dad's here. Want a ride?"

My brain screamed "Yes!" but I couldn't handle it. No way. "No, thanks. I live close."

"Okay, then. See you in art class tomorrow."

"Yep." I said, regretting that I wasn't getting into the car for five more minutes with her.

"Oh. And Mr. Rueben said we could work on the rainbow after school anytime we want. If you want to."

"Yeah, sure. Absolutely." And then I was super brave. "Can you stay tomorrow?"

She smiled. "Yeah. Tomorrow works."

I couldn't believe it. We'd made a plan to hang out (I know, we'd be painting the mural for art club, but still) tomorrow after school. And then I got greedy, over confident, and went for Thursday. This time, everything changed.

I asked, "And how about Thursday?"

She shook her head. "I can't Thursday. I have queer club."

She was in queer club. She was queer. She was queer, and I was queer. We were queer. My mouth dropped open. I had to say something.

"Okay. Well, I'll see you tomorrow." Then (and I warn you, this is super cringy), I started walking away. I turned away from this person who'd bravely admitted to a new friend that they were queer.

All the way home, I whisper-scolded myself. "Not supportive, not cool, not at all cool, you dummy."

The entire night I was a dancing mothball of emotions—floating up because I was queer and Toya was queer, sinking down because I was a dumb, stupid, unsupportive idiot. I spent a lot of time dwelling on the sinking down mothball aspects of my day. I really was the worst sometimes. I was super uncool. Here I always thought queer people were supposed to be cooler. Ha. Not me.

CHAPTER TWENTY

WEDNESDAY WAS MINIMALLY dramatic. I think because it was February, teachers and kids were too tired to stir shit up. School plodded on—teachers tried to be enthusiastic about stuff, but the kids weren't buying it. Charlie was quiet, which meant Jamie hadn't received orders to mess with me, so they left me alone. Still, I didn't see Toya until art class.

My heart started beating as soon as I walked in. She wasn't there yet, but I wandered around the room, hanging out near her table until she came in. I hoped she wasn't disappointed that I hadn't been more supportive. When she walked in, her face was sad or maybe serious about something. Then she saw me standing around because I was a dummy and gave me a big smile and came right over.

"Hey, Shay."

"Hey, Toya." The bell rang to start class. I floated on a cloud to the back of the room and my table for one.

After class, we smocked up and rolled our cart to the rainbow outside Ms. Wilkins's room. Toya still seemed down but didn't say why.

"You okay?" I finally asked.

"Oh, yeah. Sorry. I have lots going on outside school."

Okay, she wasn't too mad at me. We started painting the rainbow but didn't talk except for about the mural; she really disappeared into herself.

We rolled everything back to the art room as Mr. Reuben was leaving. "See you tomorrow, Mr. Reuben," we said at the same time. We turned to each other, and I giggled. She smiled and my face got red. My giggle must have sounded really dumb because I wasn't a giggler. I really wasn't. (You can probably tell that about me.)

Mrs. M was waiting for me as we walked out of school. Toya's dad was there too. We waved goodbye. I hoped she'd say something but she just got into the car with her dad.

"Who's that?" Mrs. M asked.

"Toya. She's in art club with me."

"Art club? That's why you needed a ride. Well, that's good, joining a club. I didn't know you were an artist."

"I'm not. Art class is cool, and Mr. Reuben said I could join."

Mrs. M was really tired. She didn't even ask if I'd gotten into any "almost fights" today. She dropped me off at Dr. Carol's, reminding me, "We're heading to the Adler's tonight after dinner to sit Shiva. You don't have to come, of course."

"Can I come if I'm not Jewish?"

"Of course."

"Then I'll come. The twins told me all about it."

She rolled her eyes. "Did they tell you they weren't allowed snacks?"

I nodded. "And they have to wear ties and keep their pants on."

She shook her head. "They really are two of a kind. I'll be here when you're done."

I went in for my appointment.

Rich White Lady was about to ask me about my week, and I hadn't prepared any story for her. I wasn't as angry at the thought of seeing her, for some reason. Maybe it was because of Toya floating around my brain all the time. I'd brought the anger journal for her to read, but she said she didn't want to.

"Then who'll read it?"

"It's for you, Shay. It's for you to kind of chronicle your experiences and track what makes you angry."

My anger. Right. My life, my anger, as told in The Anger Chronicles.

Dr. Carol jumped right in with "How was your week?"

I knew she probably already knew about the almost-fight with Jamie, so I told her about that. I told her the M's had grounded me, which was funny because I'd just been placed there, and already, I was on punishment. I made a comment about how much regret the M's must have for taking me on. Dr. Carol didn't disagree with me or anything, which was sort of sad, but also, I respected it because it was probably the truth.

I made her promise not to say anything first, then I told her about the letter to my father. She actually cared that Jamie had gone into my locker and stolen something. She was the first person who thought that was wrong too. Way to go, Dr. Carol.

We talked about how it felt to send the letter to my father and what I'd asked him. I didn't tell any outright lies to Dr. Carol today. I did omit the fact that I was crushing hard on a girl at school. I also omitted that I was planning on moving in with my father as soon as he could arrange it. But not saying something wasn't a lie, it was only leaving stuff out. That wasn't lying. At least, not in my book. Not in my Chronicles.

When the session was over, I realized I hadn't cried, definitely an improvement on the last time. Dr. Carol told me she was glad I was writing. I told her it wasn't only anger stuff, which she said was fine. I asked her if she was sure she didn't want to read it.

"Nope," she said. "You can tell me anything you want from the..." She glanced at the cover. "...Anger Chronicles. That title is quite fitting."

She asked about Consolidated Middle. I did the whole gloss-over-the-shitty-stuff that we do when adults ask us about school. I told her I didn't hate math, for once, and about Ms. Moss being a terrible teacher. She agreed it was shitty Jamie had revealed that Raymond and I were both fosters.

"Okay, Shay. That's our time. It was good seeing you again. I'm glad you came back."

Oh yeah. I'd forgotten that, last time, I had vowed not to come back. Now, it was awkward. Deflect.

"Oh. Yeah. Um, I really like that pen you gave me."

"Glides across the page, doesn't it?"

I nodded and left.

"How'd it go?" Mrs. M's question would become the standard after my sessions with Dr. Carol.

"Fine" was always my one-word response. I know she deserved more from me than that after waiting in the car for almost an hour, but I couldn't do it. I couldn't put it all back together again fast enough to casually chat about it on the drive home.

After a quick dinner, we were off to the Adlers'. The twins took turns telling me the rules and guidelines over and over until we got there. It was pretty interesting. We wouldn't knock on the door or ring the bell; we'd walk right in. The mirrors and TV would be covered, we'd sit on the floor. Sometimes, people took off their socks and shoes.

It was a school night, so we stayed about an hour. When we got home, Mr. M took the twins to put them to bed while I went right to my room. Mrs. M came in after I was in bed, reading.

"I just wanted to say goodnight, Shay."

"Goodnight. Sitting shiva was interesting. The twins did a good job."

I knew she had more important things to do than chat with me, but here she was. "Yeah, they did. I'm glad you found it interesting. Thanks for going with us." For a second, it seemed as if she wanted to say something else, but she didn't. "See you in the morning."

"See you in the morning."

I couldn't figure out what had prompted the goodnight visit, but it was kind of nice. I'd read in books about little kids getting tucked into bed. Maybe the goodnight visit was how kids my age got tucked in. I didn't hate it, to be honest. I felt terrible because I was nothing but trouble to them. They didn't deserve to be treated badly; they really didn't. I was an asshole. The sooner I was out of their house, the sooner I stopped causing them stress, the better. I lay awake for a long time berating myself for being such a problem child. I promised myself I would stay out of trouble.

I broke that promise the next day.

CHAPTER TWENTY-ONE

TOYA WAS ABSENT on Thursday, Charlie was up to her old tricks, and Jamie teamed up with Ms. Moss to almost ruin my life. Thursday sucked. I only got angry a few times, but a couple times, they were doozies. What the fuck was wrong with me?

First thing in the morning, Charlie came up to me at my locker. "What's up with you and Toya? You guys are hanging out? You know she's gay, right?" Charlie looked right at me. I stared right back.

"So what? Does it bother you?" Then I poked the bear. "What bothers you more, that I'm hanging out with her instead of you or that she's gay?"

I could tell I'd struck a nerve by saying I would rather hang out with Toya than her. She handled it by suddenly being super interested in something on her phone. Then she raised her head slowly to stare directly at me.

"I don't give a shit about Toya being gay. She's absent today. Do you miss her already? You know, you can tell me if you're dating someone."

Charlie was the absolute last person I would share dating information with. I let her know this by laughing right in her face. Out loud. "Ha ha, yeah, right."

I could tell she was super pissed. I was already super pissed. Without thinking, I shoved her into the lockers. It wasn't a hard shove, so she didn't shove me back or anything. It was over instantly with her walking away.

Someone behind me, an adult, barked, "Shay!"

Mr. Hamilton stood there, holding his clipboard with everyone's attendance and lunch orders. He'd seen me push Charlie. Was this about to become "an incident"? After my almost-fight, I was probably on thin ice as far as getting suspended. "Go have a seat, Shay."

I turned quickly to go into homeroom.

"Oh, wait. Chicken sandwich or peanut butter?"

"I packed today, Mr. Hamilton." He ticked that very important information on his clipboard, then continued taking attendance and lunch orders from the kids in line as I went into homeroom.

Marshall was already there, of course. He turned to me. "Why'd you push Charlie?"

"She was being annoying."

He laughed.

"Wait," I said. "How did you know? You were already in here."

He gestured to the front of the room, where Charlie was holding court. She was rubbing her shoulder, demonstrating our interaction, except making it appear as though I'd shoved her with the strength of a Sardaukar. She was being ridiculous, but she had the crowd's attention. Then, everyone turned to stare at me. Great. Now I wasn't only the New Kid, I was the Volatile Foster Kid. Whatever.

Marshall turned back to me, imitating a sports announcer: "To some she was a hero, to others, a villain. But Shay Turner will always be remembered for pushing Charlie Dawkins into a locker."

Mr. Hamilton came in just as the morning announcements started. "Sit down, Charlie. Marshall, turn around." This was his daily homeroom mantra as he sat at his desk, entering the all-important lunch counts and attendance. The bell rang, starting social studies, reminding me that I hadn't done my homework.

I didn't always use to be such a sucky student. I loved school when I started going. I used to play school with the kids on my block when we were in first and second grade. I was always the teacher, probably because I was bossy, but also, I didn't want other people to be in charge. Anyway, when I started having to take care of my mom, I stopped doing homework; I didn't have time. Of course, my grades started falling, followed by the calls home from school.

It was none of Charlie's business if Toya was queer. When

she tried to hurt me with it, in my humble opinion, she deserved to get pushed. Mr. Hamilton said he'd give me another day to do his homework. I was pretty sure his homework wouldn't get done, no matter how long he gave me. I think he knew it too.

Science was okay—I hadn't done the reading, but Marshall helped me finish the classwork. He gave me his phone number so I could call him if I needed help with the science and social studies assignments.

Lunch was where some more of the day's shit happened. I walked over to Charlie's table, with my lunch bag, ready to brave whatever they'd say about it. I was hungry. I was also tired of eating in the bathroom. Charlie and the Nameless Phone Faces were there. I sat down and started eating. No one said anything; they stared at their phones. Fine with me. No Jamie, which was weird as she was usually attached to Charlie whenever she could be. The decibel level in the cafeteria was deafening, but it was absolutely silent at this table. Something was up. I could tell.

At the whistle signaling the end of lunch, everyone stood up. Then it got even louder as a cold wetness ran down my back. I turned. Jamie, laughing, held an open, completely empty chocolate milk carton. I turned to Charlie and the Nameless, all of them now recording me on their phones. Everyone around us was laughing and pointing. I twisted to see. Sure enough, my back was drenched in chocolate milk.

I flew at Jamie, who backed away and ran out of the cafeteria. I tried to go after her, but one of the cafeteria aides held me back.

"No no no you don't," she said.

"Let me the fuck go!" I screamed at her, but she wouldn't. The absolute worst thing happened next. I started crying. The kids were being shooed from the cafeteria, most of them aiming their phones at me because I was covered in chocolate milk and CRYING. Blindly furious at everyone, I could have punched through a wall. A security guard I didn't know came over to wait with me and the aide. Luckily, no one tried to talk to me until Mr. Pod-nah showed up.

"Shay, let's go to my office."

"Leave me the fuck alone. I just want to go home." Mr. Stetson asked the aide to let me go, but the aide hesitated.

"You okay?" she asked. When I shrugged, she released me, adding, "Mr. Stetson, that other girl poured chocolate milk down this one's back. I saw it. Came up behind her."

"Thanks, Mrs. Smith," Mr. Pod-nah said.

I nodded to Mrs. Smith, who winked at me.

She leaned over and whispered, "Fuck them." I stared at her. She nodded at me. One of the other lunch ladies was already mopping up the milk on the floor.

"Bring her back here, Mr. Stetson." Mrs. Smith started toward the cafeteria kitchen. Mr. Pod-nah and I obediently followed her. M Mrs. Smith spoke to one of the other lunch ladies, then said, "Come back here, Shay. Mr. Stetson, you wait here."

I followed her to the very rear of the kitchen, where she handed me a T-shirt and a sweatshirt and a clean towel.

"There's a bathroom back there. Wipe off your back as best

you can. You can put your wet clothes in this plastic bag. Your pants are dry, pretty much."

I thanked her, went into the bathroom, then removed my soaked uniform shirt and bra. Luckily, I didn't really have much need of a bra, so the T-shirt and sweatshirt were fine. My pants were a little splashed but wearable. I went into the kitchen to find Mrs. Smith and Mr. Pod-nah.

"Thank you for the shirt and sweatshirt."

Mrs. Smith gripped my forearm. "Mr, Stetson, that Jamie girl is a straight-up troublemaker." Mr. Stetson tried to say something, but she cut him off. "She and her crew have run this school for years, bullying, making fun, and generally making everyone around them miserable."

"Thank you, Mrs. Smith," Mr. Stetson said.

She turned to me: "Get through this year and get to high school. It gets better."

I echoed Pod-nah: "Thank you, Mrs. Smith."

Mr. Stetson tried to say something, but she held up her hand, keeping her eyes locked on mine.

"You let me know if you need anything, okay? What's your full name?"

"Shay Turner."

"You find me if you need anything. Okay, Shay Turner?" she said and, when I nodded, turned to Mr. Stetson. "And you make sure that girl gets some punishment for what she did here today."

He also nodded. "Of course."

The next lunch group was entering the cafeteria—it sounded

like an avalanche, the volume getting louder every second.

"Go on, save yourselves," Mrs. Smith joked and smiled at me. I SMILED BACK AT HER. Mr. Pod-nah and I escaped through a side door.

We returned to his office to talk about my issues with Jamie.

"Jamie is suspended for one day," Mr. Pod-nah said. "When she comes back, the three of us will sit down and have a chat, try to resolve this issue between you."

"Charlie tells her what to do. Jamie won't resolve anything without Charlie's approval."

He shook his head. "We'll see about that. How's it going otherwise?"

"Just great."

"Come on, Shay. How's math? How's language arts?"

Sigh. Okay, Pod-nah. "Math is fine. Ms. Moss hates me because I thought she was a sub on my first day."

He laughed but tried to cover it up. "You did? Well, that's interesting. Jamie is in that class, isn't she?"

"Yes, and she sucks up to Ms. Moss all the time. She told Ms. Moss to put me at the table with the other foster kid. It was super embarrassing."

"That's not right. I'm sorry, Shay. Do you want me to change your class?"

Yes. But no. I couldn't. That would be viewed as retreat, weakness. "No, they'll find me in whatever class you put me into. I should stay. Just deal with it."

"We'll work things out together with Jamie on Monday

when she comes back from suspension."

Sure, we will, Pod-nah. Sure, we will.

He called Mrs. Morgenstern to let her know what had happened. "Here," he said, handing me the phone.

"Hello?" Mrs. M's concern was clear. I sensed disappointment too. "Shay, are you okay? I'm so angry about this. First the phone thing, now this. Are you okay? Should I come get you?"

"I'm fine. I don't want to come home. I'm mad, too, but Jamie was already sent home, so I don't have to deal with her today."

"Are you sure?"

I told her I was okay, repeating it until I thought she believed me. Leaving would be weakness, running away. I had to show my face in the eighth-grade hallway today, the sooner the better. I handed the phone back to Mr. Stetson.

He said to Mrs. M, "If she changes her mind, I'll call you. Thanks," and hung up. "Come back here to my office if you do change your mind, Shay."

I nodded. Just then, the bell rang. I stood up, a soldier going reluctantly into battle. Time for Ms. Moss and language arts class. As I made my way to the eighth-grade hallway, I wondered what fresh hell awaited.

Language arts managed to suck even though Jamie wasn't there. Wanda and Raymond practically fell over themselves patting me on the back for getting milk thrown at me. It was a lot of interaction from Raymond, which made it almost worth it. He actually appeared slightly less morose, managing to keep his head off his desk for most of the class.

He was entertained by Ms. Moss yelling at me, almost constantly, throughout class. He and Wanda kept cheering me on quietly from our table in the back, whispering "Go get her" and "Give her more shit." They said these things because my anger took over almost immediately (I'll tell you why in a minute), making me argue with Ms. Moss. Not enough to get kicked out, just enough to bug the hell out of her.

Here was what happened. I walked into class five seconds after the bell rang. I was late because apparently teachers also get bonuses for catching kids with dress-code violations. I was, of course, out of dress code. Three different teachers stopped me on my way to class to ask why I was wearing a sweatshirt. I had to show them the Official Dress Code Pass Mr. Pod-nah had written for me. They carefully scrutinized it because I looked like a kid who would forge an Official Dress Code Pass in order to wear a sweatshirt that was at least two sizes too large for me. This was why I was late to language arts.

I walked into chaos, of course, with Ms. Moss trying to get everybody to sit down, get out their journals, and complete the prompt. I wondered if anyone ever did this because I never saw anyone ever complete any prompts.

She snapped at me, "You're late." Then she noticed. "You're out of dress code!" She was already super mad at me. (You're probably thinking I got super mad back at her, but no—it's worse.)

I stood there for a second. Everyone in the class got really quiet. I was amused by her intense anger and, fully aware of what my words were about to do, said, "Calm down. I have an Official

Dress Code Pass." I held it out to her. The class erupted.

She actually sputtered and managed to splutter, "In the hall. Now."

I turned to go into the hall, realized I was smiling, then quickly made my face blank as she came storming out into the hall with me. Over her shoulder, the rest of the class, including Raymond and Wanda, crowded the doorway behind her, trying to be silent so they could watch.

Ms. Moss started yelling at me, volume ten. "You're late to class, and you're out of dress code! I don't care if you have a pass; you have detention after school today! You better get your act together, Shay. You're failing language arts. Your attitude needs adjusting too! Maybe I should call your foster parents!"

I didn't appreciate the reference to being a foster child. *This is for you, Raymond.* I asked her, "What does me being a foster kid have to do with any of this?" This caused her to splutter some more.

I glanced around. A couple other teachers stood in the hallway, craning their necks to see what the commotion was about.

"It's not about that, and you know it!" she shouted. "You're being disrespectful to me!"

In front of the witnesses, I tried again to hand her my pass. She took it and crumpled it up. I glanced around again—Mr. Hamilton and Ms. Lucy had both seen her crumple my pass. They needed to know what had happened.

"You crumpled my Dress Code pass, Ms. Moss. I need that."

She turned her head to see why I was being loud and saw the

other teachers watching us. "Back in the room," she hissed at me. "Now!"

I knew my best bet was to maintain control. Let her continue to lose her shit. As I turned to go back into the room, the kids scurried away from the door to their seats. At our table, Wanda and Raymond were both beaming at me. The whole class was beaming at me. There was nothing more entertaining than a teacher absolutely losing her shit in front of everyone.

According to the posted objectives, today, we'd be working on grammar. Glaring at me the whole time, Ms. Moss gave us five minutes to get out our journals and complete the prompt while she pretended to take attendance. I could see her taking deep breaths, counting to herself. Everyone whispered at their tables; no one would be completing any prompts today.

Ms. Moss tried to do a lesson, but I was in jerk mode now. Suddenly, I was the Participation Queen. I raised my hand for every question she asked. Sometimes, I was the only one with my hand up, so she was forced to call on me. Worst of all, I always got it right.

"Ms. Moss, the word 'curtain' is the object of the preposition 'behind.'" Then, "Ms. Moss, the verb tense is incorrect. It should be past tense, 'primed,' not present tense, 'primes.'" It was obvious I was trying to be annoying; it was also obvious that it was working.

The other kids stopped raising their hands. Then it was just the two of us. She'd ask a question, my hand would shoot up, there would be a gaping pause. She didn't want to call on me. She eventually started calling on students who didn't have their hands up. The hive mindset kicked in. No one answered any of her questions.

"I don't know," they said. "I didn't have my hand up. You can't call on me." As if that was some kind of unspoken rule.

Ms. Moss eventually stopped asking questions and gave us silent reading time. She went back to her desk in the back of the classroom.

"You broke her," Wanda whispered to me. "Nice job."

"She totally deserved that. She's not fair," Raymond chimed in quietly.

Wanda held up her fist above the desk.

Are fist bumps still a thing? "Yup." I bumped her fist, then Raymond's, which had also popped up. The noise volume in class slowly rose back to its usual level of loud.

Raymond's head eventually dropped to his arm on his desk. Wanda left our table to sit with another group. I put my head down, too, to wait out the bell.

Victory should have tasted sweeter, but I could smell chocolate milk on my pants.

CHAPTER TWENTY-TWO

ART CLASS WAS fine, even though Toya wasn't there. Mr. Reuben didn't say anything about my sweatshirt, but when I came in, he walked me back to my table.

"You okay?" he asked. "I heard there was an issue at lunch."

"I'm fine," I reassured him. To get him to leave me alone, I deflected. "Plus, I got to wear a sweatshirt instead of a uniform today."

He wasn't buying the deflection. "Nice try. Middle school is rough for a lot of reasons. Coming in midyear makes it worse. For what it's worth, I'm glad you're here today."

Yay, another pep talk. Whatever. No one was ever glad I was anywhere, so that was sort of nice. "It's really okay, Mr. Reuben. Thanks."

He waited a beat, then nodded. "Okay, Shay. Let me know if

you need anything." He waited for me to respond.

"I will, thanks."

Then he went back to the front of the room and started class.

*

CHARLIE WAS WAITING for me at my locker after school. "Nice sweatshirt," she teased. "Listen, Jamie's a bitch. She's suspended until Monday."

I stood there, willing her to leave.

"I'm sorry I teased you about Toya. You can like whoever you like. I don't care, okay?"

"Okay," I echoed.

"Don't forget about the party on Saturday. Favor says she still wants you to come. Jamie won't be there. She's at her dad's this weekend."

"Why doesn't Favor invite me herself?"

"She doesn't go to this school, plus, you don't have a cell phone. But she said I can invite you." Charlie leaned in. "Toya will be there."

I slammed my locker shut, nearly smashing her hand, which was resting on the locker next to mine.

She jumped back. "Hey!"

I noticed the kid, whose locker Charlie had been leaning on, waiting, not daring to ask her to move. I wondered how long the kid would wait. Not my problem.

"I don't care if Toya is going to the stupid party."

Charlie put her face back in her phone. "Well, if you decide you want to be cool and come, let me know. I'll give you the address." That's when I remembered I was grounded.

Charlie wandered off, and the kid finally got to her locker.

As I left school, passing the Malala mural, I realized I really wanted to go to the stupid party. I wondered if I could plead my case with the M's to forgive my grounded status for a social event. There had to be an angle they would agree to. I thought about it while walking home. Maybe, for a change, honesty would be my plan.

I spent the afternoon planning my Honesty Talk. It would take place after dinner, I decided. Perhaps we would have hot drinks in mugs while discussing my socialization, my adjustment to living here, my future at Consolidated Middle. My Honesty Talk would be real heart-to-heart, nuclear-family shit. This plan was, in my humble opinion, foolproof. At the end of the Honesty Talk, I would present my case for being allowed to go to the party.

After dinner, I asked the M's if we could talk.

They said, "Sure" and sent the twins into the study to watch TV.

"Does anyone want tea or cocoa?" I asked, filling the teapot and setting it on the burner.

They both paused, probably surprised by my thoughtfulness. Was Mrs. M trying to hide a smile? Maybe. After taking their orders, I fixed three green teas with honey and brought them to the table.

"Thanks, Shay," Mr. M said. "I'm sorry about what happened at lunch. Was it about Jamie's phone?" His question caught me off guard. I didn't want to talk about the stupid milk incident.

I took a sip of tea to buy a few seconds. It was way too hot, but I didn't react. I had to respond to his question honestly. (You know this about me; honesty isn't my strong suit—especially when it comes to sharing feelings and stuff.) This talk was my stupid idea, with honesty as the stupid theme. I started off strong, I thought, with an emotional reveal.

"I was really embarrassed about what happened at lunch today."

Mrs. M nodded. "I was glad to find out Jamie got suspended. What will happen when she comes back to school?"

"Mr. Stetson said he would talk to both of us."

"That's a good idea."

In my brain, I added, *And if she tries anything at all, I'll kick her ass.* I didn't say that out loud, of course. My level of honesty was limited by my common sense.

"Mrs. Smith loaned me her T-shirt and sweatshirt. Can I wash them later to give back tomorrow?"

"Who's Mrs. Smith?" Mrs. M asked. "One of your teachers?"

"No, she works in the cafeteria."

Mrs. M nodded. "Sure. If you want, we can bake her some cookies over the weekend as a thank-you gift."

I hadn't given a lot of thank-you gifts, but if Mrs. M thought it was a good idea, okay. "Okay, that sounds nice. Thanks."

This talk was already longer than I had mentally prepared myself for. I was already tired. The little bit of honesty I'd shared exhausted me even more. Plus, (you'll never believe this), I wanted to actually finish some homework later. (Who, me?) I made the executive decision that we'd all had enough Honesty. I told them what I wanted.

"There's a party on Saturday, and I want to go, but I know I'm still grounded. It's at this girl Favor's house. My friend Charlie will be there. Jamie won't. Oh, Charlie is a girl."

They exchanged quick glances. I couldn't read their silent communication, so I kept talking.

"I think this'll improve my social standing at school. I'm starting to make friends. I can talk to people outside of school instead of whispering in class or screaming in the cafeteria." I was basically saying the same thing over and over. Then I said HER name. "My friend Toya from art club will be there too." I picked up my tea, hoping to hide my face, which had started burning when I said her name for the very first time.

"Um, well..." Mr. M thought for a moment. "We're not saying 'no,' and we're not saying 'yes.' We'll let you know in a little bit, okay?"

"Sure, thanks. I want to get Mrs. Smith's clothes and start the wash." I left, running upstairs to grab my laundry. When I came up from the basement, Mr. M called me into the kitchen.

"Okay, Shay. You can go to the party."

I was shocked. Was it the honesty that had convinced them or the part where I told them how many friends I was making?

"There are a couple rules though. We'll drop you off and pick you up. No drinking. If there *is* any drinking there, you call us. Favor's parents will be there, right?"

I nodded all my lies. Favor's parents were out of town. There would definitely be drinking.

Mrs. M handed me a cell phone. "We had this reactivated for you. It's my old phone. Every kid your age has one, and now you can keep in touch."

I couldn't believe it. I had a cell phone again. It wasn't even a million years old, like most old people's phones.

"You're on our family plan. We can check your internet history, see your photos, read your texts." Mr. M was direct. "One complaint from a teacher at school about you using this in class, and it's gone."

I couldn't believe it. I was holding a cell phone again. I agreed to everything they said.

"You've had a cell phone before, right?" Mrs. M asked and, at my nod, continued, "Okay. The other rule is that if we call you, pick up. We won't call during school, but if we call you, pick up. If one of us texts you, text back immediately." They waited.

"I promise. Thanks for this." I was really grateful.

Mrs. M handed me a charger. I was in disbelief they were being so cool. I was going to the party with a cell phone. I didn't know what to say. It was almost too much.

"Are you okay?" Mrs. M asked.

"Yeah. I wasn't expecting you to let me go to the party, much less get a cell phone."

Mr. M said, "We just want to help you fit in."

I wasn't ever going to, but at least I could see Toya on Saturday.

"Do you need clothes?" Mrs. M asked. "For the party?"

Shit. I guessed I did. What did people around here even wear? "I don't know. I guess maybe."

"We can go out tomorrow after school if you want. I'll pick you up."

Damn. Now I'd cost them money again. "I don't want to cost you any money. I brought clothes with me."

Mrs. M shook her head. "Nonsense. We'll go to the mall after school if that works for you." She got even more excited about going after I agreed to go.

I hated clothes shopping. Hated it. Hated hated hated. When forced to go shopping, I'd get super tired instantly and cranky. I didn't have body issues or anything, I just hated that what I wore was of such great importance. I hated holding up a shirt on a hanger, then having to decide if it was a "good shirt" or if it would "look nice on me." Who gave a shit? Everyone but me, apparently.

The twins came into the kitchen. "Cool, is that a cell phone? Is it yours? Can I see it? Is that Mom's old one? Are there pictures of me on it? Will you call me on Dad's phone? Dad, can I have your phone so Shay can call me?"

Mr. M gave Eli his phone. "Go upstairs, and Shay will call you." They took off.

Mr. M showed me his and Mrs. M's numbers in my phone. Their work numbers were in there too. The lockscreen was a picture of the twins eating ice cream cones, completely covered in ice cream.

Using my new phone, I called Mr. M's phone and put on a thick British accent. "Allo, dears. It's time to get your jammies on. Cheers."

They squealed with laughter so loudly, I had to move the phone away from my ear.

Mrs. M laughed and got up. "I'll get them into bed and rescue your phone, hon."

"Thanks. I'll get lunches." Mr. M stood and got out the bread.

"I'll help," I offered.

"That's okay, Shay. You said you had homework to finish. Go ahead."

I headed to the Garret, practically sprinting.

I was excited to get reacquainted with the internet and my new phone. My phone chimed. Weird ring tone, which I made a mental note to fix. It was a text from Mr. M: *goob night shey*.

I smiled as I typed back: *Good night Eli and Nathan.*

Chime: *its omly me nathn is reading*

I typed: *Then good night Eli, from Shay.*

It should come as no surprise that I did no homework that night. I didn't read either. I spent the night on the internet with my face in my phone. It was late when I finally tried to go to sleep. That was when I realized the M's were trusting me a lot by letting me go to this party. I already knew I was going to break their rules. It was already done in my mind. I had to not get caught. That was the most important thing. Don't get caught.

Not only did I get caught, but I ruined everything.

CHAPTER TWENTY-THREE

FIRST THING FRIDAY, I traded phone numbers with everyone. Suddenly, I was cooler and everyone apparently forgot I was the chocolate milk girl. Or maybe they remembered, I didn't know, but complete strangers were smiling at me, nodding as they said, "Hey."

In homeroom, I traded phone numbers with Marshall. Charlie sought me out before the bell rang so we could trade numbers. She immediately started texting me. Then, I started getting texts from random people, who I assumed were the Nameless Phone Faces. I hadn't given my number to these people, so, thanks, Charlie, for giving it out. Charlie's and the Nameless's texts were all mean, like, *What is Fran wearing?* and *Her hair looks awful.* I fixed up the grammar for this journal. I knew Charlie played dumber than she really was, but I wasn't repeating her lousy spelling in here.

Then, I got a text from a number I didn't have in my phone. *Thanks for the day off, dummy.* I ignored it. Then, *I'll see you on Monday.* Great. Jamie. Threatening me.

"Please put the phone away, Shay."

Shit. "Sorry, Mr. Ham." I put it in my pocket, where it continued to vibrate every time I got a text, which was about every five seconds throughout the day. I checked them between classes, but they were all stupid, mean comments about people in school. I didn't respond to any of them. These were my friends?

In math, I added Olaf, Martin, and Nessa.

"Are you on "Vybe?" Nessa asked. When I shook my head, she added, "It's the new TikTok. When you get on, let us know so we can follow you. The more followers you have, the more songs and filters you can unlock."

I promised to follow them all on Vybe.

Art class was amazing. Toya gave me one of her famous (in my brain) smiles and a wave when I walked in. I went back to my table, and my phone vibrated. I surveyed the room; everyone was on their phone because the bell hadn't rung. I pulled mine out. It was a new number. *Thanks Charlie.* Probably another dipshit mean girl gossiping about someone's shoes.

Hi Shay. This is Toya. C u 2morow @ the party? (Yes, I'm repeating her text-speak exactly as received, but that's because she's cute. Her texts are automatically cute and need to be repeated. And reread a million times.)

Predictably, my face got red. I peeked over at her, but she was staring at her phone. I texted back. *Yep. Looking 4ward to it.*

She smiled when she read it, glanced over, and I boldly (so boldly) waved. She waved back just as the bell rang to start class. I was in heaven.

After class, Toya came back to my table as I was packing up. "Hey."

"Hey. How's it going?"

"Good. You?"

"Great." Sparkling conversation, I know. Then I had a conversation idea. "What do people wear to parties around here?"

"Oh, you know. Regular clothes. Jeans, hoodies, some girls wear skirts. The boys wear Thrasher T-shirts, even in winter. Then they freeze their skinny asses off all night. I'm wearing jeans, boots, and a sweater." She'd been very helpful.

"You've been very helpful. Want to walk out?"

"Sure."

And we walked out of school. Together. It was getting easier to talk to her if I didn't think too much about it. We waved as we got into our respective cars.

Mrs. M was very excited about our shopping trip to the mall. "I don't get to shop without the twins very often, I'm looking forward to this."

I didn't have the heart to tell her I hated shopping. "Me too."

I hadn't been to a mall in a very long time. Initially, it was a struggle, even though she knew where to go. I kept trying on sweaters and pants and shoes, then more sweaters and pants and shoes. I was immediately exhausted and cranky, as usual. I pushed myself to keep trying on sweaters and pants and shoes because I wanted Toya to like me. Also, Mrs. M was really enjoying herself. I'd already caused a lot of trouble, so it was nice to be able to go along with this shopping trip.

The bad thing was we hadn't gotten anything for me to wear yet.

Mrs. M said, "Let's get a snack."

We must have missed dinner. We split a huge cinnamon roll.

"This is as big as one of the twins' heads," I said.

She laughed. "Are you getting tired?"

"No," I lied.

"Well, it's almost six. I think we should keep shopping; there's a whole floor we haven't been to. But it's totally up to you. I want you to be comfortable at the party."

Wow. It was only six. I thought it had to be way later than that. More than anything, I wanted to stop shopping and go home. But she was loving this giant cinnamon roll and checking out the stores. And I really did want to wear something Toya would notice. Then I had an idea. I told Mrs. M where I wanted to go. She laughed and agreed. We finished our snack and hit three more stores, looking for specific things. We were out of the mall by seven.

Saturday, I could barely stand how excited I was. I held off on texting Toya and held my breath that she would text me. My phone blew up all day from Charlie's crew—now we were on a group text. One of the Nameless Phone Faces was complaining about her parents, Charlie was complaining about whatever popped into her head, with Jamie chiming in with more complaints from her father's house. There were a couple random phone numbers too. I remained silent all day. Olaf from math had included me in a group text about the homework, which resulted in me doing my math homework (who, me?) for once.

We were eating dinner and my phone chimed.

"No phone at dinner, please," Mrs. M said.

"Of course, I'm sorry." I took it out of my pocket. As I put it on the kitchen counter, I noticed a text from Toya. I quickly checked it and sat back down, hardly believing it. "Um, my friend Toya's dad offered to drive me home from the party tonight if you drive her to the party."

Mr. M quickly agreed. "Sounds good. I get to put my pajamas on early. After dinner, let her know it's a plan."

I managed to help clean up and calmly returned to the Garret before I texted Toya. *Sorry. We were eating dinner. Mr. M said your idea was cool, and he'd pick you up at 8. Need your address. Can't wait.* Of course, I deleted the *"Can't wait"* part of the text before I sent it. Then, I realized my text had ended too abruptly. I started hunting for a gif to send to smooth things out, but before I could find one, she texted her address. Nothing else, only her address. Welp, guessed I screwed that up. I was the Queen of Awkward Interactions, that was for sure.

I spent the remainder of my early evening going over the many other ways, many better ways, I could have communicated with Toya all day. Not listing them here, but there were about a million. I got dressed, reluctantly, because I'd completely talked myself out of my enthusiasm.

I went downstairs to the kitchen just before we were to leave.

Mr. and Mrs. M nodded approvingly at my outfit. They also smiled—not genuine—and I realized they were also worried. They didn't know me and were trusting me kind of a lot tonight.

"What's wrong?" I asked.

"Nothing. Have a good time."

Then they made me lie a few times.

"You're sure Favor's parents will be home?"

"Yes." (Lie. They wouldn't.)

"Is your phone charged?"

"Yes." (Truth.)

"You'll call us if there is alcohol there?"

"Yes." (Lie. There would definitely be alcohol there. Also, weed, vaping, maybe pills. It was a middle-school party, not a second-grade party.)

There was no guilt when I lied to them. There never was. But they didn't need to know how many choices I'd have to make to stay "safe" in their eyes. I could handle myself at a middle-school party, but they didn't know that.

Mr. M and I left to pick up Toya after I ran upstairs once more time to pee and check my stupid face in the mirror. Yep, still stupid. Toya came out of her house, her parents waving to Mr. M from the front door. She was super cute (of course), wearing a sweater and boots, and her hair was different. Also, best of all, she was smiling. So cute. I blushed, hard, and turned to her when she climbed into the back seat.

"Hey."

"Hey."

More sparkling conversation. At least there was eye contact—I didn't chicken out, and I didn't look away first. (Life Goal List, check.)

"Hi, Toya, I'm Mr. Morgenstern."

"Hi, Mr. Morgenstern."

I turned to face front as we drove to Favor's house. When we got out of the car, Toya turned me by the shoulders to face her. She peered closely at me, inspecting me up and down.

"Let's see. New sneakers, cool flannel, new hoodie. All fresh. That for me?"

I was shocked at her boldness. Then I matched it. "No. This is for you." Then I showed her my Thrasher T-shirt under my flannel. She laughed hard, an amazing, warm, deep laugh. She even got me started. My stomach flipped over immediately. Suddenly, all the other things on my Life Goals List turned into "Making Toya Laugh."

We walked into the party together, not holding hands or anything, but we were standing awfully close together. A couple people glanced at us but casually turned away. She saw some friends and invited me over to meet them.

I immediately freaked out hard because, well, I was me. Plus, it wasn't a date. (Or was it?) I sure wanted it to be but didn't know what to do on a date, so I said, "I have to go to the bathroom" because I was still the Queen of Awkward.

Toya said, "Cool. Then, come over here," before joining her friends.

I left her sitting with them. And blew everything up.

CHAPTER TWENTY-FOUR

I REALLY REGRETTED almost everything I did at the party. I really did. Now. At the time, it made perfect sense. I avoided writing all this down for a long time. Let's see if I can remember it all.

After I left Toya, I walked toward the back of the house. It was loud, hazy with vape and pot smoke, and smelled like booze. I realized most of the people were way older than me—old enough to be in college.

From across the room, Charlie screamed, "Shay!"

She came over to me, clutching a red cup, her face flushed. I smelled the alcohol before she got to me. "Shay!" she scream-repeated as if I'd forgotten who I was and was still ten feet away.

"Charlie!" I screamed back at her ironically.

She laughed—the irony didn't make it past the alcohol, which must have acted as some sort of irony filter. "I didn't think

204 | Jessie Preisendorfer

you'd come!" Again, as if I was across the room.

"Of course, I came. You invited me." I decided to have some fun with her. "We're friends!" I threw my arm around her shoulder.

"Yes!" She shoved her red cup at me. "Here!"

Here was where I made Mistake #1, breaking one of my party rules—no drinking unknown beverages. I drank from her cup.

It was delicious. Pineapple, coconut, orange, lemon... I was floating on an island of flavor. And then, there it was—vodka. Lots of vodka. Mostly vodka.

"Thanks, friend!" I screamed at Charlie, who I still stood ironically with, arm-in-arm.

She swayed as she said, "Justin made it for me." She nodded at a tall white boy in the kitchen, wearing a denim shirt and black jeans. He turned at that moment toward us. He was sort of cute and knew exactly how cute he was too. Stupidly, I made eye contact. This would be Mistake #2. He winked at me. Damn.

Favor came over, also carrying a red cup. "Hey, Shay, nice to meet you. Isn't this a great party?" She gestured with the red cup. Something sloshed out, but she didn't appear to care.

"Yeah, great party." When no one said anything, I took another swig from Charlie's red cup. That was a mistake, but I still count that as Mistake #1 because it's the same mistake as before, repeated. (Don't worry, I made lots of others.)

"Hey Favor, thanks for inviting me." I made eye contact with Denim Shirt without meaning to *again*. He started over to us.

I was thinking of Toya this whole time. I really was. I liked her. It was possible that she liked me. She'd laughed so hard at my Thrasher T-shirt. I remembered her laugh, then got nervous that I hadn't gone back to meet her friends. I should have walked away from Charlie, Favor, and Denim Shirt right then. Toya's friends were probably all like her: nice, smart, funny. They would have been nice to me, not mean to each other; we could have explained our Thrasher T-shirt joke, they would have called us cute, and then, I could have simply taken her hand.

But I didn't. I wasn't strong enough. What if it wasn't a date? What if she didn't like me LIKE THAT and I was my usual stupid self in front of her friends? What if no one thought I was good enough for her? What if I tried to take her hand but she pulled away from me? Ugh. I tried to take another drink from the red cup (Mistake #1 for the third time), but the cup was empty.

Denim Shirt stood in front of us now.

Charlie introduced Denim Shirt. "This is Justin. He's..."

Justin interrupted her. "About to make you another drink. You're Shay, right?"

I nodded. His blue eyes were interesting.

"Come with me," he said, then turned and walked toward the kitchen.

Charlie shoved me, so I followed Justin to the kitchen. (Yep, Mistake #3.)

I watched him mix us both a drink, mostly different flavored vodkas and ginger ale. This was bad. I didn't plan on getting wasted.

"So, what's your story, Shay?"

No way, Justin. You're not getting my story. "How old are you? I'm fourteen."

He didn't blink as he handed me a red cup. "I'm seventeen. Here. Cheers." He took a long drink. I pretended to do the same but only took a sip. I'd already had plenty.

He pointed to a door off to the side of the kitchen. "Let's play beer pong. You like beer pong?"

Nope. "Yep."

We went through the door, into the garage. A beer pong table stood in the center with a ton of people crowded around, all of them older. I got nervous. Suddenly, I wanted to see Toya.

"I'll be right back." I handed Justin my cup and left to find her.

I found her in the living room, sitting with some people. She jumped up when I came in.

"Shay! Come meet my friends."

I stopped at the door, so she came over to me. "There are a lot of older people here."

She nodded. "That's why we stayed in here. Favor's brother graduated from high school last year. A lot of his friends are here. You okay?" Then, "You're drinking?"

And then—and I hate this part most of all— I got angry at her. I don't know why I got angry; she was being perfectly reasonable. But there it was, my anger. Taking control, as usual. I made two mistakes in quick succession.

"That's not really your business." Mistake #4, followed by

Mistake #5—I turned and walked away.

I found Charlie in another room, kind of dancing in a group of people. I waved to them, and they waved me over. I took a drink out of Charlie's cup. The same delicious, tropical alcohol warmth ran through me. The music was super loud in here. Charlie was definitely pretty drunk.

"Is she okay?" I asked one of the Nameless Phone Faces, who waved her hands dismissively.

"She's fine. It's my turn to stay sober." That was a really fucked up way to party but whatever.

I went into the kitchen, just for a minute, to revisit my recent mistakes and gear up my courage to go apologize to Toya.

At the time, I knew I was making all these mistakes. I knew it. I sort of watched myself make them from a distance. But up close, I couldn't stop. I kept doing weak, stupid things. The weak, stupid things were my only options. As soon as I did them, I knew they were weak and stupid and most importantly, I knew they were mistakes.

I started back into the living room, where Toya sat on the couch, talking to a friend. I started to go over to her. Then, the girl she was talking to put her arm around Toya's shoulder and said something into her ear. Toya shook her head, then put her face in her hands. I didn't recognize the girl from school; she looked older. And cute. Hot, actually. Also, she was dressed up. Worst of all, she wore a rainbow scarf. Unmistakably Queer Hot Girl kept her arm around Toya as if she knew her pretty well. And Toya stayed there. With someone who wasn't me and had their arm around her. Damn. Of course, Toya could get a hot girl who knew how to dress. What would she want with me, a flannel-shirted sneaker-wearing dummy?

My whole person sank—down, down, to a dark and quiet place, everything suddenly terrible. More than anything, I wanted to leave. I wanted to go home. But not to the Morgensterns' house. My house. With my mom and grandma and grandfather, where my mom was clean, in the kitchen, cooking and laughing, with everything normal and fine. Instead, here I was in this stupid party kitchen, surrounded by loud drunk people, where nothing was normal, and everything was terrible.

Here was the part that surprised me—I wasn't immediately furious. Just sad. No, worse than sad, whatever that was. I decided to walk home. Fuck Toya. Fuck getting a ride from her dad and having to sit with Toya and probably her new girlfriend, cuddling in the back seat with stupid me sitting in the front making small talk with her dad. If I walked home, I'd be at the Morgensterns' in probably about an hour. I saw a door and went through it.

Right into the crowded garage. Shit.

Justin saw me in the doorway and waved me over. Then he turned back to the person he was talking to. I WENT OVER TO HIM BECAUSE I WAS A DUMMY. (Mistake #6.)

He handed me a red cup. "We're up next."

I stared at him.

"Beer pong." He nodded at the table. He still wanted to play beer pong. That wasn't great.

"Great," I said, taking a drink, then another. He introduced me to his friends. It turned out they were all lacrosse players (of course) and were friends of Favor's brother. It also turned out they were pretty douchey. (But that happens later.)

We started playing beer pong. I took tiny sips when I was supposed to drink and actually got some ping-pong balls into the cups. Justin and I won a few rounds, his friends cheering us on. Huh. *I can hang with high school boys.* Easier than middle-school girls, for sure. Boy, was I a dummy for thinking that.

Justin and his friends were vaping pot and kept offering the pod to me, but I turned it down. I didn't smoke pot around strangers. We kept winning, so he and his friends began betting on the games. They were making all kinds of comments, trash-talking to Justin and me. They got to be pretty rude, especially after a few rounds of vaping what they called "Cocoa Puff." After we kicked his ass, the captain of the lacrosse team came over to me. (Let's call him "Chad." And let's call the lacrosse team the "Douche Team.")

Douche Team Captain Chad said, "Okay, Shay. You against me. Quick game, only three cups on the table." He'd been doing most of the trash-talking yet couldn't sink a shot.

I agreed. And then I immediately kicked his ass.

Chad demanded a rematch. Then, "Let's make a bet. Ten bucks."

I shook my head. "I don't have ten dollars."

"I'll front you," came from Justin, watching with the Douche Team.

"Nope. Thanks anyway. This was fun." I started toward the

door into the house.

Chad stepped in my way, smelling like pot, beer, and body spray. "Hey, hey. Don't leave. You're winning. You'll probably beat me again anyway. Let Justin front you the money. It's more fun to bet."

I thought about it. I really didn't want to go back to watch Charlie get even drunker or Toya get even more snuggled with the Hot Girl on the couch.

I told Justin, "I don't know when I can pay you back."

He shrugged and set up the three cups on each side. I went first. I got my first shot in, so Chad had to drink. I missed the second. He made his first shot, so I took a sip. He missed his second shot. We both had two cups on the field. Then I sank both of mine, plop, plop, and won.

Now, more people were watching us play, in addition to the Douches. Chad was pissed as he handed me ten dollars. Huh. Easy as that, I had ten dollars.

"Again," he demanded.

Whatever. I said, "Fine. I can use the money."

Everyone laughed at Chad, who fumed. Apparently, Chad was used to winning, not being laughed at.

"Double or nothing," he insisted.

"No. If you win, you get this ten dollars back. If I win, you have to go home. As in leave the party immediately."

A hush fell. Then, the crowd erupted. The Captain of the Douches was being challenged.

His pride took over. He snarled, "Fine," then slammed the

cups into place, took a gulp, and demanded to go first. He sank his first shot, a sip for me. He sank his second shot, another sip for me. The crowd went "ooh," and he high-fived some nearby Douches.

I made both my shots, too, making the crowd roar as Chad chugged the rest of his drink. We both had one cup left. Someone handed him another drink as he lined up for his last two shots. He only had to land one to beat me and get his ten dollars back.

He lined up his first shot; it bounced off the rim of the cup. The crowd roared again. Then he took a double gulp and a hit of Cocoa Puff. The crowd cheered. The Captain of the Douches, their hero, was about to beat an eighth-grade girl at beer pong. How fucked up, right? Chad held up his last ping-pong ball and bowed to me, trying to embarrass me.

I looked right at him. He took his shot and completely missed the last cup. He got angry, but he was about to get angrier. I picked up a ping-pong ball and bowed back to him, deeper. The crowd went crazy. Then, plop, I made my shot. Game over. The crowd went wild.

I was the new hero, having defeated the Captain of the Douches. Chad handled it like the douche he was, calling me a cheater, a bitch, and a slut. First of all, I hadn't cheated; plus, I definitely wasn't a slut. Some of his douche friends on the team joined him in trying to berate me, but the admiration of the drunk and high crowd made me feel good. Justin was so happy about Chad getting toppled he kept hugging me. I let him hug me before I made Mistake #7.

212 | Jessie Preisendorfer

I kissed him. Then I kissed him again. Then he kissed me back. And then I noticed Charlie and the Nameless Phone Faces standing in the garage doorway. Their mouths hung open as they stared at me. *Probably because people are cheering for me.*

Justin tried to pull me in again, but I panicked. I didn't like Justin; I liked Toya. I didn't want to kiss Justin; I wanted to kiss Toya. If she didn't want to kiss me, then I didn't want to kiss anybody.

"I have to pee," I said.

He let me go. "Come right back."

I nodded my lie. I needed to see Toya, no matter what she was doing.

I pushed past Charlie and the Nameless, who followed me.

"Do you know who that is?" Charlie demanded, stopping me in the kitchen.

"Justin? His name is Justin," I answered sarcastically. *Was I slurring? Shit.* My phone vibrated in my pocket. My head was spinning, probably from vodka plus being an idiot plus kissing Justin plus missing Toya. "I have to pee."

I found a bathroom off the kitchen, which was free, thankfully. I checked my phone. Two texts. From Toya. Uh-oh. The first read: *My dad will be here in 15 minutes.* Sent twenty minutes ago. The second read: *My dad is here.* Uh-oh. Shit. I left the bathroom and made my way through the crowd to the front door and outside.

I stood there in the quiet for a minute, the cold air refreshing, searching for Toya's dad's SUV.

"Shay!"

There it was. I walked over, wishing she was out of the car so we could talk, but she was already sitting in the front seat. No new girlfriend in sight.

I climbed into the back seat. "Sorry. I didn't hear your text."

"No problem," came from her dad. He was silent for the rest of the ride. Toya, too. Ugh.

I didn't trust myself not to sound stupid, so I kept silent too. The drive home took forever. Uh-oh. I could smell the pot on my hoodie. Shit.

Shit shit shit. "Thanks for the ride," I said as I climbed out. Nothing from the front. I shut the door. Toya's dad waited for me, probably to go inside the house. I stared at the back of Toya's head as she stared straight ahead. I had ruined everything, forever.

The house was the last place I wanted to go, but I had to get away from her.

Inside, Mr. M was waiting up. "How was the party?" he said cheerfully. Then he got a whiff of me. "Damn, Shay. Pot? Really?"

I knew he was pissed when he cursed. "I didn't smoke any. I promise. My hoodie was in the bedroom; that's where they were smoking it. I didn't know anyone was smoking pot. I promise I didn't smoke any. You can drug test me."

"I'm glad you're home safe. We'll discuss this in the morning." He stared into my eyes, probably trying to see if I had smoked pot. "Go get some sleep. Leave the hoodie with me. I'll put it in the wash for tomorrow."

I shrugged off the hoodie, hoping my clothes didn't smell

too. He went over to the basement door, then turned back as if he wanted to say something, but he didn't. He turned away and left the room. I stood there for a minute, then I went upstairs.

It took forever to fall asleep. All I could see was the back of Toya's head in the car as we drove home. Whatever chance we'd ever had, even of being friends, was probably destroyed. By me, the Queen of Fuckups. I had certainly earned that title tonight.

If my life were a TV show, the narrator would now say, "If only she knew how much more fucked up it was about to get."

CHAPTER TWENTY-FIVE

THE NEXT DAY was a nightmare. The M's were super pissed about the pot smell on my clothes. I could tell they wanted to believe me about not smoking it, but they didn't trust me (why would they?).

"Shay, you can't bring drugs into the house. You can't." Mrs. M was practically crying. "It's not fair to the twins."

I got angry because, of course, I did. "Of course, I won't bring drugs into the house. I'm not that stupid."

Mr. M said, "No one thinks you're stupid. But you did promise you would call if there were drugs."

I had to lie. They were really angry. "I didn't know; it was in the one bedroom, and I was downstairs the whole time."

They didn't know what to do—but for starters, they grounded me again. Mr. M checked my phone, too, though I hadn't taken pictures of anything bad or posted anything online.

I spent most of the day up in my bedroom, trying to do homework but mostly trying to figure out how to repair things with Toya. Part of the problem was that I didn't know what Toya and my "thing" was. Were we friends? More than friends? I was an idiot for getting mad at her for asking if I had been drinking, when I actually had been. To make everything worse, I got into her dad's car reeking of pot. Of course, she was mad at me. Rightfully so. She probably didn't want anything to do with me anymore. Who wouldn't agree with her? So, how could I, the Queen of Fuckups, come up with any sort of decent plan? This was my day—spent dwelling on my mistakes, then beating myself up for them, over and over. Plus, science homework.

That was some bad shit I had created. Of course, worse shit started happening.

First, a text from Jamie: *Imma kill you bitch. Fukin wit my man just got you killed.*

I didn't respond—I didn't know what she was talking about. Then Jamie sent me a picture of me kissing Justin. How did she get a picture? She wasn't even at the party. Charlie or one of the Nameless had sent it to her, thoughtfully watching out for their dear friend, Jamie.

Shit. There was a picture. That wasn't great. Then random numbers started texting me. Several of the unknown numbers let me know that Justin was Jamie's boyfriend. Ah, that explains Jamie threatening to kill me.

Wow, this was bad. Jamie was going to try to hurt me

somehow, which meant trouble in school tomorrow. Also, there was a picture of me kissing a boy floating around where Toya might see it, not that we would ever be friends again, much less anything more. Lots of the texts from people called me "slut" or "bitch" or "whore" or "ho" or "hoe." Sometimes, a combination. I thought it was interesting I was the target of the slurs when Justin was the one cheating—*he* was the real "hoe." I hadn't even known who I was hooking up with, but he knew who I was and WHO HIS GIRLFRIEND WAS.

School was certainly going to be interesting tomorrow. I spent some more time kidding myself that I was doing homework. I wished I had my dad's phone number. I needed to get out of here as soon as possible. In my next letter, I'd give him my number and ask him for his so we could text. In the middle of my horrible afternoon, I was also remembering how much I missed my mom, grandma, grandpa, and the way things used to be. The memory of being in the kitchen with them had come to me the night before, the sadness overwhelming. Tears burned my eyes. I got under the bedcovers because I was freezing even though I had all my clothes on.

The texts kept coming until, eventually, I started ignoring them. I downloaded a dumb game on my phone and played that for a while, huddled under the covers. Then I saw a text from Olaf.

Hey, are you on Instagram?

No, should I be? I got a deep chill up my spine.

Yes.

Nessa texted next. *You should see what's on Charlie's IG.*

I've seen the picture. I know it's bad. The ellipses told me she was responding.

It's not just the picture.

Shit. Shit. *Is it bad?*

Then about a million hours went by while I waited for her response. When the ellipses went away, I frantically created an Instagram account using a different name. I had to ask Charlie to let me "follow" her private account. That took a million years too. Eventually, without knowing who I was, she let me onto her account. There it was. A video of Justin and me in an embrace, kissing and then kissing again.

Fuuuuuck.

This was catastrophic. The video had a bunch of likes and comments about me being a "hoe," etc. It was taken right after my beer pong victory over Captain Douche. He was super pissed off in the background as the crowd cheered. They were actually cheering for my victory, but in my mind, the world was cheering for the beginning moments of the Most Horrific Nightmare Imaginable. I had kissed a popular girl's boyfriend on camera. Of course, it had been posted online. I was doomed. Catastrophic was an understatement.

Then it all got worse.

CHAPTER TWENTY-SIX

"SHAY? WE'RE COMING up." The door was open, so they came right in. Their faces told me something terrible had happened. I thought it might have to do with Mr. M's mother, but Mrs. M had her phone in her hand.

"Shay, we just got a call from Principal Parkson. There's a video of you from the party last night. Did you know?"

Oh, shit. I nodded. "I know."

Mr. M took over. "Apparently, there is drinking and drug use in the video."

Oh shit. This was really bad. I was really fucked. I was ready to start apologizing, denying, lying, but Mr. M held up his hand.

"Don't say anything. We know you lied about the alcohol and drugs. The school administration saw the video. You're suspended tomorrow. We have to go in for a meeting Tuesday morning."

We sat there in silence for a minute.

I should have been embarrassed. I should have been sorry. My anger filled me up. I was angry at whoever took the video (probably one of the Nameless because Charlie was too drunk). I was also angry that I had been stupid and kissed Justin. I was really angry at Toya because she'd talked to that girl on the couch.

"They are trying to figure out who else is in the video and who else from the school was at the party. Principal Parkson said three or four other students would be suspended too."

I wondered who they would be. My phone vibrated in my pocket. I guessed I'd be able to find out that way.

Mrs. M said, "We want you to talk to Dr. Carol. She's already agreed to see you tomorrow. We have to report this to Ms. Rhonda too. At least you weren't using drugs or drinking in the picture. Honestly, I don't know what will happen." The M's shared a glance.

They turned to me, but I turned away. They were crushed. Who even were these people? We'd just met. They were stupid to have trusted me. So stupid. It was their fault. Naturally, I got angry at them for trusting me. I knew they shouldn't have. Trusting me was a huge mistake.

"Do you have anything to say, Shay?" The disappointment on Mrs. M's face dared me to lie to her. But I couldn't lie to her face. I was filled with anger, not regret, so I couldn't say I was sorry.

I shook my head.

Mr. M repeated Mrs. M's earlier statement. "Honestly, I

don't know what is going to happen." They left the room.

I sat there for a few minutes. I hadn't thought of what would happen if the Morgensterns decided I wasn't appropriate for their family. And I definitely wasn't appropriate. I wasn't capable of being in a regular home with a regular family. They were only now figuring this out. Maybe I was too broken. My anger made way for tidal waves of self-pity. Then my phone vibrated. What fresh hell was being unleashed?

Charlie, Favor, and the Nameless Phone Faces were all being suspended, along with two other girls I didn't know. Justin and a couple boys from the high school would be suspended too. Everyone blamed me for their suspensions, of course, even though I hadn't thrown the party, served the alcohol, used the drugs, taken the video, or shared the video. I wasn't innocent, but the punishment I was in for when I got back to school would be worse than anything I'd already been through.

"Shay! Dinner!" Mrs. M called upstairs.

I washed my face, threw my phone on the bed, and went down to do the family Sunday night dinner. As I slowly made my way to the table, I realized if social services wanted to pull me out of this placement, they could do it at literally any moment. Rhonda could show up to whisk me away, back to a group home or even to another placement. This could be my last dinner with the Morgensterns.

I sat down for Sunday night spaghetti and realized everyone was staring at me. I froze. It was silent.

Nathan saw his parents' faces. "What's wrong?" He accused

me. "Did Shay do something wrong?"

The M's started piling pasta on the twins' plates, ladling sauce, shaking parmesan out of a can. I took some pasta from the bowl, even though my stomach churned with fear and anger.

"Everything will be fine," Mrs. M said unconvincingly.

"Just fine," Mr. M agreed, handing me a piece of garlic bread.

Eli put down his fork. "What's wrong?"

Mrs. M offered an explanation. "Shay ran into some trouble with her friends last night. No one got hurt, but some rules were broken." Pause. The boys immediately turned to me.

I nodded, trying to smile, but I was sure it was more of a grimace. I opened my mouth to say something but couldn't find any words.

Eli asked, "So why is everybody so sad?"

Nathan chimed in, "Because Shay got in trouble. Again."

Mrs. M put her hand on Nathan's arm. "We're not sad. We're disappointed." I almost threw up. "Everyone makes mistakes, hon. Shay made a mistake. We'll deal with it."

Nathan and Eli both glared at me, Nathan furious and Eli— and this almost killed me on the spot—disappointed. I wanted to disappear.

"Can I be excused?" I asked, a question from my childhood springing forth from some deep recess of my mind. Without waiting for an answer, I got up, bursting into tears. I went to my room and continued crying. Ignoring texts, I watched the video repeatedly. It was gaining more and more likes on more and more people's feeds. With every like it earned, it was as if I was earning a dislike at the exact same time.

At some point, Mrs. M came upstairs with a sandwich on a plate and a glass of milk. She sat on the bed, where I lay trapped under the covers with the weight of disappointment, regret, and Spock, curled at my feet. "Peanut butter and honey. You should eat. Your appointment with Dr. Carol is early, 8:30. I'll take you after we drop the twins at school."

I managed to sit up and took a bite of the sandwich.

"We don't want you to leave, Shay. We really don't. But we don't know how to navigate dangerous behavior."

I put down the sandwich. "Thanks for the food. Sorry I got upset at dinner. I hate that Nathan doesn't like me, and I really hate upsetting Eli."

In response, she put her hand on my leg, which was under the covers, and gave my knee an affectionate squeeze. I remembered my mom or grandma making the same gesture of affection. I couldn't handle it. I was crying. Again.

"I'm sorry for disappointing you and Mr. M and the twins."

"Why? Why was it okay? To be at a party with older kids who were drinking? Doing drugs? Why?"

Because I thought I could handle all that. I was fine. I stayed in control because I didn't trust anyone. I was way safer than Charlie, who got so drunk she could barely stand. It wasn't dangerous if you could handle it, which I could.

I couldn't tell her that. I wiped my face. "I don't know why. It was okay at the time. The party was mostly me hanging out with my friends in the other room." My answer was weak and a lie, we both knew it, but it was all I could give her.

She stayed while I ate the sandwich. I told her I wasn't dating Justin. That it was a spontaneous kiss, which would never happen again. I hoped this truth appeased her desire for safety a little. I lied and told her I knew him because he was a friend's older brother. Technically, he wasn't a brother, he was Jamie's boyfriend. Jamie definitely wasn't my friend, but the bottom line was that he wasn't a total stranger. This appeased her a little more.

"The twins are playing Candyland if you want to come join us."

I shook my head. No way could I deal with those little disappointed faces tonight.

"Okay. Come on down if you change your mind. If not, I'll see you in the morning."

"Thanks. Good night."

She picked up the plate and glass and left.

I sat there, trying to read for a while. Then I turned the light off, hoping to go to sleep. I should have turned my phone off. I should have thrown it out the window. Instead, I was watching some stupid show on the internet and got a text from a number I didn't know. Again. I'd gotten a lot of messages from strangers today.

I saw the video.

Sigh. Another one of these people who were happy to watch my life decompose online. I didn't respond.

Then, *got ur number from Jamie.*

Yeah. You and most of the eighth grade. I was about to turn off my phone. I probably should have. I would have been able to sleep, maybe at least a little.

Then, *can't stop thinking bout u.*

Ewwww. Gross. Some perv was thinking about me, a child in the eyes of the law, kissing a boy three years older. And then, any chance of sleep was ruined when I found out whose phone it was.

Srsly I can't stop thinking bout u. This is Justin.

Jamie's boyfriend. Fuuuuuuck.

In panic, I turned off my phone immediately. I sat there in the dark, straight up in bed, panicking after finding out that Justin, Jamie's eleventh grade boyfriend, couldn't stop thinking about me. It was creepy and gross and dangerous and, shit, it was sexy. Sexy? What was wrong with my brain? I definitely didn't want Justin to be my boyfriend—I hadn't thought about kissing him since the party. I wanted Toya to think about me the same way Justin did. And honestly, to have someone, anyone, feel that way about me was kind of cool. I don't think anyone had ever thought about me that way. Ever.

Toya was probably texting that hot girl from the party. She probably couldn't stop thinking about her. They probably couldn't stop thinking about each other. Ugh. Then I realized that I'd have to see them at school, assuming Hot Girl went to Consolidated Middle, the Factory-Looking School, where teachers get bonuses for annoying kids in the halls and foster kids get outed and Hot Girls get together. If she joined art club, I'd drop it. Then, I decided to drop it anyway. The only reason I joined was to be around Toya; I didn't want to be around her if she was disappointed in me. Honestly, how could she not be?

I had to get to my father's as soon as I could. I disappointed the M's more every day and would probably end up back in the group home before long unless I could get to my father's. It was a freer way to think—like, no matter what happened at school, I was leaving anyway. Why give a shit about anything? Nothing here really mattered, except not going back to the group home until I could move in with my father.

I turned my phone back on after about an hour of sitting in the dark, getting more miserable by the second, but there were no more texts from Justin. He'd stopped texting after identifying himself. I spent some important quality time scrutinizing his online profiles. There were a lot of pictures of him playing lacrosse, smoking pot, and drinking at parties. There were quite a few of Jamie and him, too, with their arms around each other, gazing into each other's stupid faces. They'd started dating last year, when she was in seventh grade. Eww. He was super gross.

Cringe alert: I eventually texted him back. I wasn't planning to, especially after I saw his online profiles. Then, I don't know—late night, intrigue, danger, lack of sleep, whatever the reason—I texted back. *You're Jamie's boyfriend.* That was it. I reminded him that he was dating a terrible person.

Immediately, he responded. *U thinkin of me?*

I was instantly furious with myself for making him think that I was thinking of him, which, of course, I was.

I texted: *I'm in 8th grade. I'm too young for you.*

He responded: *lol J is in 8th grade her folks are cool*

Eeewww.

Then he texted: *party at shaun's next weekend come w me j is mad at me*

What a nightmare scenario. Quickly, I sent: *F u no. Fix it with Jamie.*

Y f u? U mad too?

I was mad but mostly at myself. *I'm grounded forever, probably. You're too old and you have a gf.*

Ur grounded? Fuck that, they're just foster parents they can't do that. And then instantly: *i want to kiss u again.* And then: *soon."*

I texted: *We'll never kiss again.* I shut off my phone.

Then I got up and put the phone in the bathroom under a stack of towels. Even though it was shut off, I didn't want some random nightmare text sneaking in and turning it on so the chime would wake me up. I lay in bed for hours and days until I fell asleep. I was such an idiot.

CHAPTER TWENTY-SEVEN

"SHAY?" MRS. M called me.

I was sound asleep, of course, having fallen asleep as my room started getting brighter, indicating the beginning of a terrible day.

"Coming! Sorry!" I yelled downstairs as I picked up my clothes from the floor and threw them on. I brushed my teeth in three seconds, checked my miserableness in the mirror (*yep, still miserable*), and abandoned washing my face or doing anything with my hair.

I raced downstairs, where the twins stood in coats and their backpacks. I grabbed my coat as Mrs. M came out of the kitchen. She handed me a granola bar and a juice box. "Breakfast." To the twins: "Let's go, people. Things to learn today."

The twins stared at me. I pretended it was because of my

messy hair, not the fact that I was a monster and made their parents upset on the reg. We all trooped out to the car and headed to the twins' school. We pulled up to a playground with lots of littles running around in coats and backpacks. It was adorable, almost too cute.

"Remember, your dad is picking you up today."

"We know, Mom."

"Learn something. Love you."

"Love you."

We pulled out of the drop off line.

Mrs. M said, "After Dr. Carol, we have a meeting at Rhonda's office. Mr. M can't make it."

"Okay."

The silence made me uncomfortable. I wasn't sure if I should apologize or offer to leave or make a joke or stay quiet. I stayed quiet because it was the least likely option to make everything worse.

When we got to Dr. Carol's, both of us talked at the same time.

"I'm really sorry about everything."

"I'll be here when you're done."

She nodded at me. I nodded back. Then I got out and went in for my special emergency meeting.

Dr. Carol offered me a water or tea as soon as I walked into the waiting room, where she was getting coffee from a Keurig.

"Water would be great," I said.

We went through a different door, into the kitchen. She

opened a cabinet and handed me a glass. "The fridge has an ice maker and water dispenser. Help yourself." She smiled at me. I got some ice water before continuing through yet another door into her consulting room.

"So, you had a weekend." She opened right at the main event. I sort of liked this about Dr. Carol. No small talk about bullshit.

"Yep." I didn't know what she knew, but I could assume it was at least about Justin. "Did you see the video?"

She shook her head. "No. I don't need to, unless you want to show me."

I definitely did not want to see it again. "Nope. And for the record, I don't like him, the boy."

"Okay. Then why did you kiss him?"

"I was curious," I responded, which was partly true.

"Shay, we're here today to find out if you have substance abuse issues or are sexually active."

Wow. Oh, wow. Brutally honest. Her directness took me aback. I didn't know what to say.

"I won't tell anyone what we talk about unless I think you are in danger or at risk of endangering someone else."

I nodded and reverted to my favorite word. "Okay."

"I know we only met a couple weeks ago, but you've already made progress. You're here. We talk. That's progress."

I definitely didn't have substance abuse issues, and I was definitely, definitely, 100 percent NOT sexually active. I relaxed a little. "Okay."

Immediately, she asked me, "Did you drink at the party?"

"I had a drink, but I definitely wasn't drunk. I don't drink at parties because I prefer to stay in control around strangers." A little lie, a little truth. (The recipe for "honesty" when talking to adults, remember?)

She nodded. "Apparently, there were lots of older kids there as well as younger kids. Were you comfortable with that?"

I was really comfortable with that. I blended in, so no one saw me. I wasn't a Pretty Girl who had to perform, and I wasn't a Bro who had to get super drunk and be extra douchey.

"I stayed mostly in the living room with my friends. Some of them were drinking. I had a few sips from one of their cups."

She took notes. Maybe she always did, but I'd never noticed before. "And the boy you kissed?"

"Ugh. Justin. He's this girl Jamie's boyfriend. I think he was trying to get her jealous."

"Did he have consent to kiss you?"

Then I was thinking of the kiss again. Damn it.

"Yes, he had my consent. I didn't know he was Jamie's boyfriend at the time, although she doesn't believe me."

"I see." And she wrote. Then, "Are you sexually active?"

Against my will, I blushed.

"Sorry, Shay. I know this is a tough question, but the boy you kissed is three years older than you. That's concerning."

I shook my head. "No, no. I'm not." Then I got mad. "He's Jamie's boyfriend, and she's my age. Is that concerning to anyone?"

She put down her notebook. "Of course. This video has created a bit of a shitstorm, if you'll pardon my language. The school is involved, and parents are being contacted. I promise you're not the only person under scrutiny."

Fucking great. Now everyone will blame me for being SCRUTINIZED.

"What?" She noticed my reaction. The anger burned me up as tears and hopelessness took over. It all spilled out.

I told her about the video and all the hate-filled comments. I told her about the hate-filled texts I got all day and night from strangers who were perfectly comfortable sending me all the slut-shaming vitriol they could think of.

"It's not fair that you're getting blamed," she said naively.

"Ha. I'm a new kid and a foster, to boot. I'm the easiest, best target for blame. It will never end. Never. Of course, it's not fair. It's middle school, and it's my life. Nothing is ever fair. So, yeah, I had some pineapple vodka and kissed a cute boy, and now everything—every, single, thing—is ruined. Forever. You want to know if I have a substance abuse problem? The question is, why DON'T I have a substance abuse problem?"

I sat back, tears and anger streaming down my face. She studied me, then put her notebook on the table. I could tell she was trying to think of something to say that would fix everything. Something that would make me want to conquer the world, despite being in some trouble.

"With your history, I don't know why you don't have a substance abuse problem, Shay. I really don't. I don't know where you get your resilience. I don't know why you're here today. You have every reason to quit. Every reason. I don't know why you don't. But you don't. Why don't you?" Then she stopped talking, waiting for me to give her the secret sauce recipe to my resilience. Why couldn't I answer the question about why didn't I have a substance abuse problem? I couldn't. I didn't have an answer.

I took a mouthful of water to stall. She reached over and picked up her coffee. We sat there. It wasn't uncomfortable, but it was a little strange as Dr. Carol waited for me to talk. I didn't have a lot of people who listened to me as hard as she did. It was weird. And then, the strangest thought entered my brain. I didn't want to lie to her. The thought, *Don't lie to her* ran from one side of my brain to the other. Why? Why shouldn't I lie to her? I couldn't explain it, but guess what? I got angry. Not at Dr. Carol—at myself. No surprise, right? Lying was my best defense and the thing I was really good at. If I didn't lie, what could I possibly say?

"You're practically daring me to start using," I said. I wanted her to know I was angry. I wanted her to know that I thought it was a little fucked up she was surprised I wasn't an addict.

"You know that's not what I mean." She gazed at me and did that "waiting for me to talk" thing again. My anger melted away as I sat there.

I had to know. "What are you going to tell the Morgensterns?"

"I'll tell them you aren't sexually active and that I don't think you have a substance abuse problem."

"Okay."

We sat for another minute. I wanted to stop thinking about the party and Justin and the hell that would face me in school. So, I thought about Toya, even though she was probably mad at me. Thinking of Toya made me happy. I decided it was Big Secret time.

"I like a girl at school. But I think she has a girlfriend."

Dr. Carol smiled. "What's her name?"

And then I told her about Toya.

THE ANGER CHRONICLES | 237

CHAPTER TWENTY-EIGHT

I REALLY ENJOYED talking about Toya with Dr. Carol. I didn't think she'd care that I liked girls, but you never knew. I'd heard stories. She made me promise to stay in art club for at least one more week. We worked out how I could apologize to Toya and maybe stay friends, how I could successfully meet with Rhonda the Craptastic later to avoid further life destruction. All in all, not too bad a meeting with my shrink. Maybe even okay.

Right at the end, Dr. Carol almost blew it when she suggested I talk to the M's about liking girls, but I really wasn't ready for that complication. I reminded her about my plan to live with my father. It wouldn't matter to the M's who I liked.

"Okay. It's totally up to you who you tell, of course. I thought it may make things easier for you to talk to them, but of course, it's 100 percent your decision." She paused to make sure I was listening. "I'm glad you told me about Toya. It must have been difficult. I respect that kind of bravery." That threw me off because no one ever respected my anything, much less my bravery.

When I got up to leave at the end of our time, Dr. Carol said, "I'll see you at the regular time, too, this week."

Oh. Okay, that was how messed up I was. Twice-a-week shrink appointments. It didn't make me angry though. Just sort of sad. I guessed I was in a pretty bad place.

I got back in the car with Mrs. M, giving her my usual "Fine" in response to "How did it go?" But then, I remembered everything I'd put her and Mr. M through. I decided to tell her a little more.

"We talked about how I can deal with Rhonda today so I don't get so mad at her."

"Oh, yeah? You have a strategy for Rhonda the—what did you call her?—the Craptastic?"

"Yeah, she's Craptastic. But if I picture her with a giant hat of flowers on her head, it's funny, which makes it easier to ignore her Craptasticness."

"Hat of flowers, huh? That's what you and Dr. Carol came up with?" Mrs. M thought for a second. "That's funny. Especially if she's allergic."

I thought a bit about Rhonda in a giant hat of flowers. "Yeah. And she sneezes all the time. But she can't take off the hat, except at night."

We talked about Rhonda in her flower hat until we pulled up outside the offices. Suddenly, my guilt overwhelmed me. Everything was terrible because of me. We checked in and got visitor's badges. Rhonda came out to get us from the lobby, fake-smiling at me, which almost got me super mad. But I thought of her in her stupid flower hat and didn't get mad. I wasn't exactly dancing with joy down the hall, but I didn't want to irritate her by asking about her failing marriage or the small hole I saw in her sweater.

We entered a conference room, where a familiar-looking white lady sat. She wasn't smiling. Also familiar. She stood up and held out her hand to Mrs. M.

"Hi, I'm Shelly Hudson. Rhonda's supervisor."

Mrs. M shook her hand. "Miriam Morgenstern."

"Nice to meet you, Mrs. Morgenstern. Nice to see you again, Shay."

I shook her hand. Her smile was fake. I wasn't surprised she was fake-smiling. It definitely wasn't nice for her to see me again. She was definitely not happy about the trouble I'd caused everyone. I'd met her a long time ago, once after Ms. Kate had quit but before Rhonda was assigned to me.

"Call me Miriam," Mrs. M said.

"Shouldn't they call you Rabbi? You're a rabbi," I said. It wasn't her fault I'd screwed up. They should treat her with more respect.

"Technically, we should call you Dr. Morgenstern, right?" Mrs. Hudson said. "She has her PhD," she explained to me.

I didn't know that Mrs. M had her PhD, so I sat there like a dummy.

Mrs. M said, "Miriam is fine," to Mrs. Hudson. She smiled at me, letting me know she knew I was defending her. I was such a dummy. She didn't need me to defend her, of course.

Mrs. Hudson started right in. "So, Shay, you were at a party where there was drinking and drugs. Is this correct?"

Duh. There's a video. "There's a video," I said, welcoming the blossoming anger in my chest. I sat forward in my chair. "Am I going back to the group home?"

Rhonda couldn't help herself from chiming in. "Shay, there's no need to be rude. Can you answer Mrs. Hudson's question?"

I opened my mouth to engage with Rhonda, who was certainly living up to her title of Most Craptastic Social Worker, when Mrs. M and Mrs. Hudson spoke at the same time.

Mrs. Hudson said, "I'll handle this, Rhonda, thanks," and Mrs. M quietly said, "Flowers," to me.

That got my attention. I realized Rhonda had been scolded by her boss. That pleased me. I closed my mouth and sat back, disengaging from the Craptastic.

"No, Shay. Putting you back in the group home isn't why we're here. The Morgensterns don't want that, and I don't think it would be best for you."

Rhonda interrupted her boss, making a mistake again. "But Mrs. Hudson, don't you think she's a danger to herself? Plus, there are two little boys in the house that she's putting at risk."

"Rhonda," Mrs. Hudson said quietly. "Thank you for your input. You and I will talk more about this later. Why don't you head out on your calls for today?"

Wow, Rhonda was being dismissed. I liked this Mrs. Hudson.

Rhonda openly glared at me as she left the conference room. I didn't want to gloat, but who was I kidding? I smirked and waved at her as she left.

"Shay," Mrs. Hudson continued. "I saw the video you referred to."

Aaaand we're back to me.

"You were at a party with drugs and alcohol, and how old was that boy you were kissing?"

Ugh. The kissing. I really regret that the most. That was the part that would continue to royally fuck up my life forever.

"Justin is a junior. He's seventeen, I think."

We sat there. They stared at me, so I knew it was my turn to keep talking. I decided to apologize even though I could totally handle the drinking and didn't do any drugs that night.

"I'm sorry I didn't call the Morgensterns to come get me as soon as I realized people were drinking. I didn't see drugs until later, but I should have called."

I waited to see what effect the apology had. Since they were silent, I kept talking.

"Justin and I had just won a game, so we kissed. It didn't mean anything. We're not dating or anything." I didn't mention that Justin had texted me about ten times already that day.

Mrs. M leaned forward. Dr. M, I should say. "Shay, you can't expose the twins to reckless behavior. They don't know anything about what happened this weekend, but we can't be sure they won't hear anything at school. This can't happen again. It can't."

She was so earnest, I got choked up, feeling really bad. Mrs.

Hudson decided to pile on.

"Shay. Dr. Carol told me she doesn't think you have a drug problem. That's good. Are you sexually active?"

Eeww. I shook my head.

"Has anyone talked to you about sex? About birth control?"

I couldn't help it; I put my face in my hands. Embarrassed, almost to death, I practically whispered, "I don't have my period yet."

It was silent.

Mrs. M said, "We'll talk about this another day, Shay. But we have to talk about it. And soon."

Grateful not to have to talk about sex and periods anymore, I nodded. I was relieved enough to say, "I won't put the twins at risk. I'm really sorry about Saturday."

"Risky behavior is a nonnegotiable." Mrs. Hudson shook her head. "We won't warn you again. Next time, you will have to leave the placement."

I put my face back in my hands.

"We don't want you to leave, Shay," Mrs. M said. "We really don't."

Mrs. Hudson chimed in. "No one does. I promise you. We all want you to stay with the Morgensterns."

I nodded, face in hands.

Mrs. Hudson continued. "One more difficult topic."

I took a deep breath, let it out, and took my face out of my hands, resigned. Now, what did I do?

"I'll talk to Rhonda about her relationship with you. You two have to work things out. Okay?"

Oh, hell, no. I wasn't agreeing with that. "No. She hates me and doesn't believe me. I told her when disgusting, pervy, grown-ass man Billy tried to kiss me and said those gross things, and she didn't believe me. I don't even need a social worker, especially a bad one."

Mrs. M was mad. "That's what happened at the Garbage Family's house? She didn't believe you?" I liked that she called them the Garbage Family.

Mrs. Hudson turned to me. "I'm sorry, but you do have to have a social worker. Right now, we're shorthanded because of the budget cuts. Unfortunately, everyone has too many cases. I can't give you to anyone else." I was a victim of budget cuts. Fuck Rhonda.

"It's fine, Shay. You won't ever have to meet with her without Mr. Morgenstern or me being there," Mrs. M said. "Thanks for apologizing again and understanding about the twins. It's important you understand how impressionable they are."

I nodded as my eyes filled up with tears. Damn it.

"It was nice seeing you again, Shay." Mrs. Hudson leaned toward me. "The Morgensterns are a nice family. I'm glad you're with them."

I wondered if she was implying a threat—"Behave or get out"—but she might have been sincere. I nodded. Mrs. Hudson and Mrs./Dr./Rabbi Morgenstern hugged goodbye.

I was exhausted. We sat in Mrs. M's car for a minute.

She started the engine. "I have to go to work this afternoon.

I can drop you at home or you can come with me."

"I think maybe I should just go home."

"Okay." And then she added, "Want to go to the diner for lunch first?"

The diner? I loved the diner. But I thought she was still mad at me. She wanted to go and eat lunch with me? Maybe the lunch offer was just a kind gesture and she didn't really want me to say yes. Then, I remembered there was pie at the diner. "Lunch sounds great."

She smiled (genuine). I knew I'd made the right decision.

CHAPTER TWENTY-NINE

AFTER LUNCH, I decided to go with Mrs. M to her work. The day care welcomed me with tiny open arms and tiny yells for my attention all afternoon. It was a good way to avoid thinking about school the next day. Jamal, my friend from the last time, saw me come in and didn't leave my side. He was always by himself, so I read a book with him. Within a few minutes, a bunch of kids had crowded around us. Later, he wanted to play with Legos, and we sat on the Lego carpet until another crowd gathered. I was sort of a rockstar, I have to admit.

I got up to get a drink of water. When I got back to the Lego carpet, my spot had been taken by Ben and Aliyah. I stood there, watching Jamal and Ben and Aliyah. They weren't playing together, exactly.

"It's called parallel play." Midge had appeared at my side.

"They play together at this age by playing next to each other. Jamal doesn't usually play near the others."

That was interesting.

Mrs. M came in. "It's three, Shay. Ready to go?"

The time had flown. I grabbed my coat, said goodbye to Jamal and his crew, and we left.

"You're really great with those kids, Shay. Jamal was adopted by his foster family when he was two. He came to us pretty shy, but he's doing a lot better lately."

Ahh, he was also a foster. Made sense why he gravitated right to me.

"I have an idea," Mrs. M said as she drove to the twins' school. "Mr. M and I had talked about grounding you, but instead, what do you think about volunteering at the day care after school?"

I thought about it. Grounding would probably be an easier punishment because no one would ever invite me anywhere again. I'd be grounded socially for a loooong time.

But volunteering at the day care didn't sound terrible. In fact, it sounded sort of fun.

"Um, okay. Every day?"

"Oh no. Let's say, two days a week. Tuesday and Thursday?"

Tuesday was art club. "Tuesday, I have art club, unless you want me to quit."

"Don't quit. How about Monday and Thursday?"

"Okay."

"Perfect. Mr. M and I will work out the transportation."

The twins were racing around the playground at their school when we arrived. We approached the monitor holding a clipboard.

"Hi, Mrs. Morgenstern." He waved as he called over his shoulder, "Eli! Nathan!"

The twins stopped, turned, and came full speed at us.

Eli saw me first. "Shay!" He barreled into me as Nathan barreled into Mrs. M.

"Hi, boys!" She gave them hugs and led us back to the car. "How was your day?" she asked, waiting for them to buckle themselves in. I handed straw-poked juice boxes back to them as they talked at us simultaneously about sketching dinosaurs or chalk drawings or something else the whole drive home.

Since I didn't have homework, I helped the boys as Mrs. M started dinner. At one point, I realized it was pretty nuclear-family stuff. I didn't hate it but reminded myself not to get too attached because I'd be living with my father soon. I thought about the fresh start that would give me in whatever school I'd attend. The nuclear-family thing kicked in again when Mr. M got home and walked into the kitchen.

"Hi, honey, I'm home!"

The twins pushed into his arms for a hug. We'd finished homework with remarkably few fights (I think only three). Now, we were drawing dinosaurs with extra arms and legs for fun.

The twins' love for macaroni and cheese made dinner twin-conflict-free. After dinner, the boys set up in the study while the M's and I rehashed the meeting with Mrs. Hudson and Rhonda and the plan for me to volunteer at the day care center. We also discussed the meeting at school first thing tomorrow to reinstate me after my suspension. We were all going to meet with the principal and guidance counselor. I could tell the M's wanted to discuss things alone, so I went into the study and hung out with the twins for a while until Mr. M came to take them upstairs.

That night, the three of us watched Mr. M's favorite TV show, which was a singing competition. Strangely, some of the songs actually made me tear up a little. I almost cried again when one of the contestants I liked got eliminated. I was confused. Where was my anger? Why was I upset? My emotions were completely unstable and unpredictable.

When the show was over, I went upstairs after saying goodnight. Spock met me in the Garret. Together, we tried to set a game plan for tomorrow, which would definitely, absolutely, without a doubt, suck.

Imagining flower hats on every person in eighth grade wouldn't be nearly enough. Justin still texted constantly until I finally blocked his number. Even though Spock was no help, it was nice having someone to bounce ideas off of. He didn't approve any of them, but I didn't either. I fell asleep without coming up with a game plan.

*

MY PHONE ALARM blared. I sat straight up in bed, instantly filled with dread. This was today's schedule:

First, a reinstatement meeting at school with foster parents, school admin, and guidance counselor. In this meeting we would relive (for the millionth time) how badly I had fucked up. Again. I'd see allllllll the disappointment on their faces. Again.

Then, I would spend the rest of my day dodging Jamie, Charlie, and the rest of humanity as my classmates and teachers silently judged the foster kid who was obviously a drug-addicted, slutty fuckup and also a whore, a ho, and a hoe.

Finally, all this terribleness would culminate with art club, which I really regretted promising Dr. Carol not to quit. Toya would probably completely ignore me or completely freak out on me, both of which I deserved, but it would be awful just the same. Maybe I could break my arm or something and have to leave school before art club.

I got dressed and went downstairs. The twins, oblivious to the nightmare I was anticipating, greeted me as they put on their coats.

"See you both at school in a bit," Mr. M said to me and Mrs. M as he herded the boys out the door.

I put my lunch in my backpack, then grabbed a granola bar, which I couldn't eat because my stomach was churning. Mrs. M and I drove to Consolidated Middle in silence.

My stomach was upset, I was on the verge of tears, and I was about to revisit all the weekend shit over and over, before spending the rest of my day in an indescribable hellscape.

CHAPTER THIRTY

WE PULLED INTO a visitor parking spot and went in. Mrs. Mozier didn't give us the same warm smile from before; she must have been disappointed too. We sat in the same conference room, waiting.

Mr. Stetson came in first with a grim smile. "Ms. Peete is coming today. The social worker. She runs the girls' group Shay belongs to."

On cue, Ms. Peete entered the room. "Hi, Shay. You must be Mrs. Morgenstern." They shook hands, after which Ms. Peete introduced herself and talked a little about the girls' group.

Mr. Stetson and Principal Parkson came in together. Yep. Disappointment everywhere, every single face. I was certainly living up to their expectations for foster kids.

"Shay," Principal Parkson started. "After a student is

suspended, we have a meeting with the guardians and the student before they are reinstated into school. We do this to make sure the student understands why they were suspended. Why do you think you were suspended?"

Everyone turned to me.

Well, duh. I was suspended because Charlie posted that stupid video. That wasn't what they wanted me to say though. I knew what they wanted.

"Because I was at a party with alcohol and drugs."

"Good. Yes. Charlie and several other students were suspended for yesterday, too. Also, for today."

I already knew about the suspensions for yesterday thanks to the millions of "helpful" texts I'd received, but they were also suspended today? That was good news—I wouldn't have to dodge them until tomorrow.

Principal Parkson continued. "Justin and several boys from the high school have also been suspended for...three days?" She turned to Ms. Peete, who nodded. "They were underage drinking and serving to minors, which means there will also be charges filed."

Oh shit.

I waited. No one said anything. I briefly thought about apologizing but wasn't sure to who or for what. Sorry for letting you down, Consolidated Middle? Sorry for not upholding the high standards of "honorable behavior" of our distinguished academic institution?

"Do you have any questions, Shay?" Mr. Stetson asked.

"Did anyone else get in trouble?" I was worried about Toya.

"Not from the Middle," Mr. Stetson said. "We notified the parents of everyone we know who was at the party. They might have gotten in trouble at home, but no one else was suspended."

It was very good news that Toya hadn't gotten in trouble. And I guessed we called it "the Middle." Cute.

Mrs. M said, "We had a meeting with Shay's social worker yesterday. She explained how risky behavior will terminate the placement. Shay had a meeting with her psychologist too. I think that Shay, you understand all this, don't you?"

I nodded, grateful that Mrs. M was attempting to end this meeting.

"Will anything change for Shay here?" she asked.

Mr. Stetson shook his head. "Nope. Back to a regular day. Shay, I have to pull you for some testing. It will take about an hour. I can do it either third or fourth block today."

Eagerly, I said, "Fourth block, please." Ms. Moss and Jamie were in my fourth block.

Too eager, I realized. *Come up with a good reason.*

"I don't want to miss math today." Math was third.

He scribbled a pass, then handed it to me. "Come to my office after you check in with Ms. Moss."

Well, this day was looking up. I'd be able to avoid Jamie too. Thanks, Pod-nah!

When the meeting ended, everyone shook hands and thanked everyone else for coming. Except me. No one shook my hand; no one thanked me for coming. I understood why, but it might have been nice. Mrs. Mozier wrote me a pass to social studies, but first, I walked Mrs. M to the front door of the Middle.

"Thanks for coming in. I'm sorry you had to waste all this time on me."

She turned to me. "Shay, it wasn't a waste of time. Not at all. This is part of being a guardian, a foster parent. I'm glad I could be there for you. You're a special kid. I'm glad you're in our lives." I swear she got choked up, but she put on her sunglasses and patted my shoulder.

Then she said the thing she always said to the twins every morning: "Go learn something." She squeezed my shoulder gently.

Then I got choked up. I nodded without saying anything. After she left, I walked into the heart of the Middle to face the rest of the day. Even without Charlie, out on suspension, and Jamie, courtesy of my get-out-of-fourth-block-jail free pass from Mr. Stetson, it was sure to be miserable and awful.

I walked into the silent social studies classroom, and every head popped up. Turns out they were in the middle of a quiz. Mr. Hamilton handed me a paper. Starting off with a quiz. Great. Oh, well. I tried to concentrate even though I could tell everyone was staring at me without turning their heads. Of course, I hadn't taken many notes or studied at all. The bell rang before I finished. I quickly bubbled in the unfinished questions and handed it to Mr. Hamilton without even reading the open-ended question.

Having bombed that quiz, I trudged off to science class. I took my seat next to Marshall.

"Heard you got Charlie and some of her crew suspended,"

he said. "You're a hero."

A hero? I shook my head. "I'm no hero."

The girl in front of us turned around. "You're Shay, right? Nice job getting those assholes suspended."

I sat there dumbfounded as the bell rang to start class. I thought Charlie and the Nameless were popular with everyone.

Ms. Winken demonstrated an experiment using a raisin and a beaker of water. We explored density, mass, and volume using raisins, paper clips, pennies, and corks in different liquids—water and corn syrup. We wrote predictions in our journals about the behavior of the raisin and our observations, according to the steps in the scientific method. After demonstrating, she let us get our materials and then turned us loose to float and sink stuff.

Marshall and I dutifully put on our safety glasses after writing the question of the day in our journals: "Why does stuff float sometimes and sink sometimes?" I thought we should try to sound a little more scientific, but he didn't want to waste time writing. He wanted to get to the floating and sinking. We made some quick predictions on what our objects would do depending on if they were put into water or corn syrup. Then, we floated and sank stuff. It was cool, especially when we combined corn syrup and water.

The corn syrup sank to the bottom of the beaker, making two layers, water on top, syrup on the bottom. The raisin sank through the water layer and settled on top of the corn syrup layer. It was very cool. We wrote in our journals and hypothesized about density, mass, and volume. We didn't talk about anything else. It was nice.

Then, as we were cleaning up, a boy from the table behind us came over. "You're the one who got Charlie suspended? She's a bully. Nice job."

"Told ya," Marshall whispered to me. "Hero."

We finished writing up our experiments in our lab journals. When it was time to turn them in, yet another kid stopped by our table, still wearing his safety goggles.

"I gotcha journals, kay?" He waited for permission to take them to the bin up front.

Marshall gestured dismissively at the journals as though they were dirty plates. Safety Goggles picked them up as though they were made of gold, nodding his gratitude at us. Just as the bell rang, he bowed and backed away from the table, which I thought was all a bit much.

"Told ya," from Marshall again. "Hero."

"Stop saying that," I said, but I was unenthusiastic. Maybe I really was a hero. At the very least, I was being treated as if I was a celebrity.

Marshall escorted me out of class like a bodyguard, putting his arm around my waist without touching me, as if to herd me. "This way. Clear a path. Make room."

No one paid him any attention, but I thought it was kind of funny.

"Have fun being a superstar for the rest of your day," he said as we parted ways to head to our different math classes.

I was about to deny my superstar status, but then he added the thing that crushed me.

"Because tomorrow it all ends."

He was right. Shit.

As soon as I walked into math, Ms. Schunk came over to me. "How are you?"

No one had asked me that in, like, a really long time. My eyes started burning. I immediately got mad. My anger arrived in my chest like a friend. It burst through the door, announcing itself, waiting for a hug. I hugged it because it was familiar and comforting.

I snapped at Ms. Schunk. "I'm fine. Can we do math now?" I know it was rude, but I had to, or I would have cried.

Ms. Schunk was unfazed. "Sure. We're glad you're here. Go ahead and have a seat. I'll show you what we're working on in a few minutes."

I joined my group.

"Martin is in the hospital," Olaf told me. "He goes in all the time. It's probably not serious, but we're making him a card."

"He has sickle cell," Nessa said. "He's getting a transfusion."

"Oh. That sucks," I said.

"Yeah, he almost died when we were in fourth grade."

"Wow. That sounds terrible. Can I help with the card?"

"Sure." Olaf pushed a sheet of poster paper toward me. It was signed by everyone in class; there were pictures drawn all over it.

Ms. Lucy came over and handed me a math worksheet. "We're going to finish this up today, Shay. It's good to have you back." She moved to the next group.

The worksheet was a review for a test. Great. More bombing on the horizon.

"Five minutes on the card, Shay," Ms. Lucy said on her way to the front.

I sat there, not knowing what to write. I didn't know Martin at all, but having sickle cell must have been scary. Then, I had an idea.

Nessa, who could draw really well, drew herself, Olaf, Martin, and me sitting at our desks in our math group, with James on the floor next to Nessa in his usual spot. I wrote the caption: "Our permutation combination is incomplete without you." I crossed out "permutation" because of the locker joke we made the first day. He probably wouldn't remember it, but I did. Martin was a nice person. It sucked that he was in the hospital.

I handed the sheet to Ms. Schunk. I shouldn't have snapped at her, but I couldn't apologize or I would have burst into tears, causing me to have to run out of the room and the school.

She saw what we had drawn and smiled. "Combination, huh? Well done, Shay. I like it, and Martin will too." My eyes started burning with embarrassment at having snapped at her. Who the hell was I? Was this a conscience? I did not like it. Not one bit. I turned and went back to the group.

We finished the review sheet, which wasn't too difficult. I'd still probably bomb the test because I hadn't been in math for a super long time. Olaf, Nessa, and I made a plan to study together tomorrow at Nessa's house. When I explained I might be grounded, they said they'd call me if I couldn't go to Nessa's house.

No one called me "hero" or even talked about the Video or why I was grounded. It was a nice break.

Next was lunch. I hadn't seen Jamie yet, though I knew she was in school. She'd probably be on the lookout for me at lunch, the Boyfriend Kisser. I had to keep my guard up, not turn my back on her. When the bell rang, off we all went. I stopped at my locker to grab my lunch, then headed to the Hellmouth of the Middle.

The cafeteria was packed. It smelled terrible. Hamburgers tasted good, but somehow, here, today, it smelled gross. I walked in, immediately getting grossed out. I stopped in my tracks, about to turn around to leave, when someone jostled my shoulder, almost knocking me over.

"Watch the fuck out," Jamie said, not seeing me because her face was in her phone. Then she looked up. I saw her at the exact same time and backed away. She screamed, "Bitch!" as she launched at me.

The cafeteria aide at the door tried to step between us, but Jamie sidestepped her, tackling me. My lunch went flying as I fell backward, landing on my butt. Jamie rolled to the side, then immediately tried to get to me. Two aides grabbed her arms and stood her up. A school security officer came over to ask me if I was okay. When I said I was, the security officer escorted Jamie out of the cafeteria.

Someone handed me my lunch as I stood up.

Marshall was there. "Come over here," he said, leading me to a table with two other boys. My skin crawled because almost everyone in the cafeteria was staring at me.

"Stop staring at me!" I shouted, which, of course, got the attention of the rest of them.

"Shay," Marshall said loudly. "You okay?"

I wasn't hurt, but I sure wasn't okay. "I'm fine."

"Have a seat," he said and nudged me after I did. "Hey. Eat your lunch. Pretend everything is normal."

I took out my sandwich. After ten years, people stopped staring.

He pointed to the boys across the table. "This is Ish and Dre."

"You're the one that got Charlie and her dumb clique suspended?" Ish asked.

Marshall shook his head. "Shut up about that."

Ish and Dre stared at me, grinning.

Dre gestured to Ish, Marshall, and himself. "We're part of a D&D group." Ish & Dre (or Ishdre, as I'd named them in my head) started talking at me about D&D, which I definitely did not care about at all but listened to because it distracted me from getting attacked by Jamie.

Ishdre resumed eating their hamburger lunches, Marshall ate his apple, so I started eating my lunch. I finished before they were done telling me about their latest adventure, which they called a "campaign." It wasn't that boring after a while. In fact, this lunch was way better than sitting with Charlie, Jamie, and the Nameless Phone Faces.

"We're almost finished with this one level; we have to figure out the puzzle to get the treasure before we can move on. The trouble is, the monster keeps regenerating every time we get it wrong."

They were all really into it. At one point, I thought of a snarky joke about nerds and girls but realized it was exactly the kind of mean-spirited joke Charlie would make, so I held back. I even started asking questions about their campaign, which apparently no one in their lives had ever done before because they practically fell over themselves answering me.

Before I knew it, lunch was over. I wasn't sure if Jamie would be in language arts, but luckily, I had a pass from Mr. Podnah to go to his office instead. In language arts, I didn't see Ms. Moss. Jamie wasn't there either. I went back to my group, who both grinned at me. Raymond actually spoke.

"You got Charlie suspended. Probably Jamie, too, after what happened at lunch."

Wanda chimed in. "And all Charlie's mean friends."

Raymond kept on enthusiastically. "They are mean to everyone. My foster brother is on the lacrosse team with Justin. He told me Justin and another kid were kicked off."

Oh boy. Oh boy. That was a lot.

Ms. Moss walked in. I told Wanda and Raymond I had an appointment in a few minutes to go see Mr. Stetson as Ms. Moss immediately came back to our table.

"We did some silent reading yesterday," she said, "and filled out our reading log. Today, we're writing thesis statements."

I had zero idea what a thesis statement was. I handed her my pass. She read it and rolled her eyes.

"So, you're missing two classes in a row? Great. Come to my room during lunch tomorrow; I'll work with you then."

I nodded like the obedient student I was, so she returned to the front of the room.

As soon as the chaos died down, Ms. Moss tried to start talking about thesis statements. Immediately, hands went up.

"Can I go to the bathroom?"

"I have to go to the nurse."

"My mom wanted me to call her after lunch."

Derailed, she wrote a bunch of passes, then tried to get back on track. She began asking questions, trying to engage us in the lesson.

I'd seen all kinds of teachers. The ones who are the most interesting are the ones you don't notice teaching. It just happens. The content doesn't matter, the room decorations don't matter, writing the objective on the board doesn't matter. When the bell rings and you don't notice that time has passed, that's an interesting class. I've found myself raising my hand to join an interesting conversation without even knowing it.

Ms. Moss was not an interesting teacher. Her room was perfect—welcoming and filled with books. Her objective was on the board every day; she had lots of stuff planned; we did graphic organizers, gallery walks, daily "do nows," and exit tickets. That stuff was enough for her, but she didn't put any of herself into any of it. Nothing was personal, as if she was trying to cross items off an Eighth-Grade Language Arts To-Do list.

Derailing her looked like fun; I wanted to join in it. I raised

THE ANGER CHRONICLES | 263

my hand. When she called on me, instead of answering her latest question, I said, "I have to leave for my appointment."

Visibly frustrated by this, she pointed to the door while continuing to try to get someone to answer a question. As I left, she called on Raymond. Raymond, of all people. I hesitated at the door to hear what he would say. Then, totally out of character, he asked her if he could go to the bathroom. I looked at him, and he smiled at me.

"Raymond, go to Mr. Hamilton's room!" Ms. Moss was kicking him out. He gathered up his things.

"That was fun," he said, walking out with me.

"Did you do that on purpose?"

"Of course not," he said sarcastically, grinning. Then he shrugged, knocking on Mr. Hamilton's door.

After he went in, I stood there in the hall for a minute, surprised at the twists the day had taken. It was about to take another one.

CHAPTER THIRTY-ONE

PRINCIPAL PARKSON WAS in Mr. Pod-nah's office when I got there.

"Shay, before you test with Mr. Stetson," she said, "we have to talk about what happened at lunch."

Mr. Pod-nah added quickly, "You aren't in trouble."

"Oh, no," Principal Parkson agreed. "We saw the video. Jamie went after you. First, are you hurt?"

"I'm not hurt. There's video?"

Principal Parkson turned her laptop to me, then pressed the spacebar. The cafeteria doorway came on screen, showing me entering, stopping, then taking a step backward into Jamie. It was obviously an accident on my part. I wasn't watching where I was going. I bumped into Jamie, she launched at me, I went flying backward onto my butt. Principal Parkson hit the spacebar, pausing the playback.

"You did nothing wrong. We want to know why Jamie went after you—if you know."

I did know. But now I had to decide if I'd tell the truth or come up with a lie. It wasn't exactly a secret that Justin was her boyfriend. I wondered if the adults were testing me to see if I'd tell the truth; they probably already knew the right answer. I never thought I'd ever admit this—lying, in this particular case, would be too much work.

A pro tip about lying: Bad lies were easy; good lies were hard. The easiest part of a lie was telling it. It was easy—just say it—but making a lie into a good one was hard. That took real commitment—coming up with one or two supporting lies or, my favorite technique, mixing in a little truth. Some people might find it hard to remember lies, but I never had trouble. When I lied, I always had a good reason. I always remembered the reason, so I always remembered the lie.

I'd already blocked Justin's number. Jamie had just tried to fight me. I had zero loyalty to either of them. Lying about why Jamie went after me wouldn't benefit me at all. Therefore, I had no good reason to lie. Also, any lie about Jamie would have to be a Good Lie. It would require at least two supporting lies, which had to be believable. The decision was easy. I made it quickly.

"You know Justin, the boy from the video?" I asked. Mr. Pod-nah and Principal Parkson nodded. "He's Jamie's boyfriend. I didn't know that when I met Justin at the party. We kissed because we won a game. Someone recorded it, posted it. Now it's a giant deal."

Principal Parkson said, "Well, that explains why Jamie went after you. Do you have any classes with her?"

"Language arts," Mr. Pod-nah answered for me. He clicked a few times on his computer. "We could switch Shay's social studies with language arts."

Now I was mad. Why did my schedule have to change? Jamie was the one with the issue. Plus, I wanted her to see me every day—reminding her about what her stupid douche boyfriend had done. I needed to stay in class with Jamie. So, I did what I did best. I came up with a lie.

"But I've made friends in language arts. Wanda and Raymond. We're in a group together. Why should I have to change my schedule?"

Mr. Pod-nah raised his eyebrows. "You're friends with Raymond? That's new for him. I haven't seen him talk to anyone since he got here in October."

"Yeah, we're both fosters, so, you know, we connected." Another lie about the connection but, mixed with a little truth about being fosters, it could successfully complete the lie. That benefitted me because I didn't want to have my schedule changed.

"Let's see." More clicking. "It would actually be easier to change Jamie's language arts."

No no no. I didn't want that to happen. I lied again. "I'd rather work things out with Jamie. She'll see me in school anyway—changing things won't stop that."

Principal Parkson said, "I agree. You'll see each other even if we change your schedules. But we can't have you two going after each other all year. We'll have to figure something out. But if you're friends with Raymond and Wanda, well, that's good for you, Shay."

She got up. "Thanks. I'll check in with you later, Mr. Stetson." To me, she said, "We have a few days to decide what to do. Jamie is suspended for three days for knocking you down. I'm very glad you weren't hurt, Shay." With that, Principal Parkson left the room.

Mr. Pod-nah turned to me. "So, tell me the truth. Do you really want to stay in language arts with Jamie?"

He thought I was lying. I actually wasn't for once. Still, I had to bolster the truth to make him believe I really did want Jamie to stay.

"Yeah, I don't care that much though. She'll stay mad at me no matter whose schedule gets changed."

He nodded. "That's probably true. Okay. I'll talk to Principal Parkson." He added, "Good for you for being friends with Raymond. He's pretty quiet and protective of himself. Good for you for getting in."

I had a twinge of guilt for lying about my friendship with Raymond, then immediately got angry at myself for it.

Mr. Pod-nah checked in with me about all my grades. Apparently, he'd found out that I wasn't exactly crushing it academically, except in math. He ascribed my slow start to being new at a school plus being at a new placement. I quickly nodded, accepting his excuses on my behalf. I'd never ever been a real student; at this point, I was too old to learn how. I needed to figure out the bare minimum required in each of my classes to stay below everyone's academic radar from now on.

Mr. Pod-nah started the testing for my education plan. At the end, he told me I'd actually improved over the last time I'd been tested. I couldn't remember ever being tested, so he showed me the report, which had been faxed or copied a hundred times.

"Um, it appears you were last tested in fifth grade," he said.

"So, you're telling me I've improved in math and reading since fifth grade?" I smiled grimly when he nodded. "Well, okay, then. I must be doing something right. Right?"

He nodded awkwardly. "Do you have any questions for me, Shay?"

His phone rang before I could answer. He picked up. "Yes? Okay. No, I remembered. I'll be right there."

To me, he said, "I have a parent meeting now. Do you want to come back after school to talk more?"

I shook my head trying to be cheerful. "Nope, I'm cool. Do I need a pass back to language arts?" We both left his office, him heading toward the main office, me toward class. Of course, I didn't go back to language arts. I had a "Get Out of Jail Free" pass that I wasn't planning on wasting. I spent the rest of the block in the library.

The last class of the day was, of course, art class, starring Toya. I'd been dreading seeing her all day. Probably, she'd be mad at me and had every right to be. But as soon as the bell rang, I couldn't wait to see her anyway. I didn't care if she yelled at me or ignored me or made faces; I couldn't wait to see her. I practically ran to class. I was almost at the door, coming around the corner, when I saw her.

What she did broke my heart.

I stopped in the hall. She stopped. I was grinning like an idiot. It was definitely a grimace or something similar because I was trying hard not to smile. She smiled, but then, in a microsecond, it was immediately replaced with blankness. Her face, her amazing face went empty. Blank. Because of me. She looked sad—my heart fell into my stomach. Her smile had been so quick, I thought maybe I'd imagined it. I was crushed. My smile disappeared, too. Suddenly, I was physically heavy as if I was about to melt into a puddle on the floor or something. I couldn't stand how angry I was with myself.

She put her head down, hurrying into class.

"Toya," I said, but she ignored me. Shit. I went into class, tried to do the work, though everything I did was terrible. It all got thrown out at the end of class. During class, I'd tried to catch her eye, but she sat with her back to me.

Art club was spectacular in its awkwardness. Toya, as the president, assigned the projects to different groups. Usually, everyone went where they usually did to work on the same projects, but today, she made an announcement.

"Mickey, you and I will finish the rainbow for the queer club. Mekhi, Brenda, you're about done with Malala, right? Finishing touches today. Don't forget to sign it. Shay, go with them please."

Everyone turned to stare at me. They all knew Toya and I

had worked on the rainbow together. It was beautiful. I saw it every day, walking into science class. Everyone was probably wondering about my demotion. They probably all assumed I couldn't help paint a rainbow. Maybe I was only good for babysitting sixth graders.

Mr. Reuben said, "Sounds good. Thanks, Toya."

Toya rolled her supply cart out of the room with Mickey in tow. I didn't see her again for days. She didn't return my texts that afternoon. I stopped after sending her three because I was pathetic but not four-text-pathetic. I didn't even realize I was three-text-pathetic. But I guessed I was.

Mrs. M picked me up after art club and, after seeing at my face, didn't have to ask how my day had been. When we pulled up to the twins' school, she said, "I'll be right back." I got out too.

Once they saw us, they came tearing over, as usual. Eli ploughed into me, Nathan ploughed into Mrs. M. I handed them the juice boxes, which launched them into a simultaneous report of their day, filled with more dinosaurs, some math, as well as a mini-argument about a game they played at recess. Mrs. M and I didn't have to talk on the short drive home, which was good because there wasn't room for us in the "conversation" anyway. It was all normal and familiar and comfortable. My heart ached; I guessed it was because the twins were so adorable. At one point, Mrs. M reached over and squeezed my hand. I realized it was because I had tears streaming down my face. I kept staring out the window, but I squeezed back.

CHAPTER THIRTY-TWO

OVER THE NEXT few weeks, my sadness took over, crowding out my anger. Occasionally, there might have been the barest hint of an angry flame, but it quickly snuffed out because I didn't have the energy it would have taken to actually get mad. I wasn't even mad at myself, just really depressed that I was stuck with myself. That realization dragged me down, down, down. All the time.

Charlie mostly left me alone. I think she knew I wasn't worth being friends with. She talked to me when we were around each other and still texted me all the time, but I hardly ever responded. Jamie came back to school but completely ignored me. Pointedly. She made a huge deal of it because I think she thought I cared. People stopped treating me as if I was a hero, which was perfect because I did not want the attention.

I continued to meet with Dr. Carol twice a week, but I didn't mind. I even practiced my Not Lying on her. I volunteered at the day care for a few weeks until they started paying me. Because I was fourteen, I got my employment papers and started working for pay at the day care, spending time thinking of other people—the kids I took care of. I enjoyed working there. Best of all, no one had seen the video.

My dad and I started texting once we had each other's phone numbers. I told the M's we were texting so they wouldn't think there was anything shady going on. I had zero contact with Rhonda the Craptastic, which was the perfect amount of contact to have with her.

I even had a math test I didn't bomb because I was allowed to go to Nessa's to study. Ms. Moss changed the groups in language arts after Raymond walked out. She probably thought I was a bad influence because he was all the way across the room from me. For a couple days, he sat with his head down on his desk. One day, Wanda and I sat at his table instead. We told the people in his group to go somewhere else. Ms. Moss didn't notice or didn't care. He picked his head up and kept it up, most days. We weren't friends or anything, but we were united against Ms. Moss. And Jamie.

Life with the M's settled into a routine. Honestly, it was kind of boring, but I was okay with that. I worked after school or saw Dr. Carol, helped the twins with their homework, sometimes helped with dinner. I started doing a little homework but was careful to keep everyone's expectations low. My grades hovered barely above the "we need to have a meeting" level, and I participated enough in class to avoid negative attention.

Toya got to a point where she was polite to me but not exactly friendly. We weren't texting yet, which I learned when I got to the two-text-pathetic level. The text-pathetic-level counter resets if there is any social interaction, in case you were wondering. I'd sent her a grand total of five unanswered texts, which put me way over the three-text-pathetic level, but as I said, the counter reset because she nodded at me once—but it might have been to the kid I was standing next to. Whatever. Text-pathetic-level counter reset.

I texted her about something dumb one of the sixth graders had said in art club while we were working on our Ketanji Brown Jackson mural. I didn't even remember what Mekhi said, but I thought it was worth seeing if Toya and I could rekindle a friendship over something dumb. Nope.

So, things had been quiet for a few weeks. No school drama, no drama at home. Then, I ruined a great day. (In fact, as you already know, I've ruined a lot of days. In fact, when there is a great day happening, if given half a chance to ruin it, I'll do it. Every time. If you want to ruin a great day, or even a mediocre day, call me. I'm the Day Ruiner.)

When I woke up Saturday, the sun was out. By the time I got down to breakfast, it was cloudy. One of my old English teachers, Ms. Brooks, would say that the sun disappearing was "foreboding" or "foreshadowing" or something. At breakfast, the boys were super quiet. I studied them. They acted as though they had school on Saturday or something. I learned this was because today was

Garage Cleaning Day.

Mrs. M was at work, so after breakfast, Mr. M took the boys and me out to the garage. Shelves lined the garage, filled with overstuffed and crumbling boxes next to piles of loose stuff. A pile of empty boxes also sat by the open garage door. Mr. M handed me a thick black magic marker.

"Your job," he said, "should you decide to accept it, is to label the boxes."

The boys would gather up the trash as Mr. M and I sorted through everything. Mr. M climbed up a small stepladder and began pulling down and lining up cartons marked "Toys" on the floor. The boys opened them and took out the contents, which were obviously intended for much younger children. They immediately started playing with the toys. Mr. M winked at me.

"That should keep them busy for a while." To the twins, he said, "Boys, take those outside. When you're done, you can keep one box of toys. Put them in the one marked 'Toys' and put the rest in those marked 'Donate.'" I figured the kids would have been in the way all day, but this idea was genius.

The boys dumped the toys outside on the driveway and began arguing and playing. I figured I'd get started and picked up a large clean, empty box. I wrote "Toys" on the side and put it by the pile of toys.

"Perfect" Mr. M said as he climbed the stepladder again.

Eli and Nathan were bouncing a Superball on the sidewalk. "Not in the street, guys," I said. They both waved back. I went back in the garage.

Mr. M asked, "They okay?"

"That Superball is going to bounce away in less than two minutes, amateur prediction."

"Not in the street, guys" he shouted.

"We knoooow, Dad!" one of them yelled back.

I took a second box labelled "Donate" and put it beside the first on the sidewalk. I drew a bouncing ball on the side of the one labelled "Toys. "Put the toys you're keeping in this one."

"We knoooow, Shay!"

I went back inside the garage.

Mr. M said, "Shay, help me with this." He was struggling to lift down a box labelled "Molly." I wanted to ask him who Molly was, but he looked sad, so I didn't.

"I keep hoping she'll come back for her things," he said. "But she won't."

I didn't say anything. I could tell Mr. M had really liked Molly.

"Molly was our other foster kid," he added. "Her mother was in jail. Her aunt lived far away, so she didn't fight for her." He stopped for a minute, then continued. He told me Molly got into a lot of trouble at school and then with the law. She got pulled over with Nathan in the car and was arrested because she was high. After a couple months in juvenile detention, the county put her in another foster home. They lost touch with her.

Wow. I was shocked. No wonder Nathan hated me. No wonder he still didn't trust me.

Mr. M continued. "We packed up her room when she went

to the other foster home. No one called for her stuff. She turned eighteen last year. Probably won't come back. But it's only one box; I'll hold on to it."

"That's messed up. She shouldn't have had Nathan in the car."

Mr. M stared at me. For a second, I thought he might get mad. Then he got even sadder. "We were pretty angry about that. I don't know if we handled it that well." I thought he maybe wanted to say more about it, but he didn't. "Let's repack, move this stuff, and put it back on the shelf." He was still pretty crushed about it.

I opened Molly's box and pulled out a few school notebooks and a framed picture of the Morgensterns with a teenaged girl. She was smiling, her arm draped around Nathan's shoulder, rings on lots of fingers. Her hair was in long braids. I could tell she was popular at school but probably not a jerk. There were a couple T-shirts, including one with the quote "Love is so short, forgetting is so long." I held it up. Mr. M smiled when he saw it.

"I remember that one. She got it at a flea market and didn't take it off except to wash it for a month."

I loved the shirt for some reason. I didn't want to like anything about her—this pot smoking, careless driving, obviously cool girl who had blown her chance at a permanent home.

Foster kids called homes "permanent" if they turned eighteen when they were there. It wasn't ever really "permanent" unless they adopted you. Which almost never happened. So, Molly could have turned eighteen, staying in the Garret, but she drove Nathan around while she was high. Then, she "aged out," as we said in juvenile detention. I guessed juvie was her "permanent" home. That sucked. It made me really sad.

So, I stood there, all sad, with Mr. M, who was also all sad.

He said, "If you want the shirt, take it. We can put it in the Planet World bag if you don't want it." The M's donated all the twins' clothes to Planet World when they grew out of them, which they did every other day. I didn't want this cool shirt to go to some stranger.

"This shirt is cool, but will you be okay if I wear it? Maybe you don't want to be reminded of Molly."

Mr. M smiled. "Of course, you can wear it. You're not like Molly at all." Which probably meant I wasn't cool in any way. But I put the shirt by the door to take inside.

He held up a brightly colored bundle. "Boys!" he called. A few seconds later, Eli and Nathan came running into the garage. Mr. M held up the bundle. "Ta da!"

"Wow! Cool! What is it?"

Mr. M unfolded it.

"Cool! Is that Molly's kite?"

"Yep, it's Molly's. Shay, have you ever flown a kite?"

Nope. I've never even seen a kite in real life. I shook my head. Mr. M thought for a minute.

"After lunch, we're going to the park!"

"Yay! Cool!" yelled the boys.

We worked until lunch. Mrs. M came home and helped for a while. When we went inside for lunch, Mr. M didn't eat with us.

Instead, he spent the entire time in another part of the house. Eventually, he came into the kitchen with a large flat package under his arm.

"Okay kids. Grab a sweatshirt. Time to go to the park." He had a plan.

Mrs. M must have known about it because she handed him a sandwich wrapped in a napkin. "You eat, I'll drive."

The Morgensterns innocently drove to the park, blissfully unaware that the Day Ruiner was sitting in the backseat, about to spring into action.

CHAPTER THIRTY-THREE

WE DROVE PAST the park to a field outside of town.

"Come on kids, while the wind is up!" Mr. M bounded out of the car. The twins and I shared a look.

"I don't know how to fly a kite," Eli whispered.

"Neither do I," I whispered back. Nathan shrugged, trying to act cool, but he was tense.

Mr. and Mrs. M had unpacked three kites, including Molly's. We watched as they got one of them aloft. Mrs. M waved me over and handed me a plastic contraption attached to the kite string.

"This is what you use to wind up the string. It's called the winder. Keep it tight, let out a little string once in a while."

And suddenly, I was flying a kite. I glanced over at the twins, who were staring at me as if I was magic or something. The kite pulled at my hands, demanding my attention.

Mrs. M said, "Give it a little string when it wants to fly."

When I did as she suggested, it did fly higher and pulled, so I let out some more string. I stared up at it. Check me out; I was flying a fucking kite.

In the distance, a second kite climbed up the sky. Across the field, Mrs. M had gotten a one flying. She was talking to Nathan as she handed him the winder. Eli came running over to me, his eyes wide.

"Dad said to give me this one, and you should go help him get the next one up." He reached out for it.

I showed him how to wind the string and how to let it out, then went over to where Mr. M held a huge, beautiful kite shaped like a bird.

"This is Molly's," he said. "It does stunts; there are usually two strings. I modified this one, so today, we'll use one string. Stunt kites can dip and loop, but let's see if you and I can get this one up. I'll take it a bit away from you. When the string is tight and there's a good gust, I'll throw it up. You pull the string to keep wind pressure on until it's up. Okay?"

I freaked a little. "Oh no. No no no. I just learned how to fly one already up. I'm not ready."

"Let's try this once or twice. If it doesn't work, I'll do this part."

He walked some distance away as I unwound the kite. When he was far enough, he stopped. "As soon as the kite pulls, step back and let out a little string." He tossed the it up. When it pulled, I did as he said. It fell. Because, of course, it did. Everyone was watching, of course. Damn.

Mr. M picked it up. Another thumbs-up, nod, toss, crash to the ground. This was terrible. I was pre-angry at Mr. M for embarrassing me but didn't want to blow up at him when he was having such a fun day.

I yelled, "Why don't we switch?"

Mr. M shook his head, yelling, "One more try." He picked up the kite, gave a thumbs-up, a nod, and tossed the kite. It grabbed the air and pulled hard against the winder. I stepped back to watch it rise a little. I gave it a little string. It dipped, but then a cool thing happened. The kite shot up, straining against the string. It was flying—a gorgeous brightly colored bird. I slowly gave it string as it pulled and pulled against me. Molly's kite was a beautiful bird against the blue-gray sky.

There was a hooting cheer in the distance from Mr. M, pumping his fist in the air, gazing skyward.

"Way to go, Shay!" Mrs. M cheered.

The wind picked up, so Mr. M gestured to me to give the kite more string. Up and up it went until I couldn't see the detail on it anymore. Mr. M took pictures of the boys, both flying their kites, along with me, flying the stunt kite. It was... (I'm trying to remember how cool this was because it all got ruined in about five minutes.) Here, flying this gorgeous bird kite, I was controlling the wind. I was free. Happy, almost.

The wind started picking up, so Mr. M told the three of us to wind in our kites. The twins needed help because the wind was getting stronger. Then it got really windy. I was having a hard time keeping hold of the winder, much less bringing in the huge amount of string I'd let loose. The kite was a million miles away and not getting any closer. Plus, it kept trying to stay up, dipping and turning and pulling hard.

Suddenly, a gust almost pulled me off my feet. An instant later, it got dead still. The kite started falling out of the sky. The string stopped pulling against the winder—I started cranking it in as hard as I could.

The kite fell into the woods that surrounded the field. We weren't near the fields at all, but it had been so far out on the string that when it fell, it reached the trees at the edge of the woods. I ran to the woods, getting to the base of a tree at the same time as Mr. M. We both peered up at the kite, Molly's kite, stuck way up in a tree. I pulled the string a little, but it was definitely stuck. Mr. M tried, too, but it was really stuck.

Mrs. M and the twins came running over.

"Wow," Nathan said.

"Yeah," echoed Eli.

My face got hot, like I was about to get pre-angry, but instead, I was about to cry. That was bad.

Mr. M's face fell as if he was about to cry too. I'd ruined everything, as usual. Then I got angry. It wasn't my fault. I didn't want to fly the damned kite in the first place. This whole day was stupid. First, there was the Molly story, where I learned why Nathan hated me. Then, I got her precious kite stuck in a tree. It was always a perfectly fine day until something terrible happened. Of course, it was my fault that everything was ruined. The Day Ruiner. Ta-dah.

Ta-fucking-dah.

Mrs. M took the winder out of my hands and began reeling in the string. "Here. I'll do this. That was a pretty strong gust. I saw you struggle. It's not your fault."

Mr. M looked at me sadly, which got me. I actually burst into tears. If I was a cartoon, the tears would have sprayed from my eyes like water from a hydrant. I was just a huge baby. Mr. M opened his arms. Bawling my eyes out, I hugged him.

"I'm so sorry" I burbled. "I ruined everything. The kite..." I was literally sobbing so hard I couldn't talk. (The actual amount of crying is too embarrassing to write about anymore, but I'm sure you get it.)

Mrs. M put her hand on my back. "Oh, Shay. It's okay. It's only a kite. Kites and trees find each other sometimes. It happens. And you"—this part she said to Mr. M—"you're not helping. You haven't seen that kite in years."

Mr. M said, "I'm so sorry, Shay. It's just a kite, and that gust was really strong. I would have had trouble winding it in. I'm not upset with you; I'm not. Not at all."

"Is it because it's Molly's kite?" Eli asked.

Nathan shoved him. "Shhh. Don't talk about Molly."

I had finally stopped blubbering like an infant. "I'm sorry. Maybe we can bring a ladder or get the fire department to bring their ladder or something."

Mrs. M gently said, "No dear. The kite belongs to the trees now. We have to leave too. It's about to storm." She was right. The sky had darkened completely. I could smell rain.

Mr. M took me by the shoulders and declared, "It wasn't your fault. And don't forget, today you flew a kite. You. All by yourself."

"Yeah. Right into a tree."

"Yeah, well I hadn't taught you how to land one. That's on me." And he smiled. (Judgment: Kind smile.)

I smiled back, even though I wasn't really feeling it.

"Nice try on the smile," he said. He judged that smile right. "But I'll take it. I don't want you to be upset about the kite. You didn't ruin anything. We had a gorgeous day. The twins flew kites for the first time too."

Mrs. M and I headed over to retrieve the other kites, which had been dropped when Molly's kite hit the woods. As we got to them, the skies opened up on us and buckets rained down. We squealed as we ran back to the car. Mr. M and the twins also got soaked, so we all shivered the whole way home.

Once we got into the house, Mrs. M said, "Pizza anyone?"

The twins cheered. "Yay!"

Mr M. cheered. "Yay! I'll make a fire."

She turned to me. "Shay, pizza?" I knew she was trying to enlist my buy-in to putting the Lost Kite Episode behind us.

"Sounds great." And I actually tried to sound sort of enthusiastic. Maybe I could try to enjoy pizza and a fire. Maybe the Day Ruiner was finished ruining days for the day.

"Terrific. You kids go change into your pajamas and meet me back in the living room. We'll do pizza and a fire and a movie tonight."

Wow. She had lumped me in with the "kids." *And I liked it.*

When I got back to the living room, Mr. M had changed into flannel pajamas. He added a log to the fire in the fireplace. The room was warm and smelled good. Upstairs, Mrs. M was helping the twins focus on changing.

Mr. M said, "Pizza will be here in fifteen. And Shay, you should know that you and Molly are nothing alike. We loved her, but she walked away from us. I don't understand why, and that part is really hard to accept. I guess we made mistakes with her. I don't know. But I want you to know that we're glad you're here. And we'll probably make more mistakes with you, but we're glad you're here."

The twins came bursting into the room chanting, "Pizza! Pizza!" Mr. M smiled and joined in. The boys were, for once, dressed differently.

"You guys aren't matching," I said.

"We don't always match." Eli retorted.

Nathan rolled his eyes. "Yes, we do."

Eli said, "Yeah. We do. It's fun when people mix us up."

Everybody laughed when Mrs. M came in because her flannel pajamas matched Mr. M's. She put her arm around Mr. M, who put his arm around her shoulders.

He said, "I hope people mix us up." They kissed.

"Gross," came from Nathan, but I thought it was kind of sweet. I wondered what kind of pajamas Toya wore. I would definitely twin with her if I knew.

The pizza was gooey and delicious, of course. The fire

blazed, everyone got under blankets, and we watched *Moana*. Everyone had already forgotten how badly I'd ruined the day. I hadn't forgotten, of course. I never would.

After Mr. M tucked the twins into bed, the three of us watched *Aliens* because it was Mr. M's turn to pick. (Judgment: Excellent choice.)

"Oh, Shay," Mr. M said as we folded blankets after the movie. "If you want to make some money, I'll pay you to help me finish the garage tomorrow." I liked money and quickly agreed.

Lying in bed, I thought it was weird how they forgot I'd ruined the day. I hoped tomorrow, I would do nothing to ruin the day. But there were no guarantees with the Day Ruiner. It could happen at any time.

As it turned out, Nathan was also a Day Ruiner.

CHAPTER THIRTY-FOUR

SUNDAY MORNING, MR. M and I were out in the garage early. He wanted to visit his mother that afternoon, but there was still a lot of work to do in the garage. Mrs. M went into her study. The twins, who were excused from garage duty because it was cold, went to their room to play. Mr. M and I headed to the garage after we bundled up.

A lot of the boxes came from Mr. M's mother's house. She had moved into the retirement home a couple years ago after insisting that Mr. M take the rest of her stuff. Mr. M had an older brother, but he lived in New York and didn't have room for all the boxes. In one, we found a complete tea set. Mr. M immediately started using a really bad British accent, calling me "old chap." We'd been watching some British detective shows (not me, I was usually reading, but Mrs. M loved the British detectives). As a result, our accents were pretty good. Top notch, even. I called him "my lord," and then we were "my lord" and "my lady."

"Shall I toss this old wooden salad bowl, my lord?"

"Dear me, yes, my lady. Chuck it right in the bin." That kind of stuff.

He got kind of quiet at one point, holding a picture in a frame. I went over. He showed me a man and woman with two young boys. "That's Ned and me, with our mom and dad. I must have been about ten here." He pointed to one of the kids.

I didn't recognize him. In the picture, he was skinny with a lot of curly hair. His brother, Ned, was probably about my age in the picture, also skinny and smiling but with braces. Very nuclear-family stuff. Mr. M put the picture by the door into the house.

"You'll meet Ned and his family sometime. He's got a boy, Mark, in college and a girl, Cathy, in, let's see, eleventh grade."

Great. Foster cousins. Forced friendship with a girl who was probably super popular and had four boyfriends, boobs, and got her period all the time. I immediately started dreading it.

When I realized he was looking at me, I applied a Custard Pie lie, "Sounds delightful, old chap," and returned to the box we'd been working on.

It was really cold in the garage, so we stopped for lunch earlier than planned. I went upstairs until then. Something was different in my room. I couldn't exactly tell what until I noticed Mrs. M had left some clean laundry on my bed—I'd forgotten it in the dryer, oops. I checked, but the notebook Dr. Carol had given me, my "Anger Chronicles," was still between my mattress and box spring. Super obvious hiding place, but there weren't exactly a million options up here in the Garret. I only hid it because I thought I should.

After lunch, we all piled into the car to visit Mr. M's mom. The twins were kind of quiet, but they'd had a huge fight before lunch. We heard it from the garage. Mr. M went in and came back out a few minutes later.

"The twins 'r 'avin' a row," he'd said with an accent so thick I almost didn't understand him. They were still pretty quiet—I guessed it had been a bad one. I tried to make them laugh by making faces at them. It usually worked, but not that time.

Dev, Mr. M's mother, was happy to see us all and loved the picture Mr. M gave her. "Oh, Rav, this is wonderful."

He beamed. "That's some fake smile on Ned. He hated those braces."

Dev laughed. "He sure did. Your father threatened to take away his skateboard if he didn't smile." They both laughed at that. She asked me, "Do you have any siblings, Shay?"

"No. Just me."

"You must have been an adorable little girl, with that smile of yours."

Instantly embarrassed, I blushed. "I don't know. I don't think there are any pictures of me little."

Her face fell. "Well, let's take one now. Rav, take our picture. Me and Shay." She leaned into me, whispering, "I'm so glad you're here."

Surprised, I turned my head just as the camera on Mr. M's

phone went *click*. "Sorry, can you take another one?" I focused on him and smiled until he got a decent shot. Then, the twins demanded someone take pictures of them—I guess they'd stopped being mad at each other. (Remember when I said Nathan was also a Day Ruiner? That part comes next.) We were scrolling through the photos Mr. M had taken. Everything was fine until Nathan spoke up.

"Maybe your dad has some of you."

No one said anything. Of course, he knew about my dad, but I had a terrible feeling about what he'd say next.

Mrs. M stepped in. "You could ask him, Shay. He may have saved some." They'd seen all the texts between my father and me because I didn't want them to think I was sneaking around. Plus, full disclosure, I didn't trust my father completely.

Nathan said, "Tell them your plan."

Eli started crying.

A chill ran up my back. My anger towards Nathan was immediate and fierce. Why did this kid try so hard to push my buttons?

Of course. He had read my journal. He knew I was planning on moving in with my father. I was too angry to speak.

Nathan announced, "Shay is planning on moving in with her father." The M's stared at Nathan. "It's in her diary." Everyone swiveled their heads to me.

I stared at Nathan. "You read my diary? You sneaky little…"

I was cut off by Mrs. M. "Is this true Shay? Are you and your father planning this? How?"

I looked at Eli, whose tear-streaked cheeks killed me. "Eli..." I started but couldn't finish because I didn't have any words for him.

"Is this true?" Mr. M said angrily. "Are you and your father planning something? Will he try to regain custody?" Before I could answer, Mrs. M spoke up.

"Is this what you want, Shay? He's only been out of prison for a few months. Do you both think he can handle being a full-time father?"

I still didn't have any words. After being betrayed by Nathan, I wasn't sure what I wanted anymore. I didn't know anything. Lamely, I said, "I don't know. We're not planning anything." I added, brilliantly, "I don't know."

Dev turned to Mr. M. "Rav, why don't you and Miriam take Shay to get some snacks. Have a talk. Boys, stay here. We'll find some *SpongeBob*."

No one wanted to do any of the things she said, but we all did them anyway. Nathan picked up the remote and turned on the TV. Eli wiped his face and nodded when his mother whispered something in his ear. He didn't look at me, which killed me again.

We sat at a table in the dining room.

"Shay, is this what you want?" Mr. M was obviously upset, but I couldn't tell if he was mad, disappointed, sad, or something else. Mrs. M was obviously sad.

"I don't know what I want. I wrote it because it was a place where I could start over. With a real family. Like you all have. With routines and things you always say and pajamas that match and pictures and a past."

The silence was terrible—heavy, filled with sadness. I really super didn't want to hurt them at all, and yet, here I was, hurting them again. Except this time, Nathan had ruined the day. Sneaky Nathan, the Day Ruiner.

"That's what the twins were fighting about," Mrs. M said. "Eli kept saying 'It's wrong' and Nathan kept saying 'I told you so.' It was a bad fight, even for them. They must have gone into your room and found your journal. I'm sorry, Shay. That's an invasion of privacy, and we will deal with it."

Mr. M said, "Is this what you want, Shay? Do you want to live with your father?"

"I don't know." I wanted to say more, but there wasn't any more.

Again, we sat in terrible, sad silence for a few minutes.

"I'll grab a couple cookies for your mom and the kids. Shay, do you want one?" Mrs. M stood up when I shook my head. "Shay, we always knew you could leave us at any time. It's difficult to handle. We'll miss you terribly, but this is part of being a foster family."

We went back upstairs with the cookies and milk for the twins.

The rest of the visit was fine, but everything was a little off, everyone a little quiet, but no one was angry anymore. There was a barrier now between me and this family that hadn't been there before the Day Ruiner went snooping.

CHAPTER THIRTY-FIVE

MONDAY AFTER SCHOOL, Nathan and Eli sat me down in the kitchen to formally apologize.

"I'm sorry we went through your stuff, Shay," Nathan started.

"I didn't go through her stuff. I told you not to," Eli said, clearly still mad, either at Nathan or having to apologize.

Nathan continued, "We won't do it again."

Eli was definitely mad at Nathan. "I didn't do it." He turned to Mrs. M. "Mom, it's not fair that I have to apologize."

"Were you in Shay's room without her permission?"

Eli dropped his head. "Sorry, Shay."

Nathan said, "Sorry, Shay." They turned to their mother. At her nod, Nathan continued. "Our punishment is we have to do your job and set the table for a week."

"Okay. Thanks, guys."

We all sat there.

"Want to go outside for while?" I offered.

"No, thanks; we're going upstairs." They slipped down off their chairs and left the room.

Ugh. The invisible wall was right there. After a minute, I said, "I'm really sorry, Mrs. M. I haven't said anything to my father. I promise. I don't even know what I want. It's nice here."

"I know, Shay. I understand. You're in a tough situation. Do you want to visit your father?"

Wow. I hadn't seen him in years. It was a weird thought. "Am I allowed?"

"I think so. I'll check with Rhonda to make sure it's okay, but we can go whenever you're ready. I'll have to contact your father first, of course. Make sure he's okay with it."

"Of course," I agreed.

So, I was maybe going to visit my father. Okay. Weird thought. What if he didn't want to see me? What if he did want custody? Ugh. What the fuck did I really want? I had no idea. This was going pretty fast. I wasn't ready for anything.

I read in the study until it was time to help Mrs. M start making dinner. When the twins came into the kitchen, they asked me to get the plates down for them so they could do my job of setting the table. Everything was fine, if slightly off-normal. The twins were slightly more polite than usual, slightly more formal. Everybody was slightly more polite than usual. They were already treating me like a guest.

After dinner, Mr. and Mrs. M told me that both Rhonda the Craptastic and my father had given the okay for a visit. Wow. That was superfast. Almost as if they couldn't wait to get rid of me. He worked nights and weekends, so it had to be during the day. Mrs. M was off this Thursday and suggested an afternoon visit. She'd pick me up during the day to go to my father's. It was up to me now. Did I want to see him?

This had all happened really fast. I didn't know what I wanted to do. I didn't want to disappoint everybody though. "Okay."

Today was Monday. Three days from now, Thursday, I would see my father. Actually, I would be *meeting* my father, since I was too young to remember when he left.

The Morgensterns couldn't wait to get rid of me. I was mad about that. Rhonda was in on it, of course. When I moved in with my father, I'd no longer be a foster. Rhonda could stamp my file "Closed" and stash it in a box somewhere with all the fosters who had found their permanent placements. Fine. They all wanted me gone. Okay, I'd go. I wondered how soon it would be after my father met me that he could gain custody. Not soon enough for the Morgensterns and the Craptastic.

I went upstairs to reread all the texts between my father and me.

I texted him: *I guess I finally get to meet you Thursday.*

He responded: *yeah you must be almost grown.*

I feel almost grown.

Do you look like ur mom or me?

I didn't reply because I didn't even know what he looked like. I didn't think I resembled my mom, but my grandma used to say sometimes, I made the same faces she did. And then my grandma would get sad. And that made me sad, thinking of my grandma being sad because her grandkid looked like her addict daughter. And I stayed sad all night.

CHAPTER THIRTY-SIX

THE NEXT DAY at school was not great. I woke up sad because I remembered the Morgensterns were practically pushing me out the door, Rhonda couldn't wait to get me off her caseload, and I didn't know what my father looked like. The good news was the day wouldn't stay sad. The bad news was the day would very soon turn into the Day of Incredibly Awkward Interactions.

Before homeroom was over, Mr. Hamilton handed a sheet of paper to each row.

Marshall turned around to pass me the paper. "I have to talk to you about the dance," he whispered.

The dance? He waved the paper we just got in my face. I studied it—a list of important dates for eighth grade for the rest of the year. There would be a dance for the eighth grade. Also, a picnic, a movie day, and a promotion ceremony. Apparently, here at

the Middle, surviving eighth grade was something to be cele-
brated. I wondered if I'd still be here for the dance, picnic, movie
day, and promotion ceremony. I would probably be living at my
father's by then. That thought made me sad too.

Now, Marshall "needed to talk to me" about the dance. Shit.
He was probably about to ask me to go with him. I didn't want to
go with Marshall; I didn't want to go at all, but if I had to, I wanted
to go with Toya, who was barely speaking to me. Damn. My sadness and anger at my stupid self filled me up. I couldn't wait to get
to my father's.

I didn't have the energy for Marshall's dance invitation,
which I would immediately have to reject. Ugh. I kept shushing
him all through social studies when he tried to bring it up. But we
also had science together. Inevitably, Marshall said he wanted to
talk to me about the dance. I tried to push him off.

"The dance isn't until May. It's only the end of March. Why
are people obsessed about it?"

He shrugged. We were working on our lab reports, but he'd
interrupted our work. He thought it was more important.

I wanted to nip this in the bud, so I initiated Awkward Interaction #1.

"Listen, Marshall. I don't like you like that. I mean, we're
friends, and you're cute and all, but I don't like you like that."

His eyebrows came together in confusion. "Okaaay," he said
slowly. "You think I'm cute?"

Oh no, was he blushing? Damn. I was about to crush this
poor kid.

"Marshall, yeah, you're cute. But I'm not going to the dance with you."

He was still confused. "Okay."

Here was the part where I demonstrated I wasn't a thinker. It was also the part where this Awkward meter topped out.

He asked me, "Do you think Toya would go with me?" That came out of the blue. (Told you I'm not a thinker. I never saw that coming.) When Marshall said he wanted to take Toya to the dance, I got super angry. Maximum anger. Instantly. Full on rage, steam blowing out my cartoon ears, furious. My sadness drained, instantly replaced with fury.

He could see I was mad. "Shay?"

Oddly, I wasn't mad at Marshall. Not even a little. He was a goofball who didn't know Toya was waaay out of his league. I was mad at Toya for being my crush. I was mad at myself for blowing everything up. I was mad at Charlie and Jamie for ruining everything. I was mad at my father for not knowing what I looked like. Mostly, I was mad at my mom. Really mad. Punch a wall mad. Ninety-nine percent of my fury was toward my mom. She had been an addict my whole life, and then she died. She was never my mom. I couldn't move. My rage had me paralyzed.

"Shay." Marshall. I'd almost forgotten he was there. "Are you okay?"

No. I was not okay. Not even a little bit. I had to go somewhere. I was about to lose my cool in a substantial way. I had to get out of this class.

I got off my stool and shoved my things into my backpack. I

went to Mrs. Winken. Calmly and carefully, I asked her, fighting back tears, "Can I please go to the bathroom?"

She studied my face. "Do you want to see Mr. Stetson instead?"

I nodded, and taking the pass she wrote for me, I left classroom and burst into tears.

I hated myself for being weak. The rainbow mural around the door to Ms. Winken's room didn't help. I didn't really want to talk to Mr. Stetson, but he was the only counselor for the eighth grade.

I paced up and down the hallway in front of Mr. Stetson's closed door until it opened. Toya came out with her head down. She didn't see me at first. Then, our eyes met. For one second, we silently commiserated about our separate miseries. She'd been crying; I'd been crying; it was quite a moment of miserableness we shared.

Ms. Peete stepped out of Mr. Stetson's office. "See you tomorrow, Toya. Hi, Shay. Come on in."

Toya gave me a small wave, which surprised me. I managed to return the gesture, which also surprised me.

"Mr. Stetson is out today; I'm filling in," Ms. Peete said. "Ms. Winken called to tell me you were upset. What's going on?"

I was relieved. Ms. Peete and I had done a lot of talking in Girls' Group about what had happened to me at the party, with the video and all. Not surprisingly, a lot of the girls had told the group about similar stuff that had happened to them. I didn't have to fill her in on my family either. She was one of the school's social workers and knew all our stories. I trusted her, which was good because I didn't have the energy to lie.

I told her I'd gotten angry about my father not knowing what I looked like. I told her about getting angry at my mom. We talked about that for a while. Well, I talked. She was a good listener. I mean, she was no Dr. Carol, but it was nice to be able to complain about my mother's shitty mothering. She complimented me for keeping my shit together in class when I got upset.

A knock on the door finally interrupted me and my running mouth. She opened it to find a seventh grader outside, crying. Ms. Peete said something and closed the door.

I stood up. "Thanks for listening."

"My pleasure. Are you okay to go back to class?"

I checked the clock. "Actually, we're at lunch. I'd rather go to the library."

She wrote me a pass. "I'll be here after school if you want to check in. You can stop by on your way out."

I thanked her again and headed to the library after stopping at my locker for my lunch.

Math class was (I really can't believe I'm writing this) fun. Again. We did board races, where we raced each other to solve problems on the board. But Ms. Schunk and Ms. Lucy let us work in teams. We had to switch problems with the other team in the middle of solving it, though eventually, we all started messing up on purpose, so the next team had to fix our errors. It got very silly because people started putting addition where there should be multiplication and then letters in where there should be numbers and then emoticons. Very silly. We ended up solving a bunch of problems, which made it actually fun.

Awkward Interaction #2 happened when the awkwardness meter reached maximum capacity again in language arts.

Here was more proof that Ms. Moss was a terrible teacher— I had an *A* in language arts. I'd been making an effort to stay off everyone's radar, grade-wise, in all my classes. I was managing a *C+* in both science and social studies, which was way better than I'd ever done. In math, I had a solid *B*, which was way, way better than I'd ever done. My *A* in language arts was way, way, way better, though it was completely undeserved.

This might have contributed to my inflated grade: Wanda, Raymond, and I shared answers constantly. All the kids in Ms. Moss's classes shared answers. We did everything as a group. Even the tests, which weren't supposed to be done in groups. She knew we were all doing this in every group, but she didn't know how to stop us. Raymond and I were both getting the first *A*'s of our lives in language arts, mostly due to Wanda, who was studious and academic and a real thinker. She was also turning into a friend.

I'd gone to Wanda's house a couple times after my punishment grounding ended. I found out she liked Raymond, who liked another girl in class (Mindy), who liked a different boy (Jason). Raymond talked to us all the time now in class. Sometimes, I saw him in the halls actually talking to other people too. One of the only good things this year was seeing Raymond come out of his shell. Of course, he was a foster, meaning he'd probably get moved to a different placement eventually, but for now, he was acting almost like a normal person.

Ms. Moss kept moving us into new groups to quiet things down because her class was usually pretty chaotic. Every time she separated us, Wanda and Raymond and I would end up together because people sat where they wanted to anyway.

So, Awkward Incident #2. Wanda was absent. We were supposed to be doing silent reading. Silent reading, in Ms. Moss's room, was where silence came to die. I didn't know how she did it, but it was louder during silent reading than it was during regular class. Maybe because she was in the back of the room, working on her computer, occasionally scolding us weakly to "Please read, people." After about five minutes of loud/silent reading, Raymond turned to me.

"I have to talk to you about the dance." Ugh. Again, with the dance.

He grinned at me. Oh no. Wanda must have been wrong that he liked Mindy. Shit. He liked me. I knew what he was about to say; I'd have to turn him down. I hated the thought of it. Raymond was coming out of his shell. I didn't want to send him back into it.

I initiated Awkward Incident #2 right away so we could minimize the Awkwardness Damage. "Listen, Raymond, you're cute and all, but we're friends, and I don't like you like that." His confusion was obvious. I realized that he, too, wasn't about to ask me to the dance. The Awkwardness Damage meter dinged at maximum. Again.

"What?" he said.

Super embarrassed, I repeated myself but made it into a

question because, as I said, I'm not a thinker. "I don't like you like that?"

He was nice about it. "That's okay. I don't like you like that either." He'd tried to make it better, but I truly deserved what he said. Then he smiled. "I want your advice on asking Mindy. I know she likes Jason, but I also know he doesn't like her."

Great. Wanda was right about Raymond liking Mindy. (And in case you're keeping score, that's exactly zero people who like me "like that.")

Raymond quickly put his head into his book, as did I. Ms. Moss was doing one of her infrequent flybys around the room, redirecting us ineffectually. I had an idea. I texted Wanda, who was home with a migraine. Wanda immediately texted back. I tapped Raymond, who leaned in.

"Listen. Forget about Mindy for now," I told him. "You, me, and Wanda will go the dance as a team. Wanda says lots of people are going without dates. You'll look popular, plus Mindy will see you there."

He thought about it for a second. "Okay, but if Mindy and I end up dating before the dance, you'll have to go with Wanda by yourself."

I nodded, relieved the awkwardness was mostly gone.

When Ms. Moss had settled back into her desk chair, Raymond said, "The theme of the dance is Broadway. What are you going to wear?"

Ugh. I hadn't thought about that when Wanda and I hatched this plan to go as a team. I briefly wondered if Toya would be there.

"Hey." Raymond poked me. "What are you gonna wear?"

"Geez, dude, I don't know. I wasn't going until five minutes ago. We'll coordinate. It's not until the end of May. Calm down."

He beamed, which made me laugh. Raymond wasn't a beamer, but there he was, beaming.

The Awkward Incidents were over. I'd done some Awkward Damage, but only to myself. I deserved it completely. Talk about ego. Why would anyone even like me "like that?" Ugh.

CHAPTER THIRTY-SEVEN

MY LAST CLASS was art, starring Toya. My only goal was to avoid any more Awkward Incidents. Survive the day. So, I had a stern talk with myself on the way. Toya and I had been almost normal outside the counselor's office earlier. I told myself to "be cool" and "not push anything."

I settled into my table in art class. My assigned seat was with a girl named Pearl, who was never in school, so I usually had the table to myself. Today, Pearl was there. We said hi and began working on our watercolor paintings. The bell rang; no Toya. Damn. That meant she wouldn't be at art club either. But as Pearl went to get our water from the sink, Toya walked in with a pass, which she gave to Mr. Reuben. Then she came right over to my table. And sat down. At my table. Where I was sitting.

Be cool, be cool. "Hey," I said. Cool, right?

"Hey."

Pearl came back. "Hey, Toya."

"Hey, Pearl. How's your grandmother?"

Pearl smiled. "She's having a good week. Here I am. In school." Pearl shrugged.

Toya turned to me. "How's your day?"

"Awkward. How's yours?"

She laughed. It was glorious to hear. "My day is also awkward. Mixed with terrible. Are you coming to art club?"

Hell, yes, I was coming to art club. "Sure. Of course. You?"

She nodded. "See ya there." She went back to her table.

I floated through class, creating joy and love and peace and happiness with every watercolor brushstroke. My ducks in a pond looked like yellow blobs on a big blue blob, but they sure were happy and joyful.

In art club, Toya announced our plans for the day. The seventh graders would repair the mural by the main entrance of the school; we would prep the ceramics unit. We walked them up to the front of the school and got them started. On the way back to the art room, Toya turned to me.

"So why was your day awkward?"

I laughed. "Don't laugh. I turned down two people for the dance."

"At least you got asked."

I shook my head. "I didn't get asked by either one."

She pressed her lips together, obviously holding back a laugh.

"Go ahead, you can laugh," I said. She did, and it was glorious again.

"You turned down two people who didn't ask?"

"I sure did. Lots of Awkwardness Damage."

I changed the subject. "Why was your day terrible?"

She stopped in the hallway outside the art room and turned to face me. "My parents are getting divorced."

I knew I should react with something akin to horror. But I didn't feel horror because my parents had never been married; my dad had never lived with us. Your parents were getting divorced but you'd still get to see both of them? Okay. Didn't sound terrible to me. I had to say the right thing though.

"I'm sorry. That must suck."

She started crying. My heart broke, seeing her cry. I almost put my arm around her, but I liked her LIKE THAT, so I couldn't. I got her some paper towels from the cart we were rolling back to the art room.

"I'm really sorry," I continued.

"It's okay," she said. "My dad will have us every other weekend. He's got an apartment near us. They're trying not to fight about everything all the time, so it's a lot more peaceful at home."

Mr. Reuben came into the hall. "Oh, here you are. It's almost time to go. I'll go get the mural crew if you two want to put everything away. We can start ceramics next week." We stood up. "Toya, are you okay?"

"Yeah, there's some drama at home. Shay was helping me. Sorry we didn't get the clay prepped." Her eyes met mine—her warm eyes. I blushed. I had helped her. Me. Helping her.

With a nod, Mr. Reuben went off toward the front of the Middle. Toya and I put everything away in silence.

"I'm still really sorry about the party and that night and everything," I said.

She turned. "It's okay. Thanks for saying that. We're cool. Oh, hey. You never told me why your day was terrible."

Ha. I had forgotten completely that my dad didn't even know what I looked like. I shook my head. "It's not important. I'll tell you some other time."

We walked out together. As soon as I got into Mrs. M's car, my phone chimed.

A text. From Toya. *Hey. This is Toya. Put my number back into your phone.* And a smiley face with the tongue sticking out.

"How was your day?" Mrs. M asked.

"Awkward and amazing," I said without a trace of irony.

"Really?"

"Really." I couldn't wipe the smile off my face.

She smiled back (genuine). Time to pick up the twins.

Of course, I hadn't deleted Toya's number. By the time we got home, she'd texted me again.

What was terrible about your day?

I quickly replied. *Tell you later. Have to do homework and break up fights with the twins.*

Ha. They're so cute.

Sometimes.

Later.

Later.

"Who are you texting?" Eli was curious.

"A friend."

"A booooy friend?" Nathan teased.

Then they made kissing sounds for about a year.

"Okay, people. I have things to do. Let's get our homework done so we can go outside before dinner." I was all business. For once, we got our homework done quickly and were outside in less than an hour. (I hadn't finished all my homework, but I'd done enough.)

Mrs. M came outside as Mr. M drove up. He opened the back of the SUV and took out a bike.

"Here, Shay."

I was shocked. "Really?"

Mrs. M came over and asked me quietly. "We didn't even ask. Do you know how to ride a bike?"

Super embarrassing question but at least I did know how to ride a bike. "Yes. I learned at the Garbage Family's house."

Mrs. M was embarrassed on my behalf. "Oh, I'm sorry, Shay."

I wasn't sure what she was apologizing for but it sure wasn't her fault the Garbage Family was garbage.

"It's really okay, Mrs. M. Thanks for the bike. I haven't ridden one in a while." To the twins: "Get your bikes, boys. See if you can keep up." They raced to the garage and returned with bikes and helmets.

Mr. M handed me a helmet. "Sorry, but the boys need to see

you wear this." He showed me how to put it on.

We rode around the neighborhood a little and pulled up to a stop in front of the M's.

"This is really nice. Can I take them around the block?"

The M's were cautious, but Mrs. M nodded. "Sure."

"Anyone want to go around the block?"

A chorus of "I do!" rang out, and then we were off.

At dinner, I thanked them again for the bike. Nathan, ever the Day Ruiner, tried again.

"Will you take the bike with you if you leave?"

"No, of course not."

When Eli put his head down, Mrs. M jumped in.

"The bike is yours, Shay. Of course, you'll take it with you when you leave."

I'd never had a bike before. I got a little choked up.

After dinner, I went into the garage to check on it. My bike. I was taking a picture of it with my phone when Mr. M and Eli came in. Eli needed to find his baseball glove.

"I never had a bike before," I told them by way of explanation. I was an idiot, taking a picture of a dumb bike.

"Want me to take a picture of you sitting on it?" Mr. M offered.

"Oh, no, that's probably way too dorky."

Then Eli shot right to my heart. "Why do you want to leave us?"

I thought about it. I wanted to give him an answer that would stop him from being sad.

"You know how you have your mom and dad and Nathan?" I waited for his nod. "They're your family, right? Well, my father is out there. He's my family. Wouldn't you want to be with your family?" He nodded again. "I want what you have. You know—family."

He paused. Then he broke my heart. "Can't we be your family?"

I had nothing.

Mr. M helped. "Shay needs to find her family. We're a safe place for her to stay while she's looking. But she needs to find her own family."

It sounded great. Eli must have been satisfied because after a second, he shrugged. "Okay." He wandered off, searching for his glove again.

"Thanks, Mr. M."

"We're glad you're here, Shay. For as long as it takes."

Eli held up a baseball glove, squealing, "Found it!"

After they went back inside, I texted Toya and sent her a picture of the bike.

She immediately texted back. *Cool bike. What's the deal with your terrible day?*

It's a long story. Are you sure?

An amazing thing happened.

My phone rang. It was Toya. We talked for an hour. I told her everything—about my father not knowing what I looked like, my mother's addiction, lots of stuff. It was easy to talk to her. She told me about her dad's drinking and her mother's new friend. Her mother was a doctor with a practice in town. Another doctor from the practice was coming over for dinner a lot now that her father had gotten an apartment.

Our lives were messed up. but we also talked about school and art (!) and books (!) and I don't even remember what else.

Mrs. M came to check on me at one point. "You okay out here?"

I put Toya on hold. "Sorry. I lost track of time. I'm on the phone."

"Oh no problem. We thought you were planning on sleeping out here with the bike."

I laughed, surprising her because I rarely did.

"Okay. As long as everything is alright." She smiled and went back inside.

"I'm still in the garage with the bike," I continued with Toya. "They were worried I was about to sleep out here."

She laughed. "I haven't even started my homework. I'll probably be up all night."

I didn't ever want the phone call to end, but I refused to be the reason she didn't make distinguished honor roll for the millionth time in a row, so I said, "Well, I'll see you tomorrow at school."

"Yep. Goodnight, Shay."

"Goodnight, Toya."

And then I went inside and told the M's that I was queer.

CHAPTER THIRTY-EIGHT

THEY HANDLED MY coming out perfectly. It turned out Mrs. M had a gay sister, so they were already versed in all the proper things to say. I also told them I liked Toya and explained how I had messed up badly at the party. They said all the right things again and, most importantly, said it didn't matter at all that I wasn't straight.

Mrs. M even made a joke about it. "Well, I guess the talk I was planning on having with you about the birds and bees will change."

I joked back. "It'll make it longer because we'll have to cover the birds AND the bees." They laughed, which made me laugh because, apparently, I laugh now.

I rode my bike to school on Wednesday. Since I wasn't walking, I got there twenty minutes early. I failed a math quiz I'd completely forgotten about. Ms. Schunk said I had to stay after school to retake it. We also had a quiz in language arts, but Wanda, Raymond, and I shared answers with the group next to us. We all aced it.

Toya and I texted on and off all day, mostly dumb stuff, but none of the gossipy crap Charlie and the Nameless Phone Faces still texted me. I only responded occasionally when I got a text from Charlie or one of the Nameless because we'd reached a truce of some kind. We pretended we were all friends so that no one said shitty things about the others. Toya texted about other stuff. Honestly, I couldn't tell what it even was, except when I saw her name in my notifications, my stomach jumped.

After school, I went to the math classroom. Ms. Schunk and I worked some of the problems I'd gotten wrong. (Most of them.) She asked me what I was reading. I told her it was some Ye Old Tyme science fiction from the M's shelves. She said she was a fan of science fiction. We actually talked about *Dune* for a few minutes. When I was leaving, I almost let her know I was really having fun in math class but didn't have the nerve. I had to leave early because I had an appointment with Dr. Carol.

Mrs. M picked me up from school and put my bike in the back. "Next time, you can ride your bike from school to Dr. Carol's, but I want you to see the way first."

Dr. Carol and I mostly talked about my impending meeting with my father. I was super stressed about it.

"How is your anger?"

I thought about it. "Still there." I described my flip out in science the day after making a plan to visit my father. She asked me if they were connected. I said they sure were. I explained that every time I got angry, I thought about my mom, even though it never had anything to do with her.

"We can work with that," she said with a smile.

I mentioned I'd come out to the M's and that my friendship with Toya was fixed.

Dr. Carol was impressed. "You've had quite a week. I'm proud of you, Shay. You're making good choices. Recognizing the source of your anger will help you address it."

I was actually pleased with myself and glad I hadn't lied to her. "Writing in the Anger Chronicles has helped, even though it's like I'm in a teen drama movie. Sometimes."

She asked me why I enjoyed journaling. I said reading old entries helped because at the time, everything appeared to be hopeless, but eventually, it all sorted out. She nodded.

The best thing Dr. Carol let me know was that I didn't have to make a decision about moving in with my father on Thursday. It would be strange for both of us. Sometimes, it took a while for the resentment and anger to fade. Plus, he might not be ready to take on full-time father duties for a while. I was glad because it meant I could stay at the M's until the end of the school year at least.

Thursday, Mrs. M excused me from school. We drove an hour to my father's apartment. The long, three-story brick building had a lot of units. As soon as we walked in the lobby, I smelled potatoes and wondered who was cooking them in the middle of the day. We made our way to his apartment. Mrs. M knocked on the door, and a skinny white guy opened it.

My father stuck out his tattoo-covered hand. I shook it. "Shay? Damn. You look like your mother."

Mrs. M introduced herself.

He shook her hand. "Come on in. Come in. Do you want something? Soda? Juice?"

When we both said no, he took us to the living room, then gestured at the couch.

The place had only one room, with a bed in the corner, a small kitchen, and a table with two chairs.

He brought over one of the chairs, placed it next to the couch, and sat down. "Um, let's see. Last time I saw you, you were maybe two. Do you remember?" I shook my head. "What grade are you in now? Fourth? Fifth?"

"Eighth. I'm in eighth grade."

He slowly shook his head from side to side in disbelief. "Shit. Eighth grade. I think you told me that in a text. Can't believe it."

I had told him. More than once.

It smelled like he'd smoked a million cigarettes already that day. He wore a shirt that was a size too large, and he hadn't shaved in a day or two.

Mrs. M asked him, "Where are you working, Mr. Turner?"

"Oh, please, ma'am. Call me Victor. I'm helping a buddy with some electrical work. Nothing regular yet."

To me, he said, "My PO will flip if I don't find something soon. But jobs are scarce right now." His hands shook. "I might get this truck driving job. It's full time. Gotta renew my driver's license and pass the drug test." His eyes flicked between the two of us. "I will pass that drug test. Two years clean. Promise."

I couldn't stop staring at his hands. How could he do electrical work if his hands shook?

He excused himself to go to the bathroom, which was right there, across the room in this little apartment. When he came back, I noticed his hands had stopped shaking. I stared at him but he wouldn't look at me. Fuck. Fuck fuck fuck. Fuck this guy.

I stood up abruptly. "I have to pee." I went into the little bathroom and closed the door. Sure enough, in the toilet tank, a half-empty bottle of vodka. Good thing my mom was an addict. I knew where all the hiding spots were. Fuck this guy.

"We have to leave now," I announced when I exited the bathroom.

Mrs. M immediately stood up when she saw my face. "It was nice meeting you, Mr. Turner."

"Victor, please," he said weakly as he also stood. "Do you have to leave? We can order some food or go somewhere."

"Nice meeting you, Victor," I tossed over my shoulder. Mrs. M followed me out without a word.

"What was that about?" she said as she started the car.

"Bottle of vodka in the toilet tank."

"Oh, Shay," she started, then stopped because what else was there to say.

"Fuck him."

She agreed. "Yup." We drove home in silence.

It was still early afternoon when we got back. "Mind if I take a bike ride for a while?" I asked.

Mrs. M shook her head. "Sure, go, of course. I'm really sorry, Shay."

"Me too. I mean, he's a complete fuckup, right?"

"I think he might be a little lost."

I rode the bike for a long time, ending up at the Middle, where I went to the side door and waited. Right on time, after queer club ended, Toya walked out.

"Hey," I said.

"Hey. My dad is here to pick me up."

"I'll walk you to the car if that's okay."

She smiled. Instantly, my day brightened. "Yes. I think it's okay. Did you leave early?"

I nodded. "I'll tell you why in a bit. First, I want to apologize to your dad."

I went around to the driver side and apologized to her father for the night of the party. He was surprised but accepted my apology.

Toya talked her dad into letting me walk her home. I told her about my dad: his crappy apartment, the vodka, my shitty plan to go live with him.

"I understand why you want to go live with family," she said. "You've bounced around so much. Plus, this year has been super shitty."

I stopped pushing my bike. She stopped. Something like static electricity sizzled between us. I swear we were about to kiss, but I couldn't make the move. She didn't either.

I said, "Not everything about this year was shitty."

She smiled and turned to keep walking.

I didn't move. "I mean..." She turned back to me. "...some things this year have been really cool." I pointed to her. She laughed.

She laughed, helping me achieve a Life Goal on this gorgeous afternoon. Even though my day had been a dancing mothball, right then, it was floating up, up, up.

CHAPTER THIRTY-NINE

THE NEXT MONTH flew by. I couldn't believe it was almost June. Toya and I hadn't gotten close to kissing again, but we hung out all the time, texting constantly. Despite the vodka in the toilet tank, I was kind of on the fence about moving in with my father. We texted occasionally, but sometimes, when he'd text, I wouldn't answer right away. Sometimes, I didn't respond at all. He'd gotten that truck driving job, but I hadn't been back to visit. He wanted to get together, but I kept putting him off. He embarrassed me. Plus, I was still pretty pissed that he'd run away when I was a little kid. Dr. Carol and I talked about it a lot—I had lots of anger toward my parents. And myself. I couldn't stop myself from believing that if I'd been a better kid, they'd have been motivated to get clean, stay sober, that at least a small part of their fucking up was my fault.

Eli had warmed back up to me, mostly. Nathan stopped talking about me moving in with my father. I'd found a much better hiding place for my Anger Chronicles. Nathan was still a little prickly sometimes. One day, something happened that helped him decide I wasn't a piece of shit. Unfortunately, Eli had to get a little emotionally bruised in the process.

I'd ridden my bike home from my job at the day care on a gorgeous Saturday afternoon. I brought home some cookies we'd baked and decorated that morning. Mrs. M was leaving just as I walked in.

"Shay, can you get the twins in about an hour at the Bisters' house? They're on a play date there, and I have to go to work. Mr. M is visiting his mother."

I agreed and, an hour later, headed five houses down the street. The Bisters had two boys, one the twins' age and the other a couple years older.

When I got there, sounds came from the backyard, so I went around the corner to where Nathan and the Bister boys were playing catch with a volleyball. They waved at me.

"Hi, Bisters. Come on, Nathan, time to go," I said. "Where's Eli?"

He dropped his eyes. "Inside." Something was off.

The older Bister kid said, "Eli sucks at everything. He can't catch, and he can't read."

My anger was immediate and fierce.

The younger Bister stared past me. There was Eli, standing at the door, his face scrunched up as if he'd been crying and was about to again.

I gestured to Nathan to toss me the volleyball, which I hurled it as hard as I could at Asshole Bister, who caught most of it with his stomach. He doubled over, gasping, and started crying.

I bent over and whispered in his ear, "If you ever say something mean about Eli again, we'll play some more volleyball." I waited. He squinted up at me, still gasping, with tears streaming down his face.

I whispered, "Nod if you understand." He nodded. I stood up.

Nathan and Young Bister were staring at me. Eli came over and took my hand. He started walking me away from Asshole Bister. Nathan joined us.

I turned. "See you again, Young Bister. You're probably a nice kid."

Young Bister cautiously waved, probably out of fear of what I'd do if he didn't.

As I walked my bike home with the twins in tow, my anger cooled quickly. I had totally overreacted, of course. The twins were silent.

"What happened?" I needed to know how badly I'd overreacted.

Nathan explained, "Eli kept dropping the ball because Tim threw it too hard at him."

Eli said, "Then he called me stupid because I'm dyslexic."

I stopped walking. "You know you're not stupid, right?"

He nodded. "I know, but Tim always picks on me." We

started walking again.

"You let me know if that asshole ever does anything again to either one of you." They stared wide-eyed at each other. Shit. I'd cursed. "Sorry, guys; you shouldn't swear."

"Swearing isn't that bad," Nathan said.

I agreed. "Yeah, but adults hate it when kids swear. Use different words, like 'shoot' and 'darn.' I'll show you— That older Bister kid is such a *dear*. Except I don't really mean *dear*, I mean asshole." Eli grinned at me. I poked him. "What are you grinning about, *dear*?"

"Nothing, *dear*," he said, grinning even wider.

"Well, that's nice, *dear*," I responded.

Nathan chimed in with, "Such a sunny day, *dear*." We did this until we got home.

Mr. M hung up the phone as we walked in. He glanced at me. Uh-oh.

"Shay, what happened at the Bisters?"

The twins started talking at once, as always. When the story was sorted out—with Mr. M satisfied I had defended Eli, but a little too enthusiastically—we all agreed I'd been a little overzealous. I promised to apologize to Asshole Bister; the twins went upstairs to play.

Mr. M said, "Thanks for standing up for Eli. Maybe less aggressively next time?"

I nodded. "I got mad that he was being mean to Eli. Eli's such a sweet kid."

His eyes filled up, and Mr. M, the softy, said, "Eli likes ice cream. Let's go out for ice cream tonight. Go apologize to that bully Bister kid and get it over with."

I headed back down the street on my bike. The Bisters were outside, still throwing the dumb volleyball. I pulled up on my bike and got off.

Asshole Bister said, "You here to apologize?"

His parents were watching us from the window. I waved to them. They didn't wave back. Whatever. I'd make nice to keep the peace with the M's. "Yep. I sure am sorry for throwing the volleyball at you."

Asshole Bister nodded. "What about threatening me?"

I glanced at the window. Yep, parents still watching. I leaned my head back and laughed, really loudly so it would appear as if we were joking around now. It was good show. Young Bister was confused, but when I winked at him, he laughed a little.

Asshole Bister didn't laugh though. I stopped laughing and gestured for the volleyball, which Young Bister tossed to me. I tossed it back to him, and we did this a few times. See Bister Parents? I was nonthreatening. I was fun. I turned to Asshole Bister. Gently and carefully, I tossed him the ball. He caught it, and I turned away from Young Bister.

Quietly, only to Asshole, I said, "I'm sorry if you thought I was threatening you. It wasn't a threat. It was a promise." I saw surprise in his eyes. (And then, satisfyingly, fear.)

I gestured for the ball; he tossed it to me. We played three-way catch for a few more tosses. See, parents? We were all friends here.

I went over to Young Bister. "You let me know if he bullies you." I held up my hand, and he high-fived me. I went over to Asshole Bister and held up my hand. He also high-fived me.

Then, he said quietly, "I'm gonna tell my parents."

"Go ahead." And I added for emphasis, "Please tell your parents." I plastered a fake but believable smile on my face, then turned and waved at the parents as I walked back to my bike. They waved back. Mission accomplished.

When I got home, no more phone calls had come from the Bisters. I checked on the twins, mostly Eli. They were playing with Legos, and Nathan asked me to help. We hadn't done Legos together since Nathan had read my journal. It was really nice. It was just like it used to be, when I wasn't a guest. We had a burping contest, which Eli won for once, and then we made a huge dinosaur with our Legos. Nathan named it "Dear."

CHAPTER FORTY

THE EIGHTH-GRADE picnic was amazing. The teachers grilled burgers and dogs, we played volleyball, and Toya and I hung out with Nessa, Wanda, Raymond, and a few of Toya's friends. It was amazing. They all talked about what they'd wear to the dance that Friday. All the girls were going to wear dresses and get their hair done. The boys could get away with nice T-shirts and jeans. Not fair. Wanda, Nessa, and Toya knew I was stressed about what to wear. They told me I could wear anything I wanted. My friends. I had friends. I put the dance out of my mind because it was a gorgeous day.

When we returned to school that day, the teachers handed us each four invitations to the promotion ceremony the following week. I put them in my backpack. After dinner, I invited the Morgensterns.

"Do you want me to see if I can get your father a ticket?" Mrs. M asked.

"No. That's okay. I'd rather you all be there."

They sat there beaming at me, and I could see Mr. M get choked up a little. Mrs. M squeezed his shoulder, and he cleared his throat.

"We'll be proud to be there," he said.

The twins stared at their father. "Are you okay, Dad?" Nathan asked, worried.

"I'm fine. I'm very proud of Shay. Do you want to go see Shay get promoted to high school?"

"Yes!" was the twins' chorus.

"We'll be there," Mrs. M said, smiling.

Mr. M cleared his throat again. "We'll be there."

Friday night, the night of the dance, I spent three hours getting ready. It was stupid to spend that much time on it because I was only wearing a white collared shirt, an old hoodie, new jeans, and my same old low-top sneakers. Mrs. M had insisted on taking me to the mall again, where I got the shirt, but I suspect the shopping expedition was more for her than me. We ate a cinnamon bun for dinner. When we'd gotten home, I spent the next three hours mentally preparing myself and putting on a shirt.

Mr. M drove me to the dance, picking up Wanda and Raymond on the way. Raymond's foster mother would drive us all home. I was grateful the M's didn't give me a speech before I left, reminding me of the last time.

Wanda was gorgeous in a beautiful dress and with her hair

up. Raymond wore a white shirt with black jeans. He also had a bow tie on, but Wanda and I made him untie it and open the top button on this shirt. He looked much cooler that way.

When we got to the dance, I immediately searched for Toya. She walked in about five minutes later. I swear, I couldn't breathe when I saw her. She wore jeans, a black shirt, and the same low-top sneakers I was wearing. She was breathtaking; I went right over to her.

"You're gorgeous," she said. To me. About me. I laughed, which made her get serious. "I mean it. You're gorgeous. I'm glad you're here."

I couldn't help myself. I took her hand. She immediately grabbed my hand back. We walked through the crowd on the dance floor to where our friends were. Wanda and Nessa smiled at us holding hands.

Raymond said, "Let's dance," and started onto the dance floor, assuming we'd all follow. We danced in a giant group—a good thing because I was a terrible dancer.

Toya and I ate pizza and danced and held hands and hung out all night. The night flew by. When the gym lights came up, my heart sank because this dream was about to end.

"My foster mom is picking us up in five minutes." Raymond came over to where Toya and I sat on the bleachers.

"Okay. I'll be right out."

After he left, I couldn't stop staring at Toya. "Text me when you get home."

She nodded. And then…she leaned in and kissed me.

I kissed her back immediately. My heart almost exploded. "Um," I said, always brilliant.

"Yeah," she agreed, kissing me again.

"Shay!" Raymond called me.

"Gotta go." I jumped up.

"Shay," Toya said. My heart really did explode. "Call me later."

I nodded because I couldn't speak because my heart had exploded. I nodded a lot. I nodded the whole time I walked across the gym to where Raymond and Wanda stood, holding hands.

THEY WERE HOLDING HANDS.

"What happened here?" I asked, pointing at their hands.

Wanda smirked at me. "I guess love is in the air." She waved at Toya.

I blushed and nudged her. She nudged me back. She was beaming. Raymond was beaming. We walked out to Raymond's foster mother's car, where she introduced herself and drove us home.

For the last week of school, Toya and I were an item. We kept it cool, of course, but everyone knew.

The morning of the promotion ceremony, I was relieved to get on my bike and ride to the Middle. The twins hadn't stopped bouncing all morning. They were excused from school, a very big deal for them. When I got to homeroom, all the eighth graders were off the charts with excitement. As a class, we filed into the gym, where our invited guests would be. I found Toya standing with some friends.

"Hey," she said.

"Hey. Big day."

"Yep."

Stellar conversation, but we were also staring at each other super hard.

During the ceremony, I made eye contact with the Morgensterns and waved at them. They all waved back, especially the twins, who waved so hard I thought their arms would pop out of their sockets. When my name was announced to get my certificate, Eli yelled, "Go Shay!" Nathan immediately yelled, "Go Shay!" Ms. Schunk was in the middle of handing me my certificate and shaking my hand. We both turned to the audience that had been asked to remain quiet until the certificates were handed out.

Embarrassed, I turned to a smiling Ms. Schunk and said apologetically, "My brothers."

My words echoed through the gym. I'd said it right into the microphone, loudly, to everyone in the room. Everyone heard me call Nathan and Eli "my brothers." Huh. I didn't hate the sound of that. I continued back to my seat, thinking about "my brothers."

After the ceremony, we all stood in a little circle. The twins oohed and aahed over the certificate of promotion, but I think they were being sarcastic, which made it funny.

"I'm glad you were here," I said to Mr. and Mrs. M.

"Of course. We'll always be here," Mrs. M said.

Mr. M, always the emotional one, cleared his throat and repeated, "We're always going to be here."

Toya and her parents came over so I could introduce the

Morgensterns.

"This is Mrs. and Mr. Morgenstern, my foster parents. This is Eli, and this is Nathan. They're my foster brothers." They grinned broadly up at me. "They are my brothers," I corrected, turning to Mr. M. Right on cue, he choked up again. Mrs. M squeezed his shoulder as she got choked up too.

Toya was smiling at me. I almost couldn't handle it.

I turned to the Morgensterns again. "There's someone important I want you to meet. Morgensterns, this is Toya. Toya, meet my family."

*

SO, THESE ARE my Anger Chronicles. I still get angry, but not as much, so that's good. I'm out of pages, so there isn't enough room to tell you HOW AWESOME MY SUMMER WAS. But it was awesome. My family went to the shore for a week—a whole week—and I got to see the ocean for the first time. By the end of the week, I was riding the waves with Mr. M, who was pretty buoyant. Best vacation ever. It was my first vacation, of course, but it still had to be one of the best ones ever. Toya and I are still an item!

Next year is high school, and I can't wait. WHO EVEN AM I?

Acknowledgements

The Anger Chronicles is about finding family, and I'm grateful to have found several in my life so far.

My original family: My mom and dad, who moved us to a house in the woods on a lake and turned us loose. Aunt Anne and her partner, Carol Sue, who drove us across the country in an RV with a big yellow dog, and my best friend, my sister, Becky. Her family: Bob, AJ, Nick, and my great-nibling, Griffin. They have all given me unconditional love, which I could not have lived without. Becky, the jokes we make at the darkest times in our lives would shock most people, but I depend on them to get through. You are the strongest, bravest person I know.

My ComedySportz Philly family: The most talented, funny people I've ever met. Working with them gave me the courage to write and perform comedy without fear. My first improv class changed my life forever. My improv teacher and mentor, the late, great, Mike Young, complimented something I said in an email once. I printed it, and it hung on my fridge for years. He had written, "Hoo-boy. That was so funny I laughed out loud." Everything I write is better because of ComedySportz, and I will always aspire to create at a "Hoo-boy from Mike" level.

My Southeast Delco School District community: One of the great joys in my life has been working with all my students and their families. The teachers are the hardest working, kindest people I've ever met (shout out to the math department). Go Knights!

The Davis family. You are all funny, kind, and welcomed me with open arms. I'm glad I married into this family. #gophillies

I'm deeply grateful to my editor, Elizabetta McKay, without whose phenomenal skills and infinite patience this book would definitely not be as good. I will also be forever grateful to NineStar Publishing. I still can't believe they took a chance on me.

Last and best, Emily. You have been a part of this process since the beginning. You helped me with plot, character, and structure more times than I can count. This book wouldn't exist without your support and encouragement. I will always be grateful for you.

About the Author

Jessie has been performing comedy in her spare time for over twenty-five years, which definitely comes in handy during the day in her job as a high school teacher. She grew up in the Poconos, in a house in the woods on a lake, with very little parental oversight. It was even more dangerous than it sounds, but it was the '70s. Jessie is a lifelong writer, and with her first novel, she is eager to contribute to the queer YA subgenre. Jessie lives outside Philadelphia with her wife, two cats, and fantasies of days spent volunteering at goat rescues after she retires.

Email

jessie.p.author@gmail.com

Connect with NineStar Press

WEBSITE: NINESTARPRESS.COM

FACEBOOK: NINESTARPRESS

X: @NINESTARPRESS

INSTAGRAM: NINESTARPRESS

BLUESKY: NINESTARPRESS

THREADS: @NINESTARPRESS

www.ingramcontent.com/pod-product-compliance
Lightning Source LLC
Chambersburg PA
CBHW060621100726
47907CB00006B/1710